Insect Summer

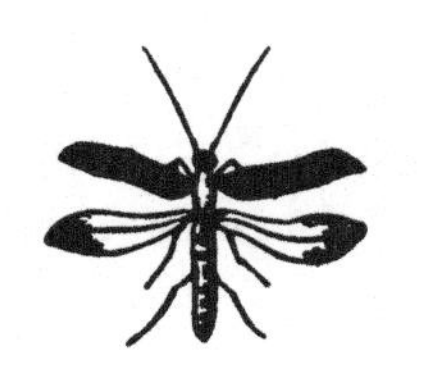

By the same author

The Sleeping Prince
Adam's Diary

KNUT FALDBAKKEN

Insect Summer

Translated from the Norwegian by
HAL SUTCLIFFE and TORBJØRN STØVERUD

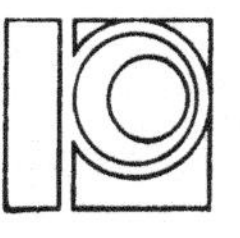

PETER OWEN
LONDON & CHESTER SPRINGS PA

PETER OWEN PUBLISHERS
73 Kenway Road London SW5 0RE
Peter Owen books are distributed in the USA by
Dufour Editions Inc. Chester Springs PA 19425–0449

Translated from the Norwegian *Insektsommer*

First published in Great Britain 1991

The endpapers are based on 'House', a wood-engraving by Rosemary Kilbourn, reproduced in David M. Sander, *Wood Engraving: an Adventure in Printmaking*, London 1979

British Library Cataloguing in Publication Data
Faldbakken, Knut, *1941–*
Insect summer.
I. Title
839.82374

ISBN 0–7206–0794–9

Printed in Great Britain by Billings of Worcester

ONE

Onan

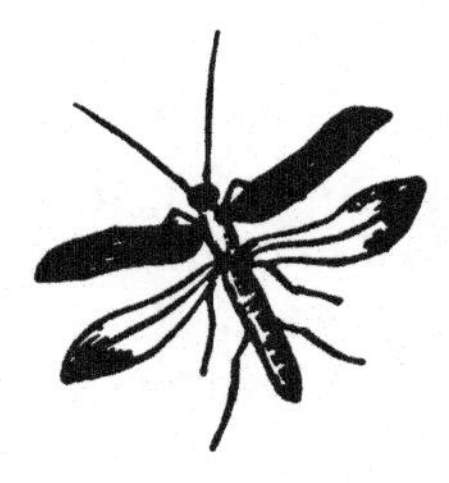

1

It was my sixteenth birthday that summer.

They said I was to spend the holidays in the country, at Aunt Linn and Uncle Kristen's, who had written with an invitation, and that was fine by me. I was even looking forward to it, though I couldn't quite get rid of the feeling that it was Mother's and Dad's idea to send me away for the summer, and they'd probably made it quite plain that they wanted them to invite me.

I had spent several summers at my aunt and uncle's, so there was nothing unusual or out of the ordinary about this arrangement. And it was true that it would be better, healthier for me to spend a few weeks in the country, rather than hang around in town with nothing to do, with all my friends away. I imagined the streets around where we lived, dozing in the dusty heat of summer, with unseeing, deserted windows, with little notes about closure for the holidays tucked in behind door-handles in small shops – the sickly sweet melancholy of hot summer days which I knew only too well from before; aimless summers, when all plans and expectations failed, came to nothing, because Mother's migraine had got worse or Dad's business had left far too little time for trips or excursions, even for normal family life, if it came to that.

No, life on a farm, that was a different story. On the farm, there was something going on the whole summer, one hectic period following on the heels of another. On the farm, everything seemed to come alive, just as everything shrivelled up here in the city, grinding slowly to a halt. I remember how, at that time, I often thought about packing in school altogether, abandoning the school career mapped out for me in favour of running a small farm, and the rude health that comes from hard toil with crops and livestock in rain and shine, through all the changing seasons. I sometimes felt like this in spring, when the pungent smell of earth wafted towards me from the nearby park; even the sight of a rotting wooden wall in a backyard, an occasional horse-drawn cart, some implement or other and even tramps, because they dressed and behaved in a way that was somehow alien to the city, all this awakened in me an enthusiasm for the robust good health that seemed to lie at the very root of life in the country. It felt safe, reassuring to think like this, and dogs, cats, neglected horses which I caught sight of on rare occasions, a flock of crows which for several winters had lived in the tall limes in the park, a down-at-heel drunkard going from door to door selling traditional Christmas sheaves for the birds each year, all of this strengthened my idea of a harmonious and pure life, in honest toil for small but inestimable rewards, far removed from the all-pervasive rottenness of the city. Such were the thoughts I had at that age, and I was looking forward to my stay at Fagerlund.

Nevertheless the thought that everything had perhaps been 'arranged' cast a shadow over my excitement. I'd got it into my head that they wanted to get rid of me, tactfully and considerately and 'for my own good', as was their habit, but a *fait accompli* all the same. Why they wanted to get rid of me I didn't know; maybe I was imagining the whole thing. Perhaps I'd started to think along these lines because my mother was more highly strung at that time, which in turn most likely stemmed from the fact that Dad had been away quite a lot that year, saying he was tired and just sitting there, seemingly unapproachable, unless of course he was arranging something or other with invisible contacts over the phone, paying no more attention to her than either of them did to me. All the same, some kind of wordless exchange seemed to be going on between them all the time, which made me embarrassed, out of sorts, because it didn't fit in with the image I had of them, placing me at the centre, as a connecting link, a sort of catalyst of the far from excessive liking and interest they displayed for one another.

I'd been thinking along these lines for the past six months or so and had derived a certain comfort from this state of affairs. It gave a sort of guarantee that an equilibrium would be maintained despite Mother's migraine attacks and Dad's business activities, which seemed to have run into trouble, since the anxiety I had experienced was quite different, more menacing than either illness or bankruptcy, much more far-reaching. . . . And it was this kind of anxiety that I felt was in the air, jeopardizing the triangle I had created to protect us, and this made me quite sick with apprehension, even if I comforted myself with the knowledge that it couldn't possibly be 'love' that held them together, nothing as unstable, as abstract as 'love'. For I'd never seen them 'do anything', display any tenderness towards one another, which might have suggested that they were anything more than two ordinary acquaintances who happened to live under the same roof. But all the same. . . .

Of course all of this could have been imagination. Maybe *I* was the one who was changing? I'd noticed that I was more prey to doubts than before, more thoughtful, subject to imaginings, able to conjure up the strangest, most bizarre and disconcerting thoughts even about the most humdrum occurrences. Bewildering, aberrant meanings could be read into everything around me, everything that happened to me. It could all come over me so powerfully that it was like performing a kind of magic: I could conjure forth things I thought up and make them real, even if they were completely irrational. In this way, I 'controlled' my surroundings by besmirching them with sometimes quite outrageous notions. And the worst of it was that even though these novel notions frightened me, they also aroused me at the same time. I had imagined many a sequence of events, many a macabre episode, at night, deep down in the safety of my snug bed with consolation so temptingly close at hand. In this way I was both cause and victim of the corruption.

I dreaded the day of judgement. It made no difference whether they drifted apart or drew closer together in this charged atmosphere; it would all come to a horrible end anyway. I always feared the worst.

I could almost have hated her when she bustled silently around him, completely at his beck and call, giving vent to her unfathomable anger in daily chores which tied her to the kitchen, from which an ominous din would emerge: I couldn't bear it, for I had a sudden flash of insight into the inverse symmetry of grown-ups' feelings, saw that the more she fussed about the living-room with an air of reproach, the more doggedly she laboured over the kitchen worktop, the more she loved him, whereas he, for his part, according to a perverse logic, grew closer to her the more taciturn and withdrawn he sat there, preoccupied with his own concerns, pretending that none of us existed.

I gathered that money had been lost, that the flat might have to be sold, that we might then have to move to another part of town which was less expensive to live in, yet this was far less important than this ominous new passion that was blossoming between them. That is, unless it was the opposite – how could one tell? On the occasions when we had guests, they made such a show of affection and concern for one another that there could be no doubt they were putting it on.

But regardless of all this, I was to spend my summer holidays at Fagerlund, at Aunt Linn and Uncle Kristen's, to give them the peace and quiet to sort out the mess they had got themselves into. That is, if this mess really did exist outside the confines of my own self-centred world.

Dad came with me to the station. He had given me a present, a beautiful new sheath-knife, just as we were leaving. I was taken aback by this, since he didn't usually give me presents unless there was a proper reason for it, such as Christmas or birthdays. He was generous all right, but the awkwardness between us spoilt the pleasure of giving and the joy of receiving. I was also taken aback by the present: a sheath-knife. What was he giving me a sheath-knife for? I was fifteen, sixteen nearly, and had secretly begun to covet a gaudy tie, trendy shoes with thick soles, perhaps even a moped in two or three years – what use was a knife to me? To me it was something you gave to small boys in order to channel them into healthy extrovert masculine pursuits. A cut finger was easy to deal with; other temptations were more problematic. Giving me a knife was an insult, an insinuation.

Yet I naturally understood that it was with the best of intentions. It always was: for my own good. And, furthermore, I knew that Dad had grown up in the country, at Fagerlund, which was now run by his younger brother, Uncle Kristen. He had once said that at Fagerlund a knife was both a toy and a tool, one of the most splendid things they could imagine. It was obvious that I would show them my new knife at Fagerlund; it was a message, a link with his own youth, full of tools, farm animals, honest labour – a healthy youth spent on a farm. In fact, it saddened me to realize this, to see through his intentions. I sat clasping the new knife all the way to the station.

Luckily there wasn't much time to spare.

'Well, goodbye then,' he said. 'Give them our love. You'll write, won't you? And look after yourself. If we have time, we'll come up there as well.' His eyes told me that he somehow wished to make up for the unfeeling words. Then we both looked away. They wouldn't come, though. I knew.

'So long, then,' I said. 'Love to Mother.'

I had said goodbye to her in the hall. She'd been in a bit of a state; there was so much to be said, so much to be done at the last moment, now that her little plan was about to succeed. A hint of the previous day's farewell meal wafted towards me as she rushed off in search of her handbag and pressed a note into my hand. A touch of powder against my cheek: Here you are, a bit of pocket money. 'Bye then Peter. It'll seem so empty here this summer when you've gone. I'll miss you. . . . Aimed at my dad rather than me. More meaningful for him than for me.

We shook hands. I jumped up on to the step. The carriage door slammed shut and I turned, glanced back, was already on the way. He was waving but his eyes were already turned inwards upon his own more pressing affairs.

So I was rid of them, and they were rid of me. I glanced at the sheath-knife in my hand, with its ornate handle, the sharp steel blade protected by the leather sheath. The present from my dad which was intended to ensure that I would fall peacefully asleep at night, would sleep soundly, undisturbed by dreams, and would awaken rested, refreshed and full of energy the following morning. An attempt to keep me as a child, to postpone puberty for one more season.

The train clattered slowly along over the joints in the rails, away from the city, out of the cutting that ran between the backyards. Every bump was transmitted to my body, to my pulse, whispering: freedom at last, freedom at last, freedom at last. The seat of my trousers rubbed against the plastic leather. I felt relieved: getting away, getting away, getting away. I could feel it coming on; I knew I couldn't stop it: my independence, my boundless youthful energy was already stiff and thrusting, clearly visible through my trousers. The lavatory was at the end of the long corridor. The mere thought of the two of them in the flat, of all that was suppressed and unsaid, sent tensions welling up inside me. A perfumed whiff of her powder on my collar. My knees trembled. I was so easily aroused. I longed for rest, peace, reconciliation, and needed scarcely any pretext. . . .

Afterwards, everything was so much better. The train had shaken off the last urban warehouses and storage yards, then patches of forest and fields, gentle wolds and distant hills came into view. The harsh light came flooding in from outside, dispelling the dark shadows of the city which I carried within me. In the reflection of the window-pane I conjured up Fagerlund, my room, the east-facing bedroom I had always had when I was there on holiday, the short, wide bed, the bedclothes that smelled different from those at home. Then I had an idea: I would ask whether I could live in the hut. It was perfectly habitable, that much I knew. I recalled how it lay there on the slope, dark with tar, the roof sagging, virtually hidden in the little wood, a mere two or three hundred yards from the farm. Just imagine if they'd let me live there! A house of my own. What a holiday that would be! From the roof of the hut you had the best possible view of the farm, the grey and brown buildings, which had stood there for nearly a hundred years. It was reassuring to think of the spacious farmyard, the barn, the large kitchen with the long table along one wall, the dark bread that Marie, the maid, baked. . . . Perhaps I'd had a bit of a crush on Marie two summers before. No, come off it – what did a thirteen-year-old know about love? I thought of the clay-coloured swallows' nests up under the roof in the barn, the willow and alder thickets by the stream, the knife, willow flutes, Dad as a boy. . . . Out there, nature flickered past constantly in glimpses and flashes of light and shade. The terrain flashed past, constantly changing, opening up and closing in on itself again.

I closed my eyes and away I went. Opened and closed them again, forwards in time, backwards in time. . . . Soaked up the sunshine. The knife lay there in my hand, reminding me of all my earlier selves.

The hours passed.

It was all a dream.

2

The dream had been so real that I'd half expected a younger version of Dad to meet me at the station with horse and cart. But it was Uncle Kristen who stood there on the platform waiting for me, and the old truck was parked in front of the station as if to provide a reminder of who and where I was, a quite unnecessary reminder, it seemed to me, even though admittedly I was somewhat disorientated after the journey, a bit dazed and tired, pleased to have got there at last.

He smiled, and it occurred to me that he bore a resemblance to Dad. They were brothers after all, but the likeness suddenly struck me as extraordinary, much greater than I remembered. Uncle Kristen looked exactly like Dad in the photograph of him as a young man which hung over Mother's bedside table. It was almost bewildering, even if he stood there in his working shirt, face brown as a berry, and so incontrovertibly my uncle. The fact that he looked so young suddenly aroused a certain unease in me, which I couldn't account for. His handshake was warm and hard and firm, quite unlike the one I had received in a hasty goodbye a few hours before.

'My, haven't you grown?'

I flinched, but at the same time was proud of the fact. I'd grown a lot the last year.

He heaved my rucksack and suitcase on to the back of the truck. We got in. The old truck lurched and rattled as we sped along the country road. We almost had to shout to make ourselves heard.

'It's great of you to have me!'

'Oh, we felt we could do with a bit of company at Fagerlund this summer too, you know.'

Aunt Linn and Uncle Kristen had no children.

'You're both OK, I hope?'

'Yes we are, thanks. Everything's fine.'

Fields, hills. Houses here and there beside the road. It wasn't all that easy to carry on a conversation.

'Jo was confirmed this spring, I hear?'

'Yes, that's right.'

Jo was the boy from the next farm, two years younger than me, whom I'd knocked about with a bit during previous holidays. I remembered that we'd sent a telegram of congratulations for his confirmation.

'Were there a lot of people there?'

'Yes, the entire neighbourhood, gossiping their heads off. . . .'

He paused, as though regretting what he had just said. Then he added: 'You mustn't pay any attention to what people say round here, Peter.' Nothing more was said on the subject of Jo's confirmation.

We drove through the village, past the filling station, the co-op, the new community hall which had been officially inaugurated with brass band, speeches and refreshments the last time we'd been here: it seemed much longer than two summers ago. All three of us had come up. Mother must have been happy that summer; she had stripped off and gone swimming in the Mill Dam, as we called the swimming place where the stream widened out, making as if to form a little lake, thanks to the dam wall left over from the days of the old mill, which had ceased working long ago. The trees of a lovely little wood reached almost to the edge of the gently sloping banks. You could count on not being disturbed there. I'd gone up there alone with my fishing-rod one evening, not to fish, just to be on my own. I'd taken off my clothes and slid into the black water soundlessly, naked as an eel – and afterwards, on the bank in the dry grass, I had marvelled at one of my first erections, a response called forth by a personified nature around me, untroubled as I was by the incomprehension of other people, who now seemed so far away. It had been so hot and had felt so wonderful to lie there naked in the tall grass. Of course I wasn't supposed to go swimming here alone; everyone said there were treacherous currents deep in the Mill Dam's murky depths. There had apparently been a number of accidents: a young lad and a girl, a newly engaged couple, were said to have drowned, but this merely served to heighten the enjoyment I derived from my modest peccadillo.

'What about the summer fête this year?'

I asked this question more than anything to break the long silence that had developed, since it was the custom to hold a summer fête and bonfire on the field below the new community hall.

'Oh, there's bound to be one,' said Uncle Kristen pensively, as he sat there holding the steering-wheel in a vain attempt to steer a straight course despite the lurching of the vehicle caused by the uneven surface of the gravel track. 'But it's another matter whether Linn and I'll be there this year. . . .'

Just as Dad might have said it, even though Uncle Kristen looked so much younger, so disconcertingly 'young'. Two summers before, we had gone down together to the fête and watched the dancing. But so much had changed since then; would I really be as keen for them to come with me to this summer's fête? Changes. I suddenly recalled the idea I'd had on the train about living up in the hut. I came straight out with it in order to steer the conversation and our thoughts on to another tack.

'I say, Uncle Kristen, do you think I could possibly live up in the hut this summer? That is, if you two don't mind. . . .'

He turned and looked at me. 'You want to live in the hut?' he asked in amazement. 'Er, well, yes, I suppose so. . . .' But he seemed none too keen. Perhaps he too was thinking of the passing years. Or perhaps he was thinking of something else altogether. . . .

'And how's Marie?'

I had to keep the conversation going, give him a hand. Something had come between us which could not simply be attributed to the two intervening years. Was it because I'd grown so much and he was now barely half a head taller than me? Was it because we could no longer go on playing 'the uncle and his pale little nephew from the city'?

There was a smell of rubber and petrol in the driver's cabin. The silence became so drawn out that I couldn't help wondering a trifle anxiously whether it was wrong of me to have asked that question. But how could that be?

At long last he answered: 'Marie isn't with us any longer.'

I looked at the grass verges flashing past, as though to ensure that everything was as before, innocent, straightforward, harmonious out here in the country, where I had spent my holidays as a boy and where I had not wanted to be troubled by my self-centredness, my suspiciousness, my fifteen-year-old's secret jiggery-pokery. But I still had to satisfy my curiosity all the same.

'Oh? Has she packed it in, then?'

'She's disappeared,' said Uncle Kristen in a tone that left no room for further explanation or comment.

A wasp or a bee, I couldn't see which, flew slowly towards us and went 'splat' against the windscreen. A summer's afternoon, of the sort I'd completely forgotten, lavished its profusion over the gentle countryside, over the truck in which we sat side by side bumping up and down. Now there was only Coombehills left and we'd be there. The fact that Marie was no longer at the farm didn't necessarily mean that anything particular had happened, but, all the same, the word 'disappeared' had an odd ring about it. This wasn't what one said of someone who had given their notice and gone away. If I'd been an adult, I could obviously have asked straight out whether she had found employment somewhere else, or maybe got married, fallen prey to wanderlust or whatever else might lead a girl to up sticks and go. However, since I was only fifteen, I just had to content myself with Uncle Kristen's terse, enigmatic comment and accept the fact that we were not going to discuss it any further. All I could do was speculate. Marie had been at Fagerlund ever since she had been a youngster and had come out of the 'home', as they called the psychiatric clinic in the neighbouring locality. Aunt Linn and Uncle Kristen had taken care of her when it had become generally acknowledged that it would be for her own good to get away from home. There was such a lot of mental instability in her family. I could remember their discussing it back at home, saying that it was taking a great risk, that it was a heavy responsibility to take in someone who was unstable on the farm. . . . But Marie had remained at Fagerlund, had almost become like their own child on the farm and there had never been any question of problems of any kind. Until now, when she had just 'disappeared'. . . . But if something really serious had happened, we'd surely have heard about it too, wouldn't we?

The dusty grass verge stretched out like a speckled ribbon, pointing the way forward. We'd be there any minute. A familiar barn wall, a clump of pine trees flashing past, indicated that everything was all right, everything was as it had been, unchanged, unchangeable. . . . Surely it was just me, allowing my frenzied imaginings to run riot. His calm profile pricked my conscience. Uncle Kristen had never been particularly talkative. His hands on the steering-wheel were so reassuring and dependable. The sun struck the windscreen like shiny metal and played on my ear. Even the weather did its utmost to show that everything was as it had been before, as it had been all the other summers. Nature, the tall birches, the fresh green foliage, convinced me . . . and I allowed myself to be convinced. Although I'd felt a hint of unease at the thought of the two of them at home, I still allowed myself to be convinced, yes, convinced.

I must have nodded off for a moment, for when I next looked up, we were suddenly at the track leading to the farm, and there were the farm buildings just ahead of us, half-way up the hillside. We drew up in front of the barn.

'Well, here we are then,' said Uncle Kristen.

A suggestion of anticlimax: I had remembered the farm as larger. The buildings suddenly seemed small and grey, dilapidated, like lichen-covered stacks of wood dotted about the grassy farmyard. I tumbled out, breathed in the sweet air, the smell: at least that hadn't changed. The soft grass gave beneath me as I walked up towards the farmhouse, squat and humble as it now appeared, despite its two floors. To the right, thirty yards below, down by the stream-bed, stood the little cottage referred to as 'Mary Cottage', which had previously been the servants' quarters and which had been turned into a place for Marie to live in. My eyes were constantly drawn in that direction as I staggered with my heavy suitcase over the grass, which yielded beneath my feet as though I was suddenly treading on something alive, having walked miles and miles on street cobbles and tarmac since I'd been here last.

A voice: 'Ah, there you are, Peter. Lovely to see you. Welcome back!'

Aunt Linn had come out on to the doorstep, smiling and holding her hand out to greet me. She had put on weight. I'd never paid attention to things like this before, hardly even noticed them. I shook hands, embarrassed: Yes, thanks, the journey had been fine, just fine, the train had been on time, everything was fine at home, and of course they sent their love.

'You must be ravenous. Come on in and have something to eat.'

The same as ever, reassuring. Gratefully, I put down my suitcase in the hall and followed her into the kitchen. Uncle Kristen followed behind with the rucksack.

'Look how he's grown!'

But even the large, low-ceilinged kitchen was different from how I remembered it. The black wood-burning stove was not in the corner where it had always stood before. Even though it was a long time since it had been in use, it had stood there as a reminder of bygone days, when there had been a larger household, more mouths to feed, more hands at work at Fagerlund. Now it had had to give way to a fridge, so new and shiny that it seemed grossly out of place in here.

She had laid a place for me near the end of the long table: 'Here you are, I thought you might like to sit here on the bench.'

My favourite place all those years. The familiar smell of meatballs. Her broad back over at the long, low worktop under the windows. So everything was more or less the same as before.

But Uncle Kristen remained standing in the middle of the floor, as though not quite sure what to do next. Tall but strong, broad, with perhaps a hint of a stoop, with thick black hair, which tumbled in a mop over his forehead. Dad wasn't quite as tall as this, and a bit heavier, and he combed his hair straight back, yet the likeness was striking all the same. A little too striking for comfort. But this wouldn't do, I'd just have to forget the town, the flat, Mother, Dad and all their crises. I was here at Fagerlund now, for the holidays.

'Well, I suppose I'd better see to the milk, then,' he said, a trifle helplessly, addressing her back.

It was so late that the milking had already been done. She probably had to take care of all the cowshed chores single-handed now that Marie was no longer there, had 'disappeared' in some way that couldn't be referred to in ordinary conversation, at least not with fifteen-year-olds present.

She was getting my supper ready and didn't reply.

'Has it been put out to cool?'

He was already standing at the door, impatient.

'It's in the scullery. There's a limit to what I can cope with, you know!' It sounded so brusque and resentful.

'Yes, of course there is,' he said, and went out.

It was the strangest welcome I'd ever had. I scarcely dared look at her. The sun was just setting. The bright evening light streamed in through all the windows, and the flies – as though at a signal – began their evening dance against the thick, uneven window-panes. There were so many of them; such a multitude and so frenzied as I'd never seen the likes of before indoors. In town we were hardly ever troubled by them. But here they were nauseating, almost frightening. I could hardly touch my food on the plate she had placed in front of me. They had had an argument. Something was up. All was not as it should have been here at Fagerlund. The flies buzzed against the bright window-panes in blind, suicidal fury.

'Did he tell you about Marie?'

All of a sudden she'd sat down at the table, opposite me, so close that she blocked out all other thoughts from my mind and prevented me from averting my eyes. She had asked whether he'd told me about Marie. She spoke in an undertone, yet intensely, at the same time unsure of herself and hesitant, as though forced by necessity to ask this question, yet at the same time not quite sure whether she dared go so far as to confide in me, to speak openly about this mysterious disappearing act.

'He mentioned that she wasn't here any more. . . .' My voice faltered and squeaked into a falsetto before I got to the end of the sentence. I blushed, looked back with longing to the events of the last summer I had spent here: fishing trips, the hectic haymaking observed from my lofty perch high up on the hay wagon, the thunderstorms. . . . So pure, fresh and fragrant, so untroubled by doubts, so straightforward: so many glowing memories from that time two years before. Now I was as tall as she was, well on the way towards manhood, yet still half-boy, half-man, with gangling limbs, who could not be sent out to play or really talked to either, an outcast with no place in this world, or that; even being proud of the fact, yet at the same time helpless, banished from the mutual hypocrisy of adults. I couldn't even give her a simple answer without my clear boyish voice faltering with complicity, percipience and dangerous insight; the breaking of the voice which I had dreaded more than anything else.

'He said she'd "disappeared",' I replied, embarrassed. I might as well throw down the gauntlet, indeed I already had done so by the way I'd shot up, by not displaying the same uninhibited joy on my arrival here. Two years before, nothing could have kept me out of the hayloft the first few hours.

'Yes, we formed a search party, combed the entire neighbourhood,' she said in a monotone, 'right up to Wildfell Marshes, but we didn't get any further than that, it was so wet, it rained so much all spring, you see. There was just no question of going any further. . . . If *she* went any further than that, she couldn't have got very far either!'

So that's what had happened. Marie had run off, disappeared into the forest, just what they had all been so afraid of many years before, when she had first come to Fagerlund, having been a psychiatric patient – there were also rumours about her mother and an aunt. . . .

I redirected my attention to the meatballs, which had always been my favourite dish, and, with an effort, forced down mouthful after mouthful. I had no appetite. I thought of the disgusting flies, of Marie who had disappeared, I chewed and swallowed, not daring to look up, not daring to ask any questions, having no right anyway to be told anything, me with my thin wrists protruding out of the arms of my jacket, slightly too short – the prim and proper grammar-school style of dress that was emphasized by the gawkiness, the freakishness of growing four inches in a single school year – long fingers scarcely able to cope with a knife and fork. How could such a creature expect to be taken seriously, expect things to be explained to him, expect grown-ups to confide in him?

The heavy food, the heat, the doziness that came over me after the long journey, kindled a gentle glow somewhere deep inside me. Again, I was at the centre of my own penetrating scrutiny; my inadequacy was a means of satisfying my curiosity. 'Why did she run away then?' I asked, as if butter wouldn't melt in my mouth, in a tone I might easily have used two years before when asking why damp hay was a fire risk, to induce her to think I was younger, more stupid than I actually was. Naïve questions have to be answered.

'Oh, I don't really know, Peter. Perhaps she'd been a bit depressed around that time. . . . I only hope it was nothing *we* did. . . .'

She sat there, leaning back, her bosom resting on her bare arms folded over her belly as though to protect herself, so heavy and sorrowful, full of self-reproach. To look like this, there had to be something on your conscience, and I sensed that in some inexplicable way this must have something to do with the fact that she had become so plump, had become 'older'. I had never thought of Aunt Linn as a woman before – breasts, belly, all such things had no real meaning in relation to her, but now I sat there secretly following the line of the mature breasts, feeling that the bulges, which she so patently regarded as a curse, a millstone round her neck, instead made her physically attractive to me in a direct, overt way, which I would never have thought possible before. At the same time as feeling that the 'fault' – whatever it was – must lie with her, I fell completely for the new, mature femininity she exuded. I suddenly saw such a clear picture of us from an earlier summer: myself running in at the door, in a hurry, a sun-tan glowing on my cheeks, wind and bits of grass seed in my hair, with a question, a request of some kind: a glass of water, a slice of bread – and her at the kitchen worktop in her apron, smiling, welcoming, accommodating my every wish. My head in her lap, my arms around her: please, oh *please*. . . !

Now I looked at the heavy breasts resting on her bare arms, the round belly that bulged slightly beneath them, becoming aware of a hot, illicit, disrespectful reaction to such thoughts and memories: my admiration of her stood hot and hard against my thigh, unless it was just the excitement I felt at speculating about what had happened, what had *really* happened here at Fagerlund.

I redirected my attention to my plate, where yet another meatball and gravy, stew and potatoes awaited the return of my appetite. For all my racy day-dreams under the table-cloth, I was outwardly only a shy, crestfallen, streaky youth, ill at ease, lanky in my city clothes, with a face in which the long nose had started to grow out of control, and the lips were thick and conspicuous, far too thick and conspicuous, in their dissolute, flesh-coloured red; hair the colour of damp hemp, unmanageable and simultaneously irresolute – like its owner – still bore the scars of the barber's excesses. At this period, the mirror was my worst enemy, though this didn't stop me from standing before it half an hour at a stretch, scrutinizing my imperfections. Yet none of this stemmed my curiosity or prevented me from believing that I was entitled to find out more. I had an insatiable appetite for everything that was dramatic, everything that I felt could give me greater knowledge, greater insight into the mysterious world of 'grown-ups', even though at the same time I was afraid of what it was I wanted to know.

As for me, I neither was anything nor knew anything. My inner world was a mosaic of lost property, 'borrowed' knowledge, second-hand experiences. I identified unreservedly with any and every idea that came my way. Everything found a response in my hazy impressions; I could choose freely from among the props, like an actor when deciding which mask best suits the role. I *was* an actor, I acted constantly and in front of everyone, acted the child among children and the grown-up among grown-ups, or vice versa, if it happened to suit my enigmatic purposes. Every time I opened my mouth, I lied, though in another context that lie could be the truth. I no longer troubled to distinguish between them.

Now I was a grown-up, or at least gave myself the airs of one, and conversed with Aunt Linn on an equal footing, acted her equal, because I had realized that she was just as bothered and inhibited about her body, her physical appearance, as I was about mine:

'When did she disappear, then?'

There was a pause, just a sigh.

'Last week.'

So it was no longer ago than that.

'The bailiff was also up here,' she added, as a kind of afterthought. 'They dragged Blackstone Pool and the Mill Dam. . . .'

So she was dead.

'So they think she's . . . dead, then?'

I could use the 'grown-up' word without feeling troubled by it, but sure enough my voice failed me, just when I needed it most.

'Oh yes, I think so. It's ten or twelve days now since she disappeared, and she'll have had nothing to eat. . . . And what if she's sunk into a bog, or fallen and injured herself. . . . No, there isn't much hope, I don't think.'

She stood up, as though to change the subject, asking me if I'd like some pudding. She'd made stewed plums. If only Kristen would come back in with the milk soon, there'd be cream as well.

I said I'd love some. She cleared away my half-eaten helping of meatballs and got cracking at the kitchen worktop. She chatted to me as she spooned out a large helping of pudding. They had had a poor spring. The sowing had been three weeks late; the warm weather had never really seemed as if it would come. . . . She walked back over to me across the floor, placed my bowl of stewed plums in front of me on the table. As she leaned over me, my nostrils caught a trace of sweat, ever so slight, and this sour little hint of her body, of an unexpected lack of personal hygiene (I'd become pathologically clean over the last year), gave me an advantage and sufficient courage to ask 'But *why*? Didn't either of you notice anything about her? Didn't she *say* anything?'

'No, she didn't. . . . She was a bit up and down, you know. We didn't talk to her much about things like this.'

She was moved; you could hear it in her voice. I thought: Poor thing, what an effect it must have had on her, yet at the same time I couldn't rid myself of the feeling that it must all somehow be connected with her plumpness, which she bewailed, this large, heavy body which had 'aged'. Irreversibly, for all to see. . . . Though might all this just be projections of my own almost pathological obsession with everything connected with the body, with everything physical, which had claimed so much of my attention of late?

'You see, it wasn't always easy, either for her or for us. She was only a young girl and, well, we're not exactly young any more, you know. . . .'

So that was the connection! She'd indicated it herself: She was young – we've grown old. . . . I pictured Marie, tall and blonde and rosy-cheeked in the farmyard, or walking along the road, or else among the fruit bushes, or with her bare white back and shoulders down at the Mill Dam, after we'd been swimming together, everyone but Aunt Linn that is, who didn't like the water. Marie had always been so young, so full of life, her cheeks like rosy apples, her eyes like two patches of blue in the summer sky. She'd already set me thinking then, two years before, when I was still unable to distinguish between elation and passion: I'd been swimming without permission – in the nude – the same evening. Afterwards, I'd lain in the grass, admiring my manhood. That had been love for me then.

'If only Kristen would hurry up, you could have some cream. . . .'

She was still pretty though, approaching middle age, pretty in a kindly sort of way, but with the advancing years had become darker round the eyes and in her hair, which she almost always concealed under a headscarf, her whole complexion had somehow grown darker, more melancholy, as though apologizing for the fact that it still hadn't faded completely. . . . But Marie had been so full of life, so spry and bouncy; I remembered how she had run down the path to the Mill Dam, stumbling over a root, falling and grazing both her knees, how she had taken hold of Uncle Kristen's arm and whimpered as the tears glinted in her bright, kindly eyes, and how the dark blood had trickled from beneath the grazed skin. I had wanted to gather her into my arms and comfort her, but I barely reached up to her shoulders. We had been on our way down for a swim. Mother was happy and Dad and Uncle Kristen were walking along chatting and I ached out of sympathy for my lovely blonde Marie and her cut and bruised knees, and was convinced that my devotion was easily on a par with any other passion imaginable. In her, I had fallen in love with everything that was happy, bright, light and cheerful. In Aunt Linn's case, it was everything that was dark, flowing, mysterious, with somehow an undertone of sorrow, which fascinated me. This was how my sensitivities underlined the differences between them, just as the vain charm of being in love found a link between young girls, older women, young and old, fire and water, hopes and disappointments: I was just such a link myself.

At long last there he was, with two cans and a mug of cream.

'Here you are,' said Aunt Linn, pouring a liberal helping of thick yellow cream on to the stewed plums. 'Help yourself to sugar, if you want some.'

I ate the stewed plums watching Uncle Kristen, who placed a can of milk in the fridge, leaving the other on the kitchen worktop.

'Have you heard that Peter wants to live up in the hut?' he said, almost cheerfully.

'What, are you sure, Peter?' she asked, almost horrified. 'I've made up the bed for you in the east-facing room as usual.'

But I'd set my heart on it.

'Oh well, I don't suppose there's any harm in it,' she relented. 'You're so grown-up now. It's only reasonable to want to be on your own.'

So that was that.

'It's high time she came to collect her milk,' said Uncle Kristen, addressing no one in particular, almost as though talking to the extra can of milk that sat there on the kitchen worktop.

'Oh, *she'll* come when it suits her, I expect. . . .'

I sat up. What was this? Who was coming here to fetch milk?

'It might be quite hard for her to get away,' he said, still as though addressing no one in particular, almost casually. 'After all, there has to be somebody there to look after the baby. She obviously can't drag the baby with her over the heath . . .'

'Well, as you make your bed, so must you lie on it.'

It sounded so hard and callous, so unlike Aunt Linn.

'Let the one who is without sin cast the first stone.' Uncle Kristen was standing by the kitchen worktop close to the can containing the milk, which had suddenly assumed such significance. 'After all, we don't really know what the poor lass has been through.'

'Not as though *that* was so hard to imagine. . . .'

I'd finished my plums, polished the bowl clean, not a trace remaining: No thanks. I couldn't possibly eat any more. It had been so good, but I was full now.

'Perhaps we ought to take a stroll up to the hut while it's still light and check that all's shipshape,' said Uncle Kristen, seemingly relieved at the thought of being outside again.

'Now, Peter, are you really sure you want to sleep in that tumbledown old shack?' Aunt Linn was holding us back. 'I've made the bed up in the east-facing room, you know. It's much cosier there.'

She was offering me her care and attention, and even if at that moment I would dearly have loved to give in to her, precisely because of this it was doubly important for me to stand by my decision to try my hand at a much lonelier, more uncertain and much less comfortable existence up in the hut; it was so much more 'grown-up' to take decisions like this, so virile to opt for self-denial rather than comfort.

'No, thanks all the same, but. . . .'

But my voice was not to be relied upon and was incapable of injecting any heroism into the proud refusal. I stood up.

'My goodness, how he's grown!' She wasn't going to let go of me, but insisted on chatting, holding me back in the warm kitchen. 'He'll soon be as tall as you, Kristen. My goodness, you were only a kid last time you were at Fagerlund.'

I blushed with pride, at the same time horribly embarrassed. Embarrassment is only a form of anger at the age of fifteen, I knew that, for I was furious with everything and everybody the whole day, was wronged, humiliated by the tiniest, most ridiculous things, the end result being merely that I gave in, retreated into my shell, overcome with self-reproach, wishing I was miles away.

'How old are you now, Peter? Fifteen?'

'Nearly sixteen,' I corrected.

'Oh yes, that's right. Your birthday's in August. We'll have to have a party like last time.'

They had organized a party for me with a chocolate cake with candles on it and pop to drink. The people from the neighbouring farm had been invited in for coffee. Marie had served us as we sat round the dining-room table. Afterwards, we had all gone out into the garden to stretch our legs, to talk or to smoke, taking advantage of the summer weather. The gentle breeze had carried our words, dispersing them in all directions so that they became unrecognizable and everyone stood there like strangers. Jo, the son of the neighbouring farmer, and I had played at cops and robbers in the barn and I had given him the slip and taken refuge in the kitchen with Marie, where there was still a piece of birthday cake left (intended for me the following day), which I managed to wheedle out of her, demanding and touchy as I was that day.

But what kind of party could we have this year without Marie in her white apron, without the disarming childishness that would permit one to beg for a piece of birthday cake decorated with str wberries in the kitchen? I suddenly longed for that distant summer, when the revealing skin around the mouth and the base of the nose was unblemished, innocent, not yet ravaged by the glandular secretions of puberty, when short trousers were the order of the day in summer and there was no need for any complexes about long, thin thighs and knobbly knees.

'Perhaps I could take the milk up,' said Uncle Kristen, as though he'd been thinking of something else and had suddenly made up his mind. 'If she's on her way down, we'll meet on the path, and if we don't, it's only a stone's throw anyway . . .'

'Yes, that's right. Why don't you start running errands up to Weasel Cottage as well!'

It sounded so sharp and bitter coming from Aunt Linn. Once more, my curiosity was aroused about this business with the milk. What was it about this woman the milk was for which upset Aunt Linn so?

'Oh, don't talk like one of those gossips down in the village.' He sounded sharp too. I couldn't recall hearing him speak like this to her before. Yet he looked helpless and somehow 'older' as she stood there upbraiding him. 'Things are surely hard enough for her as it is, so I don't see why we shouldn't give her a hand. . . .'

Then he simply picked up the milk can and went out. I followed him, not daring to look at her now. Blindly, I picked up the suitcase which stood in the hall. He had taken the heavy rucksack and slung it over his shoulder and was standing there waiting for me. Then we set off together across the farmyard, down to the gate.

Evening was drawing in, yet the light seemed reluctant to be pushed back into the shadows here between the buildings, away from the meadow, the fields which shimmered in the pale reflection of the daylight. It was mid-June; the days, now at their longest, lay merely slumbering, breathing out the smoky dew through the short nights. I had dreamed about such nights as these.

He pushed the gate aside, stepped through and I followed, pausing to put down my suitcase and close the gate. He had stopped, turned round and was waiting for me.

'So who's living up at Weasel Cottage now?'

It was a risky question, but I had to find out sooner or later and I might as well take the bull by the horns and act like a grown man entitled to know things like this. I'd nothing to lose anyway. The idyll of two years before had been seen through for what it was and then dashed to smithereens.

'Oh, just a girl with a little baby. We don't actually know her. She just turned up one day asking if we could sell her some milk. . . .'

Then he seemed reluctant to say anything more. The milk can hung from his hand. It suddenly struck me again how young he seemed out here, almost boyish. It must have been the twilight that effaced the weather-beaten aspect of his features, the deep furrows running from his nose to the corners of his mouth, yet his body also seemed lighter, his movements freer and his voice was bright and carefree, without a trace of the irritation and resignation I'd heard in the kitchen a few moments before.

'Anyway, she seemed very nice, said her name was Cathrine Stang. She's related to the Weasel family. . . .'

Weasel was a wealthy businessman who had been in the habit of spending his summer holidays in the cottage he had built up on the hill which marked the boundary of Uncle Kristen's land. I could recall paying a visit there with Dad. We were given hard little biscuits and rather sour juice. Mrs Weasel was tall and severe-looking, whereas Mr Weasel himself was portly and red-faced in his summer hat and braces. The smell of his cigar smoke had wafted over the veranda.

It was rather dark here between the trees. I let him go first and pick his way along the narrow path. It was clearly visible between the heather and the mossy outcrops of rock, the bushes, the dwarf birches, but you could never tell. The thought of Marie suddenly hit me forcefully. She had run off into the forest. But why? What had forced her to do a thing like that? I shivered. I'd never been especially courageous about the dark.

Then there we were in front of the hut. The sky stretched pale and luminous above us, framing the sharp silhouettes of the trees with mother-of-pearl. He pushed the heavy key into the lock.

'Let's see if it's habitable here, then.'

He pushed the low door open and went in ahead of me. He put down the shiny milk can on the threshold. Inside, he struck a match and lit the paraffin lamp.

'Well, at least there's a mattress,' he said.

Yet I saw a good many other things besides: a stool and a low table under the window, an enamel wash-stand, the primitive brick fireplace standing in the middle of the end wall, a little corner cupboard, a kitchen working surface on which stood two or three empty bottles, a dented coffee kettle and a jam jar. There was all I needed here. On a hook by the door hung a cardigan and an old oilskin cape. On a nail above the bunk-bed hung a coloured picture of a South Sea island, apparently torn out of a calendar, and above this, from the same nail, hung a kind of ribbon, a coloured ribbon, perhaps woven, which I had only just time to see was a hair ribbon before Uncle Kristen's large hand shot out and whipped it from the nail, unceremoniously cramming it into his trouser pocket. It all happened so fast that it was almost as though the ribbon had never hung there at all.

'Tomorrow Linn'll come and make up the bed for you,' he said with absolute composure, as though nothing had happened.

'But I've got a sleeping-bag,' I said, making a feeble protest. I'd toyed with the idea of sampling the outdoor life to the full, even though the sleeping-bag had strictly speaking been brought along only to sleep in on fishing trips, or as something to lie on in case I wanted to sunbathe.

'It's much better to sleep in a proper bed,' said Uncle Kristen, thus deciding the matter.

I sat down on the mattress, suddenly realizing how tired I

was. He stood there scrutinizing the room. Then he said cheerily: 'Well, Peter, at least you'll be completely on your own here. You can have as many dates as you like up here. Ha ha ha. . . .'

He was trying to strike a carefree, matey tone. He remained there, standing with his hand in his pocket, attempting to conceal this strange ribbon from me, yet at the same time wanting to win my confidence, to be my friend, to put us on equal terms by making dubious allusions. But why? Was it because he had suddenly become so 'young', so boyish in the twilight on the way here? I had a horror of grown-ups talking down and making themselves 'young' to get something out of youngsters. Why did he need my friendship anyway? I felt so embarrassed, hurt and humiliated by the way he was playing his cards that I was incapable of replying. All I could do was mumble 'Yes, I guess so. . . .'

And he must have understood that he'd offended me, because he said merely: 'Well, anyway, you know you can come down and live with us if it gets too lonely up here.'

'No, no,' I answered quickly, as if to wave aside any such thought. 'It's fine up here.'

'I'd better be on my way, then,' he said and went towards the door, opened it and stepped out on to the threshold. ''Night then, see you tomorrow.'

''Night,' I said.

He was still hesitating a little, standing there with the milk can in one hand, impatient to be on his way, but with something else on his mind.

'I say, Peter. Did Linn say anything to you about . . . Marie?'

I was on my guard.

'No, nothing special. She said she'd been a bit depressed and that you'd dragged the likely places and combed the whole neighbourhood. That's all.'

'Oh, I see.' He seemed quite satisfied with my answer. 'The point is, Peter, that accidents like this set tongues wagging over the whole neighbourhood, and I know she takes it to heart. That's why I asked.'

Then he said good-night and made off. He had left the low door ajar. Night insects swarmed about the hot glass of the lantern. Through the open door I could see his long back gradually disappearing from view down the path, and finally there was only a faint movement floating in the soft shadows: my uncle had changed into a wood-sprite, floating on his way to a secret meeting with a wood-nymph, the girl who lived all alone in a cottage across the heath, the one who made his voice so cheery, his step so jaunty and quick and his movements so carefree and youthful. . . .

Hypnotized, night insects flew senselessly into the lantern, dropping on the table, where they lay in their death throes with torn, trembling wings. I closed the door, feeling worn out, longing for nothing but bed, to give myself up to the darkness and the whims of sleep, the turmoil of dreams. I unrolled the sleeping-bag on the bunk, undressed, blew out the lantern and slid down into the cool cocoon. I'd thought I might masturbate, make peace with everyone, rid myself of the seamy suspicions about the people I held in esteem and who were fond of me, Aunt Linn and Uncle Kristen, Mother and Dad back in town, to put an end to ceaseless imagining and conjecturing, which merely reflected my own over-sensual relation to all the things and people in my vicinity. Yet I dozed off as I was struggling to get going, dozed off as I lay there, picturing how good it would be to meet them tomorrow without any misgivings, all speculation and all seamy suspicions simply left behind in the hut, crumpled up under the bunk in a handkerchief of shame.

3

'Peter!'

Somebody was calling my name.

'Peter!'

I woke up, or was at least awake enough to realize that it must be quite early. I opened my eyes and took in the dawn light of gentle pink wintry hues, the sheets of dusty cobwebs hanging down from the beams, and became aware of a faint smell of tar in the little hut.

'Peter!'

It was coming from some distance away, perhaps from the farm; not loud, but it carried quite clearly through the stillness, loud enough to cut through the veils of sleep. I had slept fitfully and woken up many times that first night – but who could it be?

'Peter!'

A little louder, a little more insistent, yet still I couldn't recognize the voice, couldn't fathom who it could be standing there calling my name at the crack of dawn, the first morning of my new life in the hut all on my own. . . . Then, tearing away the last cobwebs of sleep, I jumped up, threw on my clothes and ran out.

Jo was standing by the gate, Jo Bergshagen from the neighbouring farm, my pal from two summers before, from all the summers I had spent at Fagerlund. He was eighteen months younger than me, and when I'd been here last, we'd been the same height. Now I'd left him behind, that was clear, even from some way off. He was standing with his back to me, hands thrust in his trouser pockets, staring up at the house, now and then shifting his weight from one foot to the other, and was on the point of calling out again.

'Hi there, Jo!' I said.

He hadn't expected me to appear from the direction of the forest. That gave me an advantage. There had always been friendly rivalry between Jo and me. He was stronger and, besides, his had been half an inch longer than mine when we'd measured them once, though the fact that I was the elder and, what's more, came from the city, where you could go to the pictures every evening, two or three times if you wanted to, had nevertheless tipped the hairline balance of authority slightly in my favour.

'Hello,' I called out again, coming up to him.

He had turned round, caught off his guard, awkward and embarrassed. He looked at me with flint-blue eyes, half smiling, almost provocative.

'Hello.'

I was a clear half-head taller than him. That would probably not go down too well. He had short-cropped, sandy-coloured hair, which tumbled in a childish lock over his brow just as it always had, and his short, broad nose was peppered with freckles. He hadn't grown, hadn't altered in the slightest, even though he had been confirmed that spring. He had broadened out a little perhaps, but this merely emphasized a certain chubby 'childish' quality he had not got rid of. When he smiled, his teeth were small and yellow. His hands were square and tough, as always embellished with cuts and scratches and reminding me of many a defeat in Indian wrestling, finger-wrestling and other trials of strength, hands that had often alarmed me by their ruthlessness: I had watched them crush field-mice, throw stones at thrushes' nests with deadly accuracy and impale ladybirds on a needle. . . . In things of this kind I was always inferior. But when it came to playing cowboys and Indians, I was top dog. I could creep forward from tree-trunk to tree-trunk, could lie stock still in the tall grass one excruciating minute after another as he went round looking for me: my ingeniousness always got the better of his energetic but far from silent determination.

Jo was my summer friend. Our friendship was something quite special, inconstant, as capricious as the sun and the rain, but more intense, more volatile than the humdrum relationships with schoolmates throughout the year, where the monotony of the surroundings and of the daily grind dictated a similar monotony in our behaviour to each other. We had rashly bared our hearts to one another, told each other barefaced lies, swanked, exaggerated, sought above all to impress, trawled our daily existence for any mystery, any drama, squabbled, almost coming to blows when we went too far and had to defend our fantasy life against the other's scepticism and blatant one-upmanship. Yet one could never sulk for long when it was the summer holidays, with the sun shining and the grass waist-high, and the barn steeped in cool shade, full of dark hiding-places, forgotten corners where people rarely set foot, places secret enough to conjure up the most intimate thoughts, outrageous acts, indeed even to tempt forth the darkest deeds, but for the light seeping in through the cracks in the shrunken, sun-scorched planks, casting shafts of light on to our dark intentions, piercing the shameful inclination it was so tempting to surrender to. For it was here that a decisive trial of strength had taken place, here that our manhood had been quantitatively measured with Uncle Kristen's folding ruler. As it happened, I had suspected Jo of cheating a bit that time. His foreskin was more pliable than mine, he could stretch his modest pride a good bit, much more than I could mine, and he probably had done that time behind the empty grain containers in the half-light, before concluding that his was all of three and a quarter inches in length.

I had a great deal of respect for Jo. He chewed 'baccy' whenever he managed to steal a bit from his father, he could eat nettles, and never cleaned his teeth. He was the more active and, in his way, the inventive one. He had insisted on our signing a pact of friendship in blood. He had read about blood sacrifices and had dreamed up the method even before I'd given my guarded consent. He knew that there was a thrush's nest with nestlings, four of them, two each. They were to be executed on the White Stone. This stone, the height of a man, was completely white, and Uncle Kristen said it had been dragged there during the Ice Age and left behind on the pasture. For centuries it had been a landmark for people moving to and from the mountain farms. Now it was a totem for Jo and me. On one side it was polished quite smooth and even, and it was against this side that the blood sacrifice was to be made. The warm, downy fledglings weighed next to nothing in my hand. The victims were to be thrown from a predetermined distance: first he would throw, then I would, then him again, then me. The aim was to hit the same spot and then write our initials in blood. The poor wretches shot through the air, hit the stone, bouncing off as though weightless on to the mossy ground. If the faintest flicker of life still stirred in any of them, the ceremony was repeated. Then J and P were ceremoniously inscribed on the marble for all time. No doubt it could still be seen, and even now I experienced a stab of shame at the thought of a certain thrush's nest, torn asunder, a tormented ball of down and feathers, a gaping yellow beak and the white, almost transparent film where long ago, two summers before, a black, shiny, fearful eye had blinked. Before I knew anything much about good and evil, right and wrong, in the world of adults.

'I heard you'd got here,' he said.

Everywhere around us the thrushes sang in the tree-tops, from thickets and bushes. It must still have been early, as drops of dew dripped from low branches, the cool air between the tree-trunks seeping out into the sunlight. A shiver ran through me. I was still half asleep.

'Yes, I got here yesterday,' I said in a high-pitched voice. 'Quite late. I'm living up in the hut,' I added, to explain the direction I'd come from.

He'd taken one of his hands out of his trouser pocket, looking just the same as ever with his shock of sandy hair and his freckles. (As for me, I'd secretly begun to plaster my hair back with water.) He had on a check summer shirt, short trousers and wellingtons wet from the cold dew. Rather than my superior height, it was his bare knees that emphasized the advantage I had over him now.

'You're living up in the hut? By yourself?' He looked straight at me, almost smiling, but embarrassed, would no doubt sooner have challenged me to a wrestling-match. His eyes were light blue and glinted beneath fair eyebrows. 'You mean you're living up there *on your tod?*'

'Yes, I am . . .'

'For the whole summer?'

There was no doubt that he was impressed and a bit envious

as well. I could hear it.

'Sure. As long as I want to.'

'Bugger me!' he said. This was Jo's strongest form of acknowledgement.

We were standing face to face, stiff and awkward, he with his right hand in his pocket and I with my eyes drawn involuntarily towards his bare knees and my own trendy trainers and Wranglers creased from the suitcase. I had always assumed people wore long trousers after they'd been confirmed. That's what Dad had told me. It was almost pathetic to see my summer friend still dressed in this ridiculously childish way.

'You must be at grammar school now, then?'

That was another thing. He was probably still stuck at the comprehensive school.

'Yes, I've just finished my first year.'

'Bags of nice lasses there, eh?'

'You bet. . . .' I had to lay it on a bit, because the fact was that the girls in my form had been a let-down, so few, only about seven or eight, and far from as pretty or approachable as I'd imagined they would be. You couldn't count the older girls in the class above; they seemed grown-up and quite intimidating, most of them.

Jo smiled archly, as though he had some surprises up his sleeve, giving him the confidence to challenge my superiority.

'Have you seen *Roman Women*?'

I'd almost forgotten that he was mad keen on films, that I had spent hours two summers before retelling the plots of films I'd seen during the year. I thought back, but couldn't recall having seen a film about Roman women.

'They let me in and it was an X film!'

Cinema had been introduced to the local community together with the new community centre. Every Wednesday, Saturday and Sunday there was a film show in the assembly hall.

'We saw one of them's tits. They were massive, I can tell you!'

He was smirking, as though he'd noticed that he'd struck one of my weak points, even though nothing to my knowledge could have enabled him to guess this. Two summers before, he'd told me once that he had peeped at Gerd, his older sister, as she was having a bath, and had afterwards described the revelation in full detail and wanted to drag me along as well the next time an opportunity presented itself. This suggestion gave him a hold over me, because even though I said yes – and couldn't do otherwise, since cowardice was the greatest, most inconceivable sin – I could in no way match him as regards malicious cunning. Anyway, it was his idea and his sister. Apart from this, the whole thing was horribly embarrassing to me because he'd once said that Gerd had 'taken a shine' to me – how this had happened was a mystery, for I'd barely spoken to her, didn't even like her, but had noticed her *looking* at me, and realized that there might be something in it. And that made this escapade doubly embarrassing for me.

I was hiding behind the wash-house. He'd taken the bolt off the little window, so it should present no problems. I had nodded my agreement to the dirty little plot. I didn't have a sister, so couldn't comprehend how he could be so unfeeling towards his. Yet it was precisely this which confirmed his superiority. He had crept forward first, now he was waving me on, but I stayed where I was behind the corner of the wash-house, eyes tightly closed with a sinking feeling in the pit of my stomach, for I didn't feel particularly tempted by the idea of spying through the little window on Jo's sister, thickset, freckled, plain and sullen as she was, while at the same time I was almost obsessed by the thought that this was my big chance. I despaired under the weight of my own indecision.

'She's got her back to us!' Jo's whispered words sounded like thunder in my ears. He'd come to fetch me. 'She's bound to turn round in a minute! Get a move on!'

I didn't know what to say, just hissed in desperation: 'Shh! Get down. I heard somebody coming!'

The agitation inside me lent conviction to my white lie. He did as I said, and at that moment my prayers were answered by someone slamming the farmhouse door and by the sound of voices over the yard.

'Bugger me,' whispered Jo. 'That was a close shave!'

He was clutching his last surprise, his trump card, in his trouser pocket, cocksure, bursting to reveal it and making me both curious and uneasy, for I knew it could be absolutely anything, some false teeth, a mouse, a 'head-hunter's necklace' fashioned from his own milk teeth, nothing was too grisly to be excluded by Jo's passion for collecting.

In the end I had to ask: 'What's that you've got there?'

He looked at me and grinned, as though he might just try to jump me and wrestle me down, to prove that he was still the stronger, at least when he had me in that hold, but my Wranglers and his bare knees made it harder to break the ice.

'Go on, guess.'

'No, tell me!'

He withdrew his hand from his pocket and thrust his fist almost threateningly towards me. 'A rubber johnny! Never been used either,' he added in his clear, childish voice and in deadly earnest.

He unclenched his fist and held out the little pink thing wrapped in a pastel-coloured envelope towards me. I stared at it, caught off guard, slightly alarmed, for, shame to say, it was the first time I'd seen one at close quarters. I wanted to touch it and have a closer look, but my hand clutched at emptiness; he'd tricked me, the coveted object was already back in his pocket.

'I bet you've got through lots of these at the grammar school, eh?' he shouted, at the same time leaping at me, giving me a hard shove in the chest with both hands so that I fell backwards, grabbing hold of his shirt and pulling him with me. 'They know a thing or two about these, those grammar-school lasses, you can bet your arse on it!' he said.

We tumbled over each other on the damp heather. He took advantage of my unpreparedness, gained the upper hand. I fought like mad. A twig was sticking into my neck. Jo's laughter rang out loud and shrill, just as in earlier years when our strengths had been put to the test and he saw he was getting the upper hand.

'Or happen you like it better "bare-headed"?'

He was wild as he lay there pinning me down to the ground, yet there was something exaggerated, something forced in his laughter, for he no doubt sensed just as clearly as I did that the topic for this summer had now been decided, that fighting, cowboys and Indians and raiding nests were a thing of the past, that it was uncharted territory which lay before us, an area fraught with danger for inexperienced boys.

He had manoeuvred himself into a position astride me and sat with his knees planted heavily against my arms, sneering at me. I was helpless. I groaned: 'What are you going to use it for then, Jo? It's a few sizes too big yet, isn't it?'

'Bloody hell!'

He let go and took to his heels, with me after him. He was if anything a bit heavier and clumsier than me; I had long legs but tired quickly and couldn't catch up with him. We panted uphill along the path over the heath, the sound of his heavy wellingtons thudding through the hammering in my ears. My head swam, my body trembled and I felt that I'd have to throw in the sponge.

'Jo, hey, hold on!'

He ran on a further ten to fifteen yards, then stopped, turned and spat: 'Truce?'

If I agreed, it meant that he had won the first round. But I was all in. Answering as though I couldn't care less: 'OK, truce.'

'Sure? Cross your heart?'

'Cross my heart.'

We walked on up the hill side by side, in my case feeling somewhat humiliated at having made such a poor showing, despite my advantages. Yet I knew that he set less store by physical superiority than I did; for him, grammar school, several cinema performances a day, the chance to buy hot dogs, ice-cream, chocolate and liquorice at kiosks whenever you liked, counted much more. He had an insatiable appetite for news of life in the city, where he had been once, years before, to have his appendix out.

'I suppose it's a bit gloomy at Fagerlund now that Marie's gone, isn't it?'

I flinched, disliking his question. I didn't like him making a connection between Marie and what we had just been so engrossed in discussing. All the same, it provided an opportunity to find out a bit more about what had actually happened.

'Hey, I say, why do you think she did a bunk?'

In for a penny, in for a pound. Maybe he did know something, and whatever it was would no doubt come out sooner or later anyway.

'Oh, I expect she had a bun in the oven,' he answered casually. 'It's dead common round here.'

Cocky. Smug. I couldn't believe it, couldn't believe that he could spread such a story about my Marie. I fell silent, felt hurt, irritated. I couldn't find anything to say in reply. And he clearly knew that he had something over me again.

'Don't tell me you didn't know she was anybody's?'

'Oh, put a sock in it!' I glowered at him. I knew he had a filthy mind, but this was way over the top.

'Oh, for goodness' sake,' he said, condescendingly, not yielding an inch. 'Everybody knew that. She was going with several people up here – I've heard them talking about it with my own ears. Old Aage Brenden for one took her with him to Moen on his motor bike several times, and he wasn't the only one, I can tell you! There were many candles on that cake, I'll say. . . .'

Neither of us could help smiling a bit at this. But still, I was shocked and alarmed. I couldn't let these cheeky pre-adolescent remarks of his pass.

'What a load of bloody cobblers!'

'You think so? Happen you'd taken a shine to her yourself, then?'

'Bollocks!'

'Are you calling me a liar?'

'Yes, I am.'

He realized that I wouldn't let myself be goaded any further, but couldn't let his ammo go to waste.

'But there's a new one now . . .'

'What?' I hadn't been listening.

'Didn't you know there's a townie lass living up at Weasel Cottage? She's got a little nipper as well. It's a bastard. She'll be living there the whole summer like enough.'

'Oh?'

I hoped he'd go on. Most likely he'd have other interesting things to say about Cathrine Stang, if I knew him.

'It'd probably be worthwhile having a go there . . .'

'Reckon so?'

'Yes, when she has a nipper and she's not married, course it would!' He glanced at me knowingly, to see whether I'd grasped the significance of this important detail. 'Then they know what it's all about . . .'

I nodded, half letting myself be drawn into the role of would-be suitor. We walked along the narrow path side by side, bending branches back and releasing them so they whistled behind us.

'But she's not up to much,' said Jo, spitting. 'Too thin, and with that long dark hair of hers. . . .'

He seemed to like her a bit all the same, despite the fact that he was only thirteen and accustomed to the sight of his chubby ash-blonde sister Gerd. He'd not have bothered to stress his dislikes otherwise.

'Have you spoken to her?'

'Er, yes. . . .' He hesitated. 'She's been to the farm a few times to fetch milk. And Gerd's baby-sat for her a few times. . . . But she's not much to look at, that slag. . . . Pity for you though, all the same, you could have tried your luck there – she'll open her legs for grammar-school boys, sure as eggs.'

'But if she's not much to look at anyway,' I said, thereby saving both him and me from further embarrassing speculations on this topic, where ignorance was so fatal.

'Hell's teeth, no,' he said, spitting.

We had reached a place where the path forked. To the left, it descended towards Bergshagen, to the right it went up towards Weasel Cottage. Neither of us hesitated for long, faced with a choice like this.

'Hey, why don't you come home with me, so we can go in the barn?' said Jo casually. 'Dad's in the forest.'

'Sure, great.'

The barn at Bergshagen was even bigger than the one at Fagerlund, but Jo's father was strict and didn't allow us to play there.

We turned off to the left. We both felt as though we could breathe more easily on this safe, familiar old walk down to Bergshagen. It was a comfortable stroll down the gentle slope. We were relieved, in a good mood, as though we had just escaped something menacing, dangerous even. What business would we have had at Weasel Cottage anyway?

'I've got two magazines,' he said all of a sudden. He no

doubt meant girlie magazines, so-called 'art magazines' which he had bought from older boys when they'd finished with them. 'You can have one of them if you like, I mean, if you haven't already seen it.'

Of course I'd described the news-stands weighed down with the most tantalizing nude photos. But what was the reason behind this generosity? It wasn't like Jo to give something away with no suggestion of anything in return. He'd sworn he was ready to die for our blood brotherhood, but that was another story. And so had I, for that matter.

The cool morning mist had dispersed and the sun was hot even here between the trees. My feet needed no guiding on the path which was full of tufts of grass, roots, bumps, these feet which as recently as the previous evening had felt uncertain in unknown territory, accustomed as they were to tarmac, straight streets, symmetrical pavements.

'Are you going to the summer fête?' asked Jo out of the blue, scrutinizing me.

'Maybe. Yes, I think so,' I said, hesitating only when I remembered Uncle Kristen's strange resigned comment in the truck the day before. Yes, I wanted to go; I wanted to retrace my steps and find the summer again, a summer which was steadily slipping from my grasp.

'You can have *both* magazines,' he said, 'if you'll do something for me.'

He had something unpleasant on his chest now, I could sense it.

'All right.'

At least this gave me the upper hand.

'I . . . er, wondered whether there was any chance. . . . Whether you could teach me to waltz?'

'To *waltz*?'

'Yes, just for daft.' He hurried to cover himself. 'I've got a gramophone and some records . . .'

'Sure, yes. . . . Course I can.'

'Thanks a bundle.'

He was clearly relieved. He prodded me in the back. 'I say, do you know what they call her?'

'Who?'

'That slag up at Weasel Cottage.'

As though I hadn't guessed.

'Cathrine Stang. Cathrine with a "c". Can you credit it? But you like swanky lasses with long black hair, don't you?'

He prodded me in the back again and ran off down the path, with me behind, feeling superior: now it was I who had the upper hand.

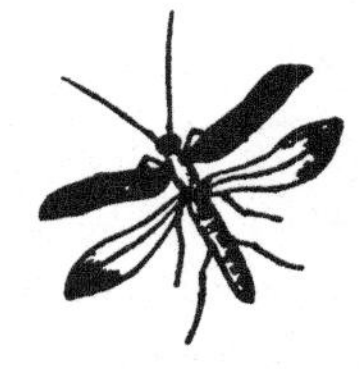

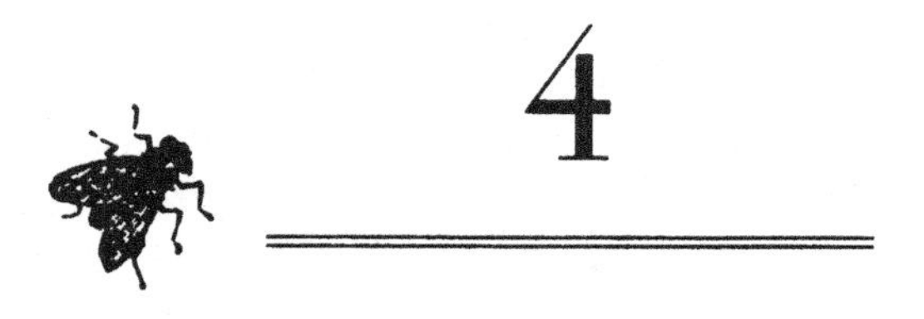

4

'This is how you do it,' I said. 'First, right foot forward, then swing your left foot out to the left, bring your right foot together with it. Pause. Then left foot forward, swing your right foot to the right and bring your left foot together with it. Pause. One-two-three, one-two-three. Zigzag forwards.'

'OK, hang on a tick, let me try,' said Jo impatiently.

I had wanted to demonstrate it, to give him some idea of the steps, now he was impatient to have a go, to get it learnt, to get this embarrassing episode over and done with.

We stood there in the middle of the hayloft. The portable gramophone glinted in a corner. The waltz record lay on the turntable, ready. But first some instruction on the steps: one-two-three. One-two-three. I called out, full of bossy authority. He moved across the plank floor as though on skates, over-eager, too forceful to realize that a dance was something for two people, a game of precision played between you, your partner and the music on the basis of practised movements in time with the rhythm. But that wasn't all there was to it. One of the girls in the advanced group had suddenly stood there before me at the dancing school ball the year before as a result of the complicated partner-changing routines. We had danced a tango and I had felt a hint of her thigh against my trousers. Her hand held mine tight and warm. For a moment it was as though we were melting into the lilting music and flowing along with it. She was flushed in the cheeks and wet-lipped and as tall as me. I had lost sight of her afterwards in the crush for soft drinks, was scared stiff, relieved, as I had no idea what on earth to say to her. But that night I lay awake mulling it all over, experiencing it all again, all the whirling in my body, just as I had experienced it with her, conjuring up the tango melody in my head over and over again. And the following autumn, I had found a pretext for not starting lessons at Mrs Wangen's dancing school again. I didn't want to be moved up to the advanced group.

I was thirteen then, the same age as my desperately eager pupil was now. It wasn't very long since. Yet it seemed an eternity.

'You look as though you're pushing the plough!' I shouted. 'What do you think the girls are going to say when you shove them around like that?'

'I couldn't give a tinker's cuss what *they* say,' he snorted. He wouldn't brook any criticism from me, but in this area he had to acknowledge his limitations: either you could dance or you couldn't.

The bright light of day percolated in through openings high up in the walls and through cracks between the planks, yet there was a dim, protective immunity in the half-light here in the barn. We had reached the next stage in the lesson, the waltz record had been placed on the turntable and we were about to dance together. The opening notes of the 'Blue Danube' sounded shrill and tinny. We stood there facing one another in the subdued light of the barn, but couldn't get going properly. He was supposed to 'lead', as he was the one who was supposed to be learning, but I was so much taller than him and had never danced the 'girl' before. It all seemed so unnatural. He still had his wellingtons on. The 'Blue Danube' grated on. Then I took hold of his left hand with my right, slicing through the embarrassment; he placed his arm firmly round my waist and we started to dance, tight-lipped, as hostile as fighting cocks, counting the beat between clenched teeth.

He learned fast, as he was quick on the uptake and worked hard at it, wishing to keep his martyrdom as brief as possible. I had asked him why there was such a hurry, but he was reluctant to say. He thought it gave him that much more 'chance' with the girls on the dance floor. Nevertheless, I had my suspicions it was the summer fête he had in mind and perhaps in particular Miss Stang up at Weasel Cottage, of whom he was so contemptuous. Still, the sum total of what I had learned at the dancing school and which two years before had been completely pathetic, was now really in demand.

The 'Blue Danube' faded away in a hoarse rasp.

'Well, was it OK then?'

He was impatient to have done with our session, in which he was cast in such an inferior role.

'Yes, OK, but there's a lot more to it.'

He wasn't going to get off so lightly.

'A lot more?'

'Yes, now you have to learn how to turn.'

'Hell's bells!' Anger showed in his narrowed eyes. 'Do I have to?'

'Look, you can't waltz as though you were tramping along a furrow, for goodness' sake. Just watch. . . .'

I showed him. 'You swing round on your toes instead of moving straight ahead. Then bring your right foot out and together with your left one, like before. Now move your left foot *backwards* and round on your toes again. Get it?'

'Yes, yes. . . .'

But this took longer to learn. We tortured the 'Blue Danube' over and over again with blunt needles. We shuffled our wellingtons and trainers over the barn floor, counting the beat through clenched teeth as we panted with the effort, allowing the dancing positions to degenerate into a silent wrestling-match, as our feet struggled laboriously to keep to the graceful arcs of the waltz.

Eventually we were both so cheesed off with the whole thing that we ground to a halt. We'd achieved our aim – well, all but: Jo had more or less learned to waltz, though laboriously and clumsily, and would never be able to improve on it much. The podgy gawkiness of his little boy's body was totally bereft of elegance, lacking all form or proportion. Whereas in my own imaginings I had recently discovered a predilection for the slender, the esoteric, the flowing. I could sit for minutes at a time looking at my own fingers, in my mind's eye letting them loose on various kinds of instruments and becoming completely engrossed in their imagined mastery. Of all my limbs, it was my hands alone which were able to give me any feeling of being reasonably well proportioned, perhaps attractive and even handsome. Jo's clumsy body, his coarseness, even his intrepid, unrestrainable temperament, which had always impressed me before, now offended my newly discovered aesthetic criteria.

He packed up the gramophone, removed the rags we had considerately stuffed into the sound-box, so the noise wouldn't be noticed by other people (and especially his sister). Then the 'Blue Danube' was put back into its worn cover. I had climbed up on to one of the beams under the sloping roof and sat there looking down at him. It was so warm up here. You could almost hear the sun beating down on the roof a few inches above my head. There was a smell of dry wood, of dust, of hay from a tuft left behind in a nearby corner. The swallows were going busily about their tasks under the gable. I could hear insects, a wasp, two or three perhaps, buzzing round a wasps' nest somewhere out of sight. I had been stung the summer before last, when we had raided the wasps' nest under the storehouse floor. We had wanted to see what was inside. And even though my hand throbbed from the four stings I'd received, it was impossible not to admire this neat, symmetrical construction, even after we had exterminated all the inhabitants with DDT.

Everything alive in the barn reminded me of summers gone by. I felt my body return to that of an innocent child as I sat there on the beam, light-headed, hungry, suddenly remembering that I'd forgotten breakfast, as though in a trance, in which my senses were abnormally acute. Even my long, thin, Wrangler-clad thighs and legs could not quite bring me back to a definite, unmistakable here-and-now. All the many surprises and unanswered questions of the past twenty-four hours, Jo's nasty remarks about Marie and the well-nigh incomprehensible fact that we had just been dancing together here in the barn, was like a suggestion of an ache at the nape of my neck, like a slight itch under the foreskin, and if I'd had the chance to be alone for just five minutes, two or three practised hand movements would have been enough to bring me relief from this last remaining strand of unease, suspicion, reproach and doubt, the last precocious scruples, and enabled me to merge into a remembered, untarnished summer mood here in the dim light of the barn.

But here was Jo. He was walking across the barn floor towards me and was clearly up to something, as betrayed by his smile, which shone with such intimate and comradely malevolence, and his piercing blue eyes.

'Here comes the waltz champ!'

I was on my guard. I could sense that he'd figured out something which would give him the upper hand again after the ignominy of our dancing together.

'Shut it!'

He clambered up and sat beside me. His knees looked naked, young, almost indecently vulnerable sticking out next to my long legs concealed in corduroy, but his face was a picture of smugness as he asked: 'You know what?'

'No, what?'

'Well no, I'm not supposed to tell.'

'Come on, spit it out.'

'No.'

'Oh, come on, let's hear it. Who's it about?'

'Your uncle. . . .'

Uncle Kristen. What could Jo 'know' about Uncle Kristen? What could anybody 'know' about a man like him?

'What about him, then?'

'I had to promise not to tell, not to tell *anyone*.'

He had me hooked now and was enjoying it.

'I won't tell anyone else, cross my heart. Go on, tell me.'

'Only if I can have one of the magazines back.'

The payment for the dancing lesson.

'You can have both of them, just tell me what it is!'

He would have liked to draw the suspense out a bit longer, but was bursting to tell his sensational bit of news.

'He was having it off with Marie.'

That was too much. He saw I was cross, as he hastened to add: 'At least, that's what folk are saying . . .'

'What a load of utter crap!'

I was so cross that my voice slid into a falsetto.

'Everybody says so.'

'What a load of crap! Who's spreading these lies about people?'

'Lies? Who's lying?'

'You, for a start!'

'Oh, yes?'

'Yes, you!'

'Happen you'd like to know who I heard it from, then?'

'I couldn't care less what bloody gossips you listen to.'

'They were snogging away in the porch at my confirmation party. Both Gerd and Mother saw them, so there!'

'Silly bloody old biddies!'

'Is my mum a silly old biddy, then?'

'You bloody bet she is!'

'Oh yes . . .?'

Now he was cross too. We jumped down to the floor together, feeling the need for more room.

'Take back what you said about Uncle Kristen!'

'Pooh – everybody knows what *he* was up to . . .'

'Only bloody gossips like your mother!'

He glared at me, seething. 'Take back what you just said!'

'She's a bloody gossiping old bag!'

Whereupon he flew at me. I was weak at the knees with anger, but parried the attack with my outstretched hand. Without aiming at anything in particular, I hit him with my fist under the eye. He swung out a foot and caught me on the calf. Tears struggled with my intense anger, but I couldn't give up now. I gave him two clouts in the face and shoved him as hard as I could, so that he fell, tumbling backwards over the dusty barn floor. I saw a cut open up on his knee, saw the dark blood trickle slowly down the skin towards the top of his wellington. I turned on my heels and fled from the scene. Already I was sorry, hadn't been *so* cross with him after all, shouldn't have struck him in the face. I clenched my numb knuckles and fled, barely able to breathe, barely able to run properly because I was about to break down and blub. I got across the farmyard, up the slope, allowing my legs to carry me back home, swallowing back hoarse sobs. It was ridiculous, ridiculous that everything I fantasized about came true. Hadn't I been the suspicious one the evening before, pointing the finger at Uncle Kristen because he had acted strange and 'boyishly' up in the hut? Imagined all manner of complications just because of the tension between Aunt Linn and him, because of the milk can and because of Marie's disappearance which they could not talk about? And now – an affair between Uncle Kristen and Marie. His broad hand which had snatched the mysterious hair ribbon from the wall yesterday evening bore this out. Something about their behaviour was suspect. Something wasn't quite as it should have been. . . . And Marie, my Marie, with her thick golden plaits, had been mixed up with several, with a lot of men . . . the thought, however inconceivable it seemed, excited me beyond words.

My headlong flight had almost petered out. Even the woodland smells, the sounds, the pale shafts of warm sunshine that filtered down through the branches sparked off my lewd imaginings. Marie. . . . My Marie, whom I had had a crush on all these years without even realizing or acknowledging it, the gentle flame of a child's love that is akin to shyness, remoteness and indifference, until a wood-grouse is startled into flight and fear awakens hatred – and self-loathing. For nothing is more terrible than one's own depths. But now the dream had become flesh: Marie had had a whole host of lovers and Uncle Kristen might be one of them. The mere thought of it sent indescribable notions through my mind. . . . I sauntered away from the path into the shadows, where all of this overwhelmed me even more forcefully: I had to make amends for my fantasies, my shameless ideas, which made me an accomplice, indeed directly implicated me in their lewd deeds, but I knew of only one way of banishing infected 'adult' thoughts.

I knelt down on the soft carpet of moss beneath a tall spruce and carried out my act of self-aroused penance with my Wranglers round my knees, eyes tight shut, spilling out my pale sin on grass and plants, watching it drip from leaf to leaf in heavy drops until it soaked into the forest floor.

5 

At dusk, Aunt Linn invited us out into the garden. She had laid the round table there, put out waffles, jam and sour cream. It was really such a nice evening. It had been so warm, almost too warm all day, though it was perhaps unfair to complain now that summer was here at long last after such a late spring. The milking had been done, there was contentment in the sound of the cowbells from the pasture. A starling perched on its look-out post atop the aerial sang out over its territory. The last swallows swooped straight up into the white sky.

We sat round the circular garden table eating waffles, sour cream and strawberry jam, talking about the same things as we had talked about at dinner-time, more or less the same as we had talked about the evening before, the first evening. I thought that this was how it always was: you talked about the same things, like water emptied from jug to mug to cup, so there was less and less till in the end it had become only a lukewarm mouthful which one drank without actually being thirsty any more. But this meant that one came to master the things one talked about, and one could thus even slowly alter truth itself, because what was referred to as 'real' was not something fixed and static but depended on repetition, on a consensus about the way it was articulated, which in turn ensured the same consensus in thought. On the other hand, very little was needed to topple this construction, just a false note in the harmony, just a doubt as to whether the mechanics worked and were valid, was enough to call forth its justification. I sat thinking about the many layers of truth that lay beneath 'the truth'.

'Hasn't he grown! I've never seen anything like it. . . .'

We sat round the table eating waffles, sour cream, sweet red jam and talking. Peace and contentment. I had fastened my new sheath-knife to my belt, and, sitting there on the white garden bench, I felt the branches of a lilac tree tickling my neck as I watched the swallows disappearing like black specks into the vast whiteness. The coffee-cups clinked against the saucers, the teaspoons rattling as people stirred their coffee, their voices sounding light and lively, just as they ought to sound, the way I remembered them as an accompaniment to waffles, sour cream and strawberry jam, which were my absolute, all-time favourites.

'Yes, you'll soon be as tall as me, Peter. Just fancy, you're fifteen already and going to the grammar school. . . .' There was almost a note of longing in Uncle Kristen's voice. They sat side by side on the opposite bench. Man and wife. There was no sign of any tension now. She sat there, so at ease in her summer frock, dreamy, concealing her gaze in the shadows; he sat leaning earnestly towards me, elbows on the table, his shirt-sleeves rolled up and his collar button open, wanting me to say more about what it was like at grammar school. He was strong, vital, full of energy; she was formless, timeless, all at once. There was still no sign of disharmony between them.

'That's a lovely knife you've got there,' he said out of the blue. 'Did you buy it in town?'

'Dad gave me it,' I said proudly, withdrawing it from the sheath and handing it to him across the table. Boyishness radiated from me; I was innocence and naïvety itself this evening. He took hold of it, weighed it in his hand, measured it with his eyes, tested the blade approvingly.

'A very fine knife. Solingen steel. I almost thought they'd stopped making them now. Look – it's razor sharp. . . .'

He placed his bare forearm flat on the table and with the point of the knife quickly drew a line across the thin skin. When the sharp steel blade got down as far as the wrist, it paused momentarily, pressed harder and the blade pierced the skin, not very deep, but deep enough for blood to trickle out in a dark droplet.

Uncle Kristen laughed and held out his arm: 'Here, want a lick?'

Startled, I drew back into the lilac bush, not understanding what he meant, what he was driving at with this bizarre invitation, and was upset that he wanted to turn this surprisingly brutal action into something intimate, to try to get me to lick his skin. The very thought sent a shiver of disgust down my spine. But he was still laughing, his strong teeth flashing under a clear-blue gaze and a dark wave of hair flopping down askew over his forehead. Dad combed his hair straight back. Dad looked much older, though the age difference between them couldn't be more than seven or eight years. Dad's arms were soft and white, the few sparse hairs looking as though they'd been planted there. The sight of Uncle Kristen sitting there so virile, so wiry and boyish, wounded my pride.

'There's nothing to be afraid of,' he said, smiling. 'We used to do this as boys. Blood-brothers we called it, tasting each other's blood. It made us brothers like, only for fun though, you know. . . .'

But I was mesmerized by the shiny droplet on his skin. He was offering to make me his blood-brother. My own uncle, whom I'd known for as long as I could remember. Why wasn't our ordinary kinship enough for him? What extra closeness was he aiming at? What unconventional form of intimacy? I was on my guard: a grown man does not make suggestions like this to a fifteen-year-old. My fifteen-year-old's insane distrust saw straight through him. My aversion to all dissimulation, all hypocrisy on the part of grown-ups, was fanatical.

'Well, how about it?'

The arm still lay there with the droplet of blood glistening on the skin. The repugnance I felt was intense, yet at the same time I was warm, excited, flattered almost by this strange gesture which actually made him so vulnerable, laid him open to my fifteen-year-old's contempt, invited my supercilious rejection. Why was he, a grown man with large, sure hands, strong arms and a calm gaze, play-acting like this for me? What was he hoping to achieve from a spotty (two or three big new ones had come out during the night; I kept a careful watch on them) and confused adolescent? I was only too cruelly aware of my handicaps and could not forgive anyone for failing to respect my feeling of isolation, for seeking to treat me like a normal naturally endowed person, and thereby robbing me of the tiny spark of individuality I was at such pains to create.

The evening drew in with its verdant reveries. The mosquitoes danced. Large, graceful mosquitoes, like the finest threads held together in the middle by a delicate knot of a body, hung suspended over the table-cloth in a dance, hovered over Uncle Kristen's naked forearm with its drop of blood.

'Come on then, Peter lad,' he coaxed. 'Happen you're not used to the likes of this in the town. It's man's stuff, you know.'

He laughed. He was in a good mood. He persisted, his white teeth, the whites of his eyes shining in the twilight. I was so weak. My will flitted hither and thither between us like the mosquitoes dancing above the table, attracted by the warm arm, the blood, contact with his naked skin, with this human being, and at the same time I was scared to death, scared of being caught, squashed. . . . I shivered, even though it wasn't cold at all. The warm dusk, which had brought out the mosquitoes from the foliage, from the grass and set them dancing, also enticed me to give in, to seize his hand and do as he wished, degrade both of us, but Aunt Linn intervened and saved me.

'Don't keep on like that, Kristen. Surely you can see Peter doesn't want to!'

He was still smiling but no longer as sure of himself. Finally, he withdrew his arm, embellishing his retreat with fancy knife tricks, making the steel suddenly appear like lightning between his fingers, getting the knife to spring up and make loop after loop in the air before landing point first in the grass beside his shoe.

'Women don't like the sight of blood, you see, Peter. It makes them feel faint, you know, weak at the knees. . . . But you'll find that out soon enough.' He was still trying to be matey, dynamic, assertive. 'Isn't that right, Linn?' He turned suddenly towards Aunt Linn, who sat there as though in a shadow, almost motionless and barely speaking. 'D'you remember how well you looked after me that time I hacked myself with the axe?'

'For goodness' sake, Kristen,' she said, embarrassed, but with a smile in her voice. 'Don't let's talk about that, it's a thing of the past. . . .'

A spider came abseiling down an invisible thread and landed on his white shirt-sleeve, scurried immediately from the sleeve down on to the cloth, continued to the edge of the table and launched itself down into the shadows. Of course I knew the story of the accident he'd had in the woods, when he'd hacked himself with the axe on the leg, but I'd never realized that this had meant anything special to their relationship. The thought of it made me if anything even more uneasy.

They drew closer to one another on the bench.

'Oh, but you were good to me that time, Linn.'

'I thought you'd bleed to death.'

'You watched over me . . .'

'Oh, come off it!'

He had moved right up to her, placed his hand in her lap, squeezing her thigh. She was heavy, shy and reluctant, but willing all the same. Her eyes were almost concealed by shadows. The thick black hair was piled up in a bun on top of her head, making her seem 'older'. Before, she had let it hang down loose over her shoulders.

'There was nothing you wouldn't do for me then. . . .'

He was as eager as a schoolboy, sitting there with his hand resting in her broad lap, caressing her thigh, half teasing, though not friendly, not joking, or at least not *only* joking, his hand moving up and down her placid thigh slumbering under its own weight beneath her dress. I was on tenterhooks watching them, attentive to the slightest development, to every detail, yet without attracting any attention to myself. The worst of it was not that they sat there exchanging small tokens of tenderness so openly but that he sat there squeezing her, looking for all the world like a young lad on his first date. He laughed, he smiled, there was something awkward, almost painfully inadequate in his advances, but it seemed to be just this that was the whole attraction for him. It was almost as though he could hardly refrain from winking knowingly at me, indeed it was most likely for my benefit that he'd started this whole performance, as if to emphasize the contact he was seeking to establish because, by acting the 'boy', green and awkward, he wanted to underline his own questionable 'youthfulness' to enable him to identify with me, a fifteen-year-old. But she just sat there resting in her own shadow, observing the scene from a distance, allowing him to pursue his childish courtship, going along with it, even allowing herself to be coaxed into smiling, into taking part in the game, more or less. . . . She was as patient as a mother with him. She was old, he was young, and this made the flirting between them so excruciating for me, as this was the essential false note that permeated everything which was done or said, and for that matter, life as a whole at Fagerlund. His hand on her thigh was as indecent as mine would have been, because he was so charming, so full of beans, so 'young' and unable to acknowledge his age, while she sat there so lovely, so buxom, so wistful, almost amorphous in her plump fullness, her every gesture, her every breath betraying regret for the years that had left their mark on her. There was nothing to hold them together any longer. When he sought peace and reconciliation, by laying his hand on her thigh, it was indecent, almost perverse.

Marie had also been so young, so fair, so radiant. And she and Uncle Kristen . . . if I was to believe Jo's malicious tongue. Yet it 'fitted', that was what was so unbearable to contemplate; the way it looked to my fevered imaginings, it did 'fit', this business with Uncle Kristen and Marie. They were both so 'young' – that was the link between them. And that girl up there over the heath, to whom they gave milk – Cathrine Stang – was also young. And all of it was bound up with Marie's disappearance.

But it was terrible to think such thoughts! I had to dig up more facts. I had to ask the only people able to answer.

'Did she leave any letter?'

They stared at me as though they had no inkling what I was referring to.

'Marie, I mean. If she disappeared. . . . You often find letters. . . .'

The threadlike mosquitoes drew closer and closer in their random and intricate dance and my own thoughts flitted about just as erratically. I saw Uncle Kristen pull his hand away, realized that I should not have raised the subject of this tragedy, regretted having done so, could have bitten my tongue off, but I'd said it now. They sat there like strangers beside one another.

The soft June darkness rose up from the grass and descended like a dim cloud between everything and everyone. We were transformed into shadows round the faint white outline of the garden table. The mosquitoes danced as though possessed, a counterpoint to my dire imaginings: a letter meant suicide. Why on earth hadn't I thought of it? And even now no one knew for certain that there hadn't been an accident. No one knew *what* had happened. . . .

'No, there wasn't any letter,' said Uncle Kristen at last. 'We did look, though, and so did the bailiff.'

'And a good job too,' said Aunt Linn, barely audible. 'It would have been dreadful to sit here knowing why or knowing who was to blame . . .'

'Oh, don't talk like that, Linn,' he said. 'No one's to blame, I tell you.' He sounded almost brusque. But she was older, wiser than him; she knew what she knew, what that heavy body of hers knew, but she didn't reply, just sighed. Dear oh dear.

It had grown late. It was time to turn in.

'I think we should go in,' he said, standing up.

She cleared the table, gathered up the cups and dessert plates on a tray, carefully folded the cloth. All colours had faded into grey and black. They stood there side by side hesitating, separated by the dusk, the mistrust which was my handiwork. Something had to be said to bring matters to a conclusion. The seconds ticked by.

'You don't find it lonely up there in the hut, do you, Peter? You can sleep here in the east room if you like. . . .'

She cared about me, bless her heart. How I longed for company and yet how I dreaded contact and the proximity of other people.

'No thanks,' I said. 'I'm fine up there.'

Uncle Kristen bent down and picked up something which was sticking into the ground. The knife. I'd forgotten my knife. 'It's a very fine knife, Peter,' he said. 'Maybe I could borrow it one of these days?'

'Er, yes,' I said hesitating. 'Sure you can, but not just now. I'll be using it tomorrow.'

'I meant later,' he said. 'Another day. Next week maybe.'

'Yes, yes of course,' I said. 'Whenever you like. Next week.'

A small rust-coloured mark on the pale skin below Uncle Kristen's wrist reminded me of the offer of peace, of reconciliation and trust I had rejected. Had felt compelled to reject.

6

I had to make peace with Jo. At least we were the same age, or almost. He was not very reliable maybe, but it was easy to see through him, and his mischievous nature, his contrariness and his monumental irreverence could always be relied upon. I'd worked out a plan. I would make a clean breast of it, tell him I thought Uncle Kristen was behaving oddly, maybe come up with something out of the ordinary, soften him up and then coax out of him every last particle of what he knew, all the gossip, all the sordid insinuations. I had to establish a sound basis for my self-righteousness, which flared up when Uncle Kristen tried to get close to me, tried to act 'young'.

Just after breakfast the next morning I went over to Bergs-hagen, but Jo wasn't in. Instead I met Gerd in the farmyard, the last person I had any desire to meet. I wished I was a million miles away but couldn't leave without saying hello. She didn't seem to have grown much, but was bigger in a disturbing way. Her hair had grown so that it reached down to her shoulders, but two garish mother-of-pearl clasps held it back from her fore-head, and her nose stuck out confident and freckled in the middle of her round face.

She blushed deeply when she saw me.

'Hi.'

She blushed even more.

'I heard you'd arrived.'

'Yes, the day before yesterday,' I said, just to say something, perhaps blushing a bit myself. The thought of Gerd and of Jo's spying on her – the 'big chance' I'd thrown away – always made me slightly embarrassed; his shabby horse-trading with his own sister just to get the upper hand over me who, after all, lived only four streets away from the cinema.

'Jo said so. He's gone with Dad into the woods.'

'Oh, I see.'

I wanted to leave but couldn't quite think what to say to put this across. She stood there looking at me as though she would have liked me to stay a bit longer, but I couldn't think of anything to talk to her about. And, anyway, she surely couldn't expect me to stay just for *her* sake, could she?

'They won't be back till later . . .'

'Oh, I see.'

She was wearing jeans and a check sports shirt, was nearly as tall as me and nearly three years older. Perhaps she had been 'in love' with me that time two years before, at least she'd *looked* at me, yet at the same time she'd been unfriendly, even hostile almost. I had thought 'this was love' and had steered clear of her. Jo had pulled my leg and put the fear of God into me by painting a picture of what she looked like with nothing on, when she was having a bath. It had been a convincing picture too; not a thing had escaped Jo's attention.

'So how're things, then?'

I answered haltingly, hoping my voice could be relied on not to crack. 'Fine, thanks.'

She smiled. Gerd, whose most secret places were known to me, smiled, stuck her hands in her jeans pockets and smiled. Her blushes coloured her neck just below the ears. I was painfully aware of my own long nose which sported two new spots.

'What . . . er, what are you doing with yourself these days, then?'

'I've been at the domestic science college.'

'Oh? Did you like it?'

'Yes, it was OK. . . .'

She giggled suddenly, covering her mouth with her hand and blushing again. What was there about the domestic science college to make her blush? And why on earth these insinuations? Was she still foolishly 'in love'? I thought all of a sudden, hoping the ground would open up and swallow me. Yet at the same time I felt my curiosity aroused: *she* didn't know that I knew. . . .

'I say, Peter. . . .'

My gaze settled on her shirt buttons below her neck. Two of them were open, revealing a patch of skin, white where the sun had not brought out the freckles. Her sports shirt stretched taut over her breasts and I remembered Jo's scornful descriptions. . . .

'Peter, do you know who's living up at Weasel Cottage now?'

'No, yes, I mean I've heard there's a girl living up there . . .'

'Cathrine!' She was well and truly launched now. 'She's called Cathrine Stang, the girl who lives there. I know her. I told her you'd be coming . . .'

'Oh?'

I didn't know what to think: the mysterious Cathrine Stang already knew of my existence almost before I'd had time to come to any definite conclusion about hers. Where was all this leading?

'Yes, and she said she thought she knew someone who knew you.'

The plot was thickening. At any rate, I was sure I'd never heard of her before. And there stood Gerd Bergshagen looking at me and smiling as though the fact that Cathrine Stang and I might know someone in common was a source of huge personal satisfaction to her.

'But I don't think I know her . . .'

'No, she didn't say *that*, she said she maybe knew someone who *knew* you. . . .'

This mild reproach of hers was couched in so many smiles that I didn't know what to think.

'Oh yes . . .'

'So you'll have to come up to the cottage some time,' she went on, not to be stopped, her neck and throat aflame. 'She said she'd like to meet you. . . .'

But it was her, Gerd Bergshagen, who was inviting me. She was still 'in love' with me. I saw it now.

'What's she like then, Cathrine?'

'She's great.' Gerd's melancholy eyes shone. 'She's really nice and dead easy to get on with. . . . And very pretty! She's just fantastic!'

She was still 'in love' with me. That was why she was eager to arrange this meeting between me and the perfect Miss Stang. This was what it was like when you were 'in love'. That's how complicated 'love' was.

'Yes, well I can pop up there one of these days. . . .'

I felt my knees trembling slightly with pride and embarrassment all at once. I had never believed my company could be so much sought after, but at the same time the thought of paying a visit to Weasel Cottage sent a shudder of cold fear through me. What on earth would I find to say to that girl, who, apart from being several years older probably, had also had a baby, and therefore. . . . Jo's spiteful insinuation was still fresh in my mind; of course it was easy enough for him, a mere boy, to speculate. No one would dream of suggesting that *he* should have a go himself, regardless of what the chances of success were, so he could stir things up to his heart's content. . . . But where I was concerned, it was different; with my day-dreams, my gangling legs and clammy hands, I was involved in other ways, more dangerous ways, compromised by the potential of this unpredictable body.

'Will you be coming tomorrow?'

'Er no, I mean yes. Maybe. I can't say for sure. I might have to give Uncle Kristen a hand with something. . . .'

Better not tie oneself down. Better not commit oneself to anything definite. The way she looked at me, the way she smiled, restored some of my self-confidence. It was such a strange feeling to stand here right in front of a girl and know that she was 'in love' with you.

'I'll pop in when I've got a moment.'

'OK, Peter. Shall I say hello to Cathrine from you and let her know?'

'Yes, why don't you?'

I felt so elated, stole a glance at her shirt, the round breasts: just fancy that it was me she was 'in love' with. I felt completely humbled by this; it might even make me change my whole attitude to the girl. Gerd was maybe not that bad, all things considered, at least she'd got rid of her chubbiness and shapelessness. Not that I found her all that attractive, and I was still far from sure that I *liked* her all that much, but the fact that she stood there blushing, smiling and was so 'in love' gave me a feeling of self-respect, of wielding power over another human being, and this was so much the more captivating because *I* wasn't the least little bit in love with *her*, and was therefore under no obligation, was free to derive whatever benefit I chose from this major insight of mine.

And what of the mysterious Cathrine Stang who was going about saying that she as good as knew me? It might not be such a bad idea to drop by at Weasel Cottage after all!

7

After dinner, I took up a vantage-point behind a sturdy pine tree on the hill and kept watch on the farmyard. I wanted to spy on them, check on everything that moved on the farm, take note of anything that might be of assistance to me in my speculations about what was happening and what wasn't at Fagerlund.

Curiosity tingled inside me with voluptuous pleasure. I had lain down on my side vaguely toying with my suspicions, as though stimulating them was all that was needed to set in motion the bizarre enactment of my own fantasies down in the farmyard.

I couldn't see anyone. Not a thing stirred. Perhaps they were having an afternoon nap. It was still quite early, about three o'clock perhaps, and it was hot. A trail of dust lay over the road after the postman's moped. He called every day at lunch-time. A hint of coolness, fresh and refreshing, as though emanating from the ice deep within the cold bedrock, slowly permeated my shirt and trousers. It was so quiet I could hear the sun baking the bark up and down the broad trunk of the pine tree. Everything around me slumbered in perfect peace. Not the slightest breath of wind, not a blade of grass stirred; a mossy outcrop, a slab of rock covered with bilberry bushes, the small hollow between two sturdy roots where I lay, everything slumbered away undisturbed, as though it had lain like this since the dawn of time and would carry on doing so just as I saw it now for ever.

But then I became aware of an ant scurrying over the root of the pine tree; it crawled sideways across the rock and disappeared behind the mossy outcrop. Then another, and another. It was swarming with them up and down the slender root, and suddenly I noticed their narrow path under the bilberry bushes;

it was as if the whole forest floor was suddenly creeping and crawling. And it wasn't just ants, I noticed now; small gnats flitted between the tightly packed leaves of the bilberry bushes. On a slender stalk of grass there hung a little caterpillar, and a spider was spinning its web from one dry twig to another with fanatical precision. The insects were everywhere around me, masses of them, alive and moving on what a moment before I had thought of as immobile, inalterably static. It was as though they were undermining the entire landscape with their tireless activities, just like my own thoughts about the 'true' and the 'real'. If one looked closely at the 'true', one discovered many peculiar things creeping and crawling about on the surface, perforating and altering the entire structure of 'the truth'. There was always something moving, something one didn't see at first glance, but which was constantly there as a reminder that not everything is what it appears to be, that nothing remains exactly as it once was, and that the 'true' and the 'real' constantly change their form and expression. And my own thoughts and ideas, my fantasies, crawled about on the 'truth' like these insects, transforming it and sowing doubt.

A door was softly closed. I heard it as though the gentle sound had been amplified tenfold in the dry afternoon stillness. A figure came out on to the steps. Now perhaps – at long last . . .! I yearned to participate in what was going on beneath the day-to-day play-acting.

But it wasn't Uncle Kristen who came out on to the steps as I'd anticipated. It was her, Aunt Linn! Aunt Linn in a neat and practical apron, her hair gathered in a bun, who made her way purposefully across the lawn towards the shuttered Mary Cottage. At the door she paused and fished something out of her pocket. The key. Then the door swung open and she disappeared into the semi-darkness, but glanced back over her shoulder as she stepped over the threshold. Inaudibly, the door swung to behind her.

I'd expected it to be Uncle Kristen. He was the one under suspicion, the active one, the one who was so anxious to be matey and throw me into confusion. I had sat scrutinizing him at dinner-time, noted how he used his knife and fork, how they became sure instruments in his steady hands, how he got them to do his every bidding, shovelled down two portions of meat and veg, while I struggled to hold back the nausea of defeat and could do no more than pick at the indigestible fat on the plate. His very gluttony seemed to reveal an insatiable appetite for life itself, as though he wished to increase his strength, his healthy optimism, his 'youthful' vigour, by shovelling down helping after helping of yellow split pea soup and lumps of beef and pork. It fairly turned my stomach. His greed put paid to my appetite, already weakened by the sight of the enormous pan of soup, the steam on the newly cleaned window-panes and the smell of his favourite dish.

'We mustn't forget to take another can of milk up to Weasel Cottage today,' he said, as he stood heaping thick, yellow split pea soup on top of the mound of potatoes from the pan on the stove. Beads of sweat stood out on his nose, his arms were bare and covered in embarrassingly dense hair (compared with my own pathetically sparse little crop where it mattered), and of course those blue eyes of his shining beneath his quiff. It was as though the very thought of going up to Weasel Cottage made him even more full of beans, more unashamedly 'macho', while I sat there, all gangling limbs, gaucheness, contrariness and high-minded principles, and envied him.

But it was Aunt Linn who'd come out on to the steps, hurried over the farmyard and gone into Mary Cottage. There was something fishy here. I reassured myself with the thought that she no doubt had some business there, legitimate woman's business, clothes to wash, cleaning, rooms to be aired; even cases of tragic disappearance created a need for tidying and cleaning. For I couldn't imagine Aunt Linn had anything but legitimate business there. Nevertheless, the sight of her in this unexpected situation had set my nerves tingling with excitement.

And here was *he* now. Here was Uncle Kristen as well! I lay pressed to the ground, feeling the damp seep through my trouser knees. My compulsion to investigate stood stiff as a poker. What would Uncle Kristen do now?

He walked towards the barn with long, sure steps, one hand in his trouser pocket. Involuntarily my thoughts went back to the first evening when he'd snatched the hair ribbon from the nail on the wall, and I trembled with excitement. He went round the corner, waded through the forests of withered nettles behind the hen-run and stopped where the manure from the cowshed overflowed, its imposing pyramid of dark brown dung spreading out over the waste ground behind the cowshed waiting to be carted away and spread on the fields on steaming, late winter days. What on earth was he doing here? He paused in front of the midden, stood legs apart, half turned away, took his right hand out of his pocket and began slowly and deliberately to do something I couldn't make out because of the way he was standing, though it wasn't hard to guess what it was, and my heart sank, for this was nothing unusual, wasn't suspicious or in the least noteworthy: a bright, sparkling stream from my Uncle Kristen's middle splashed down on to the midden, and from my vantage-point I could see the steam rising where his relief mingled with the dark dung. I thought suddenly that I could catch the scent of manure right up here where I lay hiding. But to be honest, what could possibly be deduced from this? True, standing there like that with his legs apart as he went about his business was provocative, but everybody was allowed to take a leak and that was all there was to it.

Yet he remained in the same position. He ought to have finished by now, still there he stood, legs slightly apart, his right hand busy with essential manoeuvres. But it was taking ages. Yet he remained there, legs apart, doing something in front of him with his right hand. Then it dawned on me what he was *actually* up to: my Uncle Kristen was standing behind the cowshed masturbating!

So engrossed was I in observing this scene that I had failed to notice Aunt Linn, who had suddenly emerged and was standing in the farmyard in front of Mary Cottage. The door was closed behind her and she stood there motionless, as though about to set off, as though she was expecting unpleasant surprises from every direction, before setting off back across the farmyard towards the open kitchen door. She ran clumsily and heavily, buxom as she was, her arms held out slightly from her body, her feet never raised more than an inch or so above the ground, knock-kneed, the sluggish weight swaying slowly from side to side, as though the energy was being used up by the body's very swaying to and fro, and nothing was left over to propel her forward. She glided over the green grass as though weightless, her limbs engaged in a rhythmic beat, as though she were swimming through the still afternoon air, floating slow and soundless, her apron billowing about her broad, honey-white thighs. Agitated? Alarmed? Flustered? At any rate, outside the confines of her customary day-to-day rhythm and dignity. My Aunt Linn, whom I discreetly cultivated and admired in my solitude, captured here in an irredeemable second, an eternal moment, an illusion, which would keep her like this for always, frozen and at the same time in flight across the green lawn in the afternoon sun, with all her weight, all the mature fullness age had endowed her with, all her voluptuous charm, so sparsely enveloped in her apron, charitably displayed by the generous law of gravity and by her own determined but futile efforts to reach the kitchen door. So long as my adulation, my rapture in catching her off her guard like this reared up hot and throbbing and my untiring manual dexterity drove my curiosity to bursting-point, I had to keep her like this, she must keep on running, running slowly through the afternoon stillness, her arms and legs moving rhythmically, her apron drawn up over her heavy thighs and her weight, her years, her mature years, her resignation, swaying in gentle sinus curves forwards, backwards, slowly oscillating, ineffectual and distracting despite her actual intention, the straight flight towards the kitchen door, the saving manoeuvre my fanatical fixations forbade. I had to hold her thus till it was all over and the tableau was concluded, till my devotion, my loneliness, my determination had a chance to spill out over a picture it had fashioned itself of her, weightless, floating, gliding along, her apron flapping about her plump body, her limbs in slow and cumbersome co-ordination, an unrecognizable, unfettered revelation of a woman dancing between the old buildings at Fagerlund: my Aunt Linn. And all this while *he* stood there, legs apart, behind the cowshed wall, feverishly perpetrating his adultery, his 'youthful sin' against her. What further 'proof' did I need? What else was there to learn on the subject of his 'youthful' energy, lack of moral fibre, unreliability, deceitfulness? And what of her? What better proof of her unassuming and irritating female secretiveness? My painfully suppressed love, my capitulation, my persistence exploded as she reached the kitchen steps; as my Uncle Kristen carefully wiped off the drops of his self-gratification, the ritual he used to rediscover his 'youthful' freedom, regaining his wanton independence, the cord snapped and I slid over the point of no return into nothingness. All my passion dripped down on to the bilberry bushes and from there down on to the ants in the moss.

I heard the kitchen door click shut. I heard Uncle Kristen tramp through the wilderness of last year's nettles.

I took out my handkerchief and carefully rubbed away the dark spots on my Wranglers. The feeling of joy and all other feelings were gone. I had found the confirmation I'd been looking for.

TWO

Pan

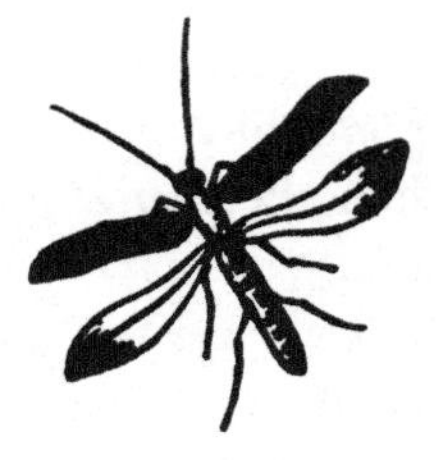

8

I no longer had any desire to spy. I felt hollow and empty. It was so depressing and futile attempting to observe other people's private affairs, which in all probability were not all that unusual or sensational anyway. I was fully aware that the lives of all grown-ups were a tissue of lies, ambiguities and pretence, but when no blissful thrill pulsed through my body, this did not excite me, merely filled me with distaste and aloofness, as though all this no longer concerned me. If there had been something between Uncle Kristen and Marie, and Aunt Linn held this against him, that was their affair; it was too pathetic, too contemptible, too demeaning for me to concern myself with it. At least, not for the moment.

I looked around me, inhaled deeply, enjoying the stillness of the afternoon. I felt like one of the pine trees on the hill, every bit as proud and dignified. I wanted to think I was above taking any part in the endless untruths on the farm, no longer wished to follow up my suspicions. I had other more worthwhile things to attend to: my self, my ego, my individuality. I perceived and experienced things more purely and profoundly than they did. I wanted to emphasize this, set an example, make them take notice of me and value me as I deserved to be valued, and this I would best achieve by paddling my own canoe. I did what so many poets have done, sought out nature and my own salvation when the contemptible world of humankind became too problematical.

I had always felt a mysterious unity with nature. Of late, I had been afraid it might have left me, believing it must belong to a more 'childish' phase to think in such terms, but now, at this moment, I felt my joy at being here in the forest as strong as ever; it was so much easier to find confirmation of oneself in these protective surroundings. Here I *was* someone, here among the trees which stood so green and beautiful, their branches interwoven, there was also room for me; here I was safe from other people's attacks and violations. And the heat, the light that fell across the tree-tops and branches, the colours of the shadows along the path as I walked, reinforced this feeling of security. Here I was free. Here I had an inviolable, independent existence at the same time as being at one with the foliage, the branches, the moss, the heather, the endless majestic mystery of the forest. I paid no attention to Uncle Kristen's fence where it ran alongside the path, as though to remind me that just now my endless forest covered an area of only three to four acres, so absorbed was I in my communion with the Spirit of the Forest, my utterly splendid unity with nature. . . .

That is, until I came face to face with another spirit of the forest. This one had short trousers and close-cropped hair with a forelock tumbling down over his brow, a snub nose, freckles and a conciliatory grin revealing yellow teeth: Jo.

'I heard you'd been round,' he said, testing the water.

'Yes. You were out though. . . .'

Bad luck to bump into *him*, especially just now of all times. It was impossible to keep a grip on esoteric concepts, to explore sublime moods under the scrutiny of his stony gaze.

'Had to go with the gaffer into the forest,' he said gruffly. 'A heifer'd got stuck. Bloody nuisance!'

'Yes, so Gerd told me,' I said, immediately regretting it as I saw his grin.

'Aye, we got a right lugful about her meeting you!' He grinned triumphantly. 'She can't talk about anything else. It's Peter this, Peter that, how tall Peter's got, how grown-up he seems. . . .' He laughed menacingly. 'I think you'd best go canny with her. She's been at the domestic science college, you know. She lived in as well, at Kvamme. . . .' Meaningfully, as though it marked out his sister's behaviour for ever. 'And last summer she had a job at the Tourist Hotel and was mixed up with an English bloke. But I bet she's just as gone on you as she was before. And there's a good bit more growth on her bush now, too. . . .' He laughed again in that malicious way of his. 'I've had an eyeful all right, even though she's been so careful about it recently like,' he added vindictively. 'Bloody dames! They can damn well rot in hell!'

I drew back almost, as his meaningless blasphemy seemed particularly brutal here in such chaste surroundings, yet, all the same, part of me envied him his childish crudity and thought his oaths impressive.

He thrust a hand inside his shirt and pulled out a tattered magazine. 'Here. The mag I owe you.'

I could just make out a title, *Pin-up Sexpots*, but the woman who was featured on the cover clad in a tiger skin was hard to make out properly, so often had Jo's cherished property been folded this way and that.

'Not bad is she, this one? Here, on page fourteen. . . .'

He seized the magazine, thumbed eagerly through the pages. On page fourteen there was a picture of the same woman without the tiger skin, but with one hand concealing the place on which all interest centred. The model had long black hair and was smiling vaguely at some far-off point to our right. I couldn't help thinking of Gerd Bergshagen having a bath.

'Fab, isn't she? Just look at her tits! I got these from a farmhand who'd ordered them from Sweden.'

'Yeah, not bad,' I said without meaning it. It suddenly made me sick standing here with this little squirt gawping at a picture of a naked woman in an unnatural pose. It didn't go with my new-found identity, my dignity as a free, aesthetic being in the forest. But embarrassment was not something that troubled Jo. He spat on to the path like one of the lads, flicked through the magazine with a practised hand, pointing, leering, laughing out loud, then suddenly he asked: 'D'you do it every day?'

'Do what?'

'Play with it.'

'Depends. . . . Now and then. . . . Not all that often. . . .'

Why on earth did he have to bring this up now? Of course it was true that, during the past year, I'd done it at all times, day and night, in all imaginable places, whenever an opportunity had presented itself, but that was over now, I'd decided, I'd reached a stage when there were other things to think about, and I didn't like being reminded of my onanistic existence which had ended barely half an hour before.

'I do it every day,' he said, pleased with himself, 'three or four times at least. Once last winter I did it six times!'

Obviously he was exaggerating. No doubt he still imagined he had an advantage over me because his had been longer when we'd measured them that time.

'Feel like doing it now?'

For Christ's sake! I thought, recoiling.

'No, I . . . er, I'll have to be getting back for tea now . . .'

'Oh, you're yellow, are you?'

'Don't be daft!'

His might well have been longer two years before, but I was nearly sixteen now. I'd grown a whole head taller since the previous summer and my pride and joy was five and a half inches long. I'd been a late starter, but now I was completely sure of my attributes, of my unruly member's size and willingness. I could conjure up an erection at any time whatever, regardless of circumstances; my imagination brimmed over with the most bizarre personal aphrodisiacs, I could press a button in my mind and day-dreams would envelop me, unnatural, unmentionable. . . . There was nothing Jo could teach me where self-abuse was concerned.

'*Saving* it, are you, scared you'll wear it out . . .?'

He nodded vaguely up in the direction of the heath, and I realized whom he was referring to. I hadn't forgotten my rash decision to drop by Weasel Cottage, though I'd no idea how it would come about in practice, what pretext I could use, for just going up to her and saying Hello, here I am, was out of the question regardless of what Gerd had said. And here stood Jo in front of me ruining everything with his smutty insinuations. My attitude towards Cathrine Stang had suddenly altered. I visualized her long dark hair and imagined I detected something mysterious, retiring, perhaps melancholy permeating her entire being; something which fitted in with living alone in a cottage in the middle of the forest and with my own attitude of mind, my longing for harmony and oneness with nature, with everything around me. . . .

'Well, I think I'll have to be getting back for tea now,' I said, to put an end to this aimless banter. We were both standing on the path. He was my ally in everything that was coarse and vulgar, in what was 'boyish', but there were other things that separated us, a gap in ages – he was thirteen and a half and I fifteen – and there was so much he didn't understand, couldn't understand.

'I say, Peter,' he said. 'D'you think you could teach me a bit of tango as well? So I can do a bit more than just waltz . . .'

'Er yes, sure I can.'

'But I haven't got any tango records.'

'Then we'll just have to hum the tune.'

'OK.'

'Come up to the hut, then.'

'All right. Tomorrow?'

'OK. Tomorrow morning.'

'All right. See you.'

''Bye.'

He left. It was a relief for both of us to be rid of the other's scrutiny. Neither of us had referred to our little scuffle in the barn. It was as though respect, a kind of mutual regard, forbade us to bring this up again, embarrassing as it was for both of us.

I wended my way back to the hut with my unaesthetic reward screwed up in my hand. On the way, it occurred to me that what I wanted to do was burn the magazine or tear it up, scatter it in tiny pieces, unrecognizable and harmless. But I did neither. I unfolded the magazine and placed it neatly sandwiched between my mattress and the bed-boards. There was no telling when it might come in handy. This compromise with strict principles was a much-needed concession and made me feel so much more at ease in my splendid isolation. The shaft of sunlight that fell slanting across the table with its yellow plastic cloth set my thoughts wandering. In the doorway, frantic flies flew hither and thither paying not the slightest attention to me. All I could see from where I sat were the trees that pressed in around the cramped hut. I felt so utterly contented here in my own little house. I would buy food at the local shop, bread, margarine and jam, and manage on my own. I didn't want to be a burden to them. I would go hunting. Who knows, I might well catch something edible, a capercaillie, for example, maybe even a hare? I would lead a healthy, natural and wholesome life, run, go for hikes, build up my muscles, be my own master, independent of everyone else. Too bad what they thought at Fagerlund.

Nevertheless when I heard a voice from below calling out that it was tea-time, hunger sent me bounding down to the farm. After all, it was far too late to go and buy food tonight, and besides, the kitchen at Fagerlund was the nicest place I knew when the sun shone bright and the shadows lengthened. And I felt sure the Spirit of the Forest was strong enough not to allow himself to be corrupted by a bit of food.

9

After the evening meal, the longed-for opportunity suddenly presented itself.

I was sitting in my usual place on the bench watching the sunset through the window and scarcely noticed Uncle Kristen go out only to return a moment later with the milk cans he'd fetched from the cooling sink. Then the little drama commenced, just like the first evening. The large can was placed in the fridge, while the small one was placed on the worktop. Uncle Kristen stood there restless, ill at ease. Aunt Linn had cleared the table and was washing up, if anything a bit more energetically than usual, but with her head bowed as though in mourning. In the window the flies had calmed down somewhat, but a perplexed wasp (my guilty conscience) kept on launching itself pointlessly at the shiny window-panes. I took all this in without really noticing it, lost as I was in my own thoughts about the sunset and the harmony of nature, but their remarks to one another gradually began to break through into my day-dreams.

She: 'You've got something to see to, haven't you, before it gets dark?'

He: 'Er, yes. Yes, I have that. She asked whether I could pop up there if I had a moment. It's not so easy for her to get out. You know how it is . . .'

'I thought Gerd Bergshagen could baby-sit for her. She's up there practically all the time, so I've heard.'

'Oh, I don't know about that. Any rate, she asked me to. There's nothing wrong in that surely, is there?'

'Nothing wrong in it! You know what folk are saying though, don't you?'

'Oh, for goodness' sake, Linn. Surely we can't bother our heads about what folk say.'

'You could pay a bit of heed, all the same.'

'Who to? Those gossips down in the village?'

'No, to me.'

'But Linn. You mustn't take on so. Seeing as there's nothing in it.'

'Nothing in it. Nothing in it for you either?'

'No, nothing! I should think not . . .'

'So Peter can go then, can't he?'

Whereupon I was torn from my day-dreams. Now I was involved, a buffer in the conflict between them.

'Yes of course he can. If he wants to, that is . . .'

'You've nothing against a little evening constitutional, have you, Peter lad?'

'No, course not,' I said as obediently and dutifully as I could, to stifle the stabs of fear that made my voice tremble with uncertainty. To Weasel Cottage tonight, already! What could be worse than having one's dream, one's greatest desire, fulfilled just like that, without any chance to prepare for it? 'Yes, I quite fancy a stroll actually.'

So there I was all of a sudden walking along the path in the balmy evening air, horrified, scared out of my wits, and yet cocky, since I had a watertight excuse, even though I hadn't the faintest what to say to her. I strode along, hoping I looked like a true forester, along the path up over the gently sloping hillside, through the forest which now, in the twilight, became the willing instrument of my imagination and presented obstacles and dangers which my determination to act could only just overcome. Though not particularly heavy, the milk can handle made deep grooves in my soft grammar-school fingers, fanning thoughts about self-sacrifice and valour: I was going to Miss Stang's to deliver the milk which she must already be waiting for. And but for my magnanimous gesture there wouldn't be any. The fact that it was probably her baby the milk was mostly for was something I ignored for the moment, as I couldn't quite see how an illegitimate baby could fit in with my heroic adventure. I saw babies as nothing but the focal point of oodles of extravagant emotion and showy sentimentality, women being the major culprits, and these sham outbursts of feeling could strike me so forcibly that just being near a baby could make me physically sick. Likewise, the sight of a blind person, a cripple, the mere thought of the poor, the needy, even animals, a budgerigar in a cage, a sparrow in the gutter, kittens, a lame dog, rodents in sawdust-lined cages in petshop windows, made me feel quite sick, because all of them made demands upon my emotions, which I possessed in such abundance that they could bowl me over at any time. I felt as if I might go completely to pieces if I really gave in to them. It was absolutely vital to be strong and detached. I would have preferred to forget that Miss Stang was a mother as I strode boldly along, defying dangers unseen and unheard, enduring the strain of the tension and the anticipation, all for her sake.

Weasel Cottage was one of those traditional log cabins, creosoted and low-roofed. From the path I could already see the slate roof above the birch thickets covering Birch Hill. I went on, my heart pounding in my ears. There was still time to turn back, hide the milk can, think up some excuse – anything would do – there was still time, it would still be easy to wriggle out of the tight corner I had been so arrogantly fantasizing about only a few hours before, and then naïvely allowed myself to be lured into. There was still time, but I went on along the cart-track the last few hundred yards, hoping the ground would open up and swallow me. I couldn't even countenance the thought of knocking at the door and saying what I'd come for. What if she was already sitting there waiting for me? Me! What if she'd already spoken to Gerd Bergshagen and heard I might turn up any time? Goodness knows what she'd been told, for Gerd was capable of anything, 'in love' with me as she was and therefore keen to dream up any story she could about me, however little truth there might be in it. That much I did know about the mixed-up feelings of love.

I'd expected that the darkness would be a help, allowing me to float the last few yards across the lawn, blending in with the twilit forest itself right up to her door, just to knock and stand there like a vision emerging from the balmy evening, hand her the milk can and be gone like a breath from the forest. . . . But of course it wasn't dark enough yet. High over the hilltop the sky formed a lofty vault of white streaked with eggshell blue and salmon pink, a reflection of which hung suspended between the tree-trunks. Out here on the open path, all surfaces reflected the luminosity that hung in the air like dust; silver flowed from deep wheel ruts and disappeared under the grass at the side of the track, leaves turned by the breeze glittered white towards the west, and my own hand was as white and shiny as the confounded aluminium milk can, which was to blame for everything. I couldn't see a light in any window, and anyway it was still too early. Not a sign of life, of her, in the silent cottage, but if she looked out it would be easy for her to see me, tall and lanky, on the cart-track. I broke out into a cold sweat at the thought that she might already be observing me from behind the dark, shiny window-panes.

But she was surprised when I arrived. She peered at me, not understanding who I was, gazed in surprise at the milk can which I handed to her without a word, far too nonplussed, far too surprised to manage even a customary greeting, because she was so different from what I'd imagined. She was much smaller than I'd thought she would be, and her hair wasn't dark at all, but fair and full of waves and curls. She gave a gentle, slightly nervous smile, saying 'What's this?'

'The milk,' I stammered. 'From Fagerlund.'

'Oh, the milk. Of course. Thanks a lot.'

'He couldn't come himself,' I said.

'Oh, I see.'

This implied that it was him she'd expected.

I still couldn't quite grasp that she was so young, so small, so trim, with curls falling in a mass around her thin, pale and slightly delicate face. She was anything but dark and exotic as Jo had said. On the contrary, her large eyes were blue and friendly, her mouth broad and smiling, so how could Jo . . .? Then I realized that he'd obviously never set eyes on her. Jo had never met Cathrine Stang, had only heard what his sister had reported and formed an imaginary picture with the help of his pin-ups. That was the explanation.

'Well, come on in, then.'

She said this so naturally. I could never have asked anyone, let alone a girl I didn't know, to come in in such a natural-sounding voice. Her invitation thus became something everyday, reassuring, yet at the same time far more meaningful than a mere invitation to come in.

'So you're staying at Fagerlund with your aunt and uncle, are you?' she said, when I'd eventually made up my mind to sit down somewhere, on the stool by the fireplace, since it was so important to maintain a distance between us, and above all to steer clear of the sofa like the plague.

'Yes, well actually I'm living up in the hut. . . . But it's them I'm staying with.'

Putting it like this didn't exactly win me any Brownie points for living on my own. I was scared stiff that my highly unpredictable voice might suddenly shoot up into a falsetto.

'Gerd told me about you. You go to Hammer School, don't you?'

So Gerd had managed to sniff this out, had she? Further fuel to fan the flames of my embarrassment. What else had Gerd said? She scarcely knew me.

'Yes. I'm just about to move up to Form 3. . . .'

What a lie! A stupid childish fib, so easy to check up on, easy to see through. To be fifteen is to be a barefaced liar about things that cannot be lied about.

'I had a girl-friend who went to Hammer two years ago.'

'Oh?'

So this was the 'mutual acquaintance' whom Gerd had conjured up. I felt my anger rise against poor Gerd, who had said such a lot of strange things on account of being 'in love' with me. I felt seriously compromised.

She picked up a packet of cigarettes from the table and offered it to me: 'Smoke?'

'What? No – no thanks. . . .' I shook my head feebly.

The two or three times I'd tried it on my own had resulted in a coughing fit and made me feel sick. No, this was something I couldn't risk. She lit a cigarette and blew the smoke casually out into the room. She must be at least nineteen.

'So how long will you be staying here?'

'Till the end of the summer holidays.'

'It's pretty dead round here,' she said. She talked as though she hadn't noticed that I was sitting there tormented half to death by my own inadequacy. She was natural, gentle and friendly. This alone caused my cruel limitations to degenerate into paralysis. I couldn't blame Gerd Bergshagen as I sat here dispirited and awkward to the point of immobility: I was my own worst enemy.

'Oh, time passes quickly enough up in the hut,' I said, just to say something, and she gave me a look of such gentleness and interest that I was forced to continue, even though my head was empty of all reason, of anything that might be interesting to talk to a girl about: 'There's so much you can observe and study – in nature, I mean.'

'Such as what, for example?'

She had me there. What observations in nature could I, a fifteen-year-old, have made that were worth mentioning to a girl who was four or five years older and sat there blowing cigarette smoke into the air as if it was the most natural thing in the world, and looked me in the eye so completely unabashed and open? The answer was that it was *me* I observed in nature, metaphors for my own life, echoes of my feeling of helplessness in the world of men. . . . Then I had a sudden brainwave.

'Insects! Take insects, for example! Think of all the different species and varieties. Think how clever they are, think how they build, collect food in complicated traps, work all hours of day and night, everywhere. . . . Almost like us humans!'

This thought struck a chord in her too.

'Yes, imagine if we were insects. Imagine if all people were insects!' She laughed. It wouldn't have surprised me if she'd applauded as well, her laughter was so infectious. 'Imagine if we'd been wasps and mosquitoes and beetles. . . . Which d'you reckon there are most of?'

'Flies,' I said with assurance. I pictured them crawling about on all kinds of filth, cheeky, clever, always quicker than those trying to catch them and get even with them, repulsive creatures. . . . Yes, people were all flies. At least, almost all of them.

'Ugh, they're disgusting!' She screwed up her delicate nose and stubbed out her cigarette. 'I think most people are bees, actually. Bees or ants. Imagine how absorbed they are in their own little tasks, how they labour to get what they need, slaving away day and night. . . . Think what *boring* lives most people lead, and *put up* with it year in year out. . . .' She sighed, looking as though the idea of associating people with insects had depressed her all of a sudden. I took in every feature in her narrow face. 'Still, you're right,' she said after a while. 'There are flies too, bluebottles, really disgusting. Which would you have been if you'd had the choice?'

'A spider,' I said, still sure of myself. The spider was the quintessential loner, an artist. It operated completely alone, could catch other insects in its web and torment them without emerging from its hidy-hole. In this way, it was superior to all the others. It was my favourite insect.

'What an imagination you've got!' she exclaimed. But she was interested, I could tell. I'd been fortunate in my choice of an insect identity.

'So what would you have been, then?'

Now it was her turn. I'd already imagined her as a butterfly.

'Oh, me . . .' she said and made as if to laugh, but didn't quite bring it off. 'Perhaps I'd have liked to be a ladybird if I'd had the chance. Ladybirds are so beautiful and dependable somehow, so innocent. . . . But actually, a moth would suit me best.'

'A moth?'

'Yes, you know, the ones that flit about when it's dark, and fly into the flame and get burned . . .'

'Oh yes. . . .'

Suddenly the atmosphere between us became charged with meaning. It was as though she'd wanted to say so much more, had half begun to take me into her confidence, as though there was so much she wanted to get off her chest now there was someone here to talk to (it just happened to be me, that was all there was to it, I realized that). Yet still she held back. She was perhaps still not sure it would be worth the effort, whether *I*, a gormless fifteen-year-old sitting on the stool by the fireplace, with his hands folded round his knees to stop them from sticking out and attracting attention, was worth bothering with, worth taking into her confidence. Nor could I blame her. How could she have seen into my soul, where all the possibilities lay ready, if only someone would give them a helping hand? Or at any rate, take the trouble to try.

'No, it's a long time since I was a moth, a creature of the

night,' she said. She had lit yet another cigarette with long, slender fingers. There were flakes of pink nail varnish on her oval nails. 'Now I've become an ant too, I suppose. At least, I soon will be . . .'

'How long will you be living here, then?'

It had grown dark enough now to hazard such a question.

'Oh, I'm not rightly sure – till the autumn, I think, till they've found a job for me somewhere where I can take Hanna with me. . . .' Hanna. The baby. Her daughter. All these realities which made me seem so small.

'It's no joke getting in the family way and bringing shame on my relations, I can tell you. At least, not on *my* family!' She grimaced and blew billows of smoke up towards the ceiling. Her hair hung down over her cheeks, making her face so small and narrow, childlike, young, so easy to identify with. And at the same time, this unfathomable distance was a fact. That is, unless she went out of her way to reduce it by treating me naturally, like an equal, as she was doing now.

'It's so damned *stupid*, so idiotic to try and hide me up here to avoid gossip! So I could "have a rest", can you credit it. . . . The fact that he was a married man obviously made everything a lot worse, it was somehow twice as shame-making for them. You should have heard them when I said it was too late for an abortion. And then they did their damnedest to talk me into having it adopted. Somehow they couldn't grasp that I wanted to keep my baby. And before you could say "Jack Robinson", they'd spirited me away up here. . . .'

She talked in a quick, staccato way, as though afraid I might check her, even though I sat quiet as a mouse, not daring to reveal by any sound or gesture that I was completely on her side, that I was well aware of the hypocrisy and stupidity of grown-ups. That I could identify so fully and whole-heartedly with everything she said.

'Anyway, it was a good thing he was married,' she went on. 'Otherwise, they'd probably have forced me up the aisle. But I don't want to get married, that's for sure! Besides, they can't force me to do anything. I'm of age now, even though people say I don't look it. Till I get a job though, I'm well and truly tied to their purse-strings. . . .' She paused, puffed angrily at what little remained of the cigarette before stubbing it out in the ashtray. 'Of course it was silly of me to get mixed up with a married man. I knew it couldn't work, but it's just one of those things. He worked at the firm where I was a secretary. We were so head over heels in love, but I knew he wouldn't leave his wife. Then one time we were careless, so. . . .'

So this was the moth, the night creature Cathrine. And she was over twenty-one. She'd been to bed with a married man, probably over thirty. Hell's bells, Uncle Kristen was only just over forty. . . . A knot formed in my chest. But how could she speak so *naturally* about all this, confide these scandalous things in me, as though it was the most normal thing in the world for her to discuss her private life with fifteen-year-olds. Surely she must see that. . . . I was still horrified when I thought of that married boy-friend of hers. But the fact that she treated me normally and talked to me as though it was a foregone conclusion that I understood the significance of all kinds of erotic complications gave an enormous boost to my self-esteem. Did it mean that such freedom was within my grasp too? Did it mean that one day I too could be free and happy and sure of myself? For surely that's what happiness was, not allowing others to destroy anything in oneself; being able to stand up for oneself, that was happiness for a fifteen-year-old. And Cathrine must be happy despite all she'd been through. Perhaps I too could learn to be happy – with her help.

'How dark it's got,' she said, getting up to fetch the lamp from the mantelpiece just three feet away from me, removing the glass and lighting the wick with the small lighter she'd used with such sophistication when smoking. The yellow glow and the fact that I could see her features clearly again put paid to some of the smugness I'd been feeling. It would no doubt be a long while before I could dream of emulating her, as I sat there trying to show off my new Wranglers and trendy trainers. It was Jo I was more like – sex on the brain, dishonest and at the same time scared stiff. Pathetic, that's what I was, and the mere fact that she bothered to tell me about her experiences with candour and honesty gave me a sort of *raison d'être*.

She stood by the table in her short summer frock, partly turned away from me, one hand resting against her cheek as though deep in thought. Then she went over to the window and looked out towards the dark forest beneath a sky which was still ivory. 'Ugh, it gets so chilly as soon as the sun goes down,' she said. 'Don't you think so? I suppose we could've lit the fire, but of course there's nothing to chop wood with in this place, not even a decent knife. . . .'

The knife. Of course. I should have brought it with me. Wasn't I a man of the forest? Wasn't a sheath-knife an essential tool in the forest? And I, idiot that I was, had left it at home so as not to seem 'childish'.

'Your uncle helped me to get the fire going the other day. He managed it with just a few twigs he found outside. He's so clever . . .'

'Shall I. . . .'

I was already on my way out to fetch some twigs. If he could do it, so could I. And he'd wanted to borrow my knife yesterday. . . .

'No, no – it's not worth bothering. It's not that cold anyway. It's just that it's so cosy with the fire going.'

So there I sat perched on my stool again, thoroughly humiliated because *he* was so dextrous and could turn his hand to so many things. . . .

'Why don't we play cards?' she said. 'Poker. Can you play?'

But I couldn't play poker. I'd got as far as whist, but no further. At that moment I'd have given my right arm to gain an insight into the mysteries of poker. But she wasn't put off by my ignorance.

'I've got some dice. We could play yatzy.'

Yes, I could play yatzy. She took out the dice and a notepad. Then we played. Luck was on her side from her very first throw. I was less fortunate, but didn't let this bother me. I couldn't keep my mind on the game, only on her sitting there opposite me, keen, concentrating, enthusiastic. Not even my annoyance at the fact that it was my fault we had to sit here playing this childish game could cast a cloud over the intense happiness I felt when she accidentally brushed my hand once when reaching for one of the dice. She beat me hands down the first round. I lost no time in asking for a return match.

'Anyway, he's very kind, your uncle,' she said suddenly, as though wishing to take up again where we'd left off earlier. 'He gives me almost more milk than I need and he's helped me with bits and pieces here in the cottage. He's a real handyman. . . . And he's so fond of Hanna too. I've never met a man so fond of children.'

A strange feeling of loyalty towards Uncle Kristen suddenly welled up in me, completely contrary to what I'd planned and against my better judgement. Obviously I knew he was a threat and a danger to me and to my independence, and I was pathologically jealous of all his exemplary qualities, his manliness, his self-assuredness and his level-headed calm. Yet at the same time it did me good in a strange way to hear this girl praising him as though his being my uncle was something to be proud of. And before I could say 'Jack Robinson' there I sat singing his praises as well. Forgotten was the embarrassment of the degrading act I'd witnessed that afternoon.

'Yes, he's a nice bloke, Uncle Kristen. And he's no softie either. I've seen a scar he has on his leg from when he once hacked a chunk out of himself with an axe in the forest. It's as long as your arm. But he struggled home, even though he practically bled to death.'

'Good grief, did he?' she said, looking shocked out of her wits.

'Yes, he's a real tough guy,' I said. 'He was always getting into scraps when he was a lad. He was cock of the parish.'

This was an exaggeration, though Dad had once said that Kristen had been a bit of a fighter when young.

'I say, how exciting!' she said with a smile – was she having me on a bit? – 'Well, he's kindness itself where I'm concerned . . .'

'Yes, he likes helping you. He said so. . . .'

But this was going too far. Way over the top. What the heck had come over me?

'Did he now?' was all she said.

She won the second round too. I had no reason to stay here any longer now. It had grown late. It was all but dark outside. I'd done enough damage as it was with my impulsive boasting about Uncle Kristen. I stood up. 'I think I ought to be getting along now,' I said.

'Already?'

She seemed disappointed, genuinely wanted me to stay a bit longer, but this only hardened my determination.

'Yes. There's something I have to see to.'

Something which was more important than the chance to sit here with her. I had to show her that there was more than one man in the family.

'Oh well, if you have to.'

I had stood up, walked towards the door, wanting to spin out the time as long as possible, at the same time sticking to what I'd said. She stood up too and followed me, so slim she was almost frail, birdlike. Her frock was short-sleeved and I could see a suggestion of goose-pimples on her arms even though it was far from cold in the room. I was a good head taller. That was something in my favour at least. But the thought that she was over twenty-one and such a freer, more self-assured and happier person than I nevertheless made me embarrassed and miserable. I stood there dumb and gormless, still not wanting to open the door, waiting for a miracle to happen. I looked at the floor, up at the ceiling, shrugged my shoulders theatrically right up over my ears, dug my hands deep into my trouser pockets to convey an impression of my single-mindedness, my sense of responsibility, profound thoughts about so many matters far weightier than her in the cottage here, than us, our friendship, which I still couldn't be quite sure had actually begun. But, in reality, I stood there cursing my over-hasty decision to leave. In point of fact I'd nothing else to do, I had no one else to talk to and I would have liked to play endless rounds of yatzy, even though it was actually beneath our dignity and even though, strictly speaking, I'd have been happy to play snap, gin rummy and black two to avoid going out into the dark. But I was man enough to stick to my decision and opened the door.

'Well, thanks for the milk,' she said.

'Oh *that*. . . .' I'd clean forgotten the milk. 'Oh, that's nothing.'

'It's been lovely to have a bit of company. I don't have very many visitors, you know. It gets really lonely living here by myself.' She laughed as though to conceal the serious note underlying what she'd said. She had white teeth, which appeared large in her broad mouth, itself seeming large in her narrow and young-looking face. You'd almost have thought we were the same age.

'I . . . I can call by another time!' I stuttered in my eagerness to help her out in her loneliness, comfort her, support her in whatever way I could and at the same time receive confirmation of the fact that she genuinely wanted me to visit her again.

She gave an even broader smile, came closer, laid her hand on my shoulder and brought her face up to mine; then I felt her soft cheek against mine, her lips as quick and warm as a moist breath of wind. 'You're a funny one, you are,' she said, almost in a whisper, and laughed again. 'I like you. Yes, come again some time when you're not so busy, won't you?'

I realized that she had seen through me and held on for dear life to the thought of making my retreat as honourable as possible. Meanwhile, I had actually already started to fumble for her hand, her arm, to pull her towards me and make this into the sort of embrace the situation demanded, as a man was supposed to do. But it was impossible to get hold of her; she was so close, yet ducked out of my grasp, laughed, pushed me good-humouredly towards the door, which I'd opened: 'Here, don't forget the empty milk can.'

I thought I'd perhaps better leave so as not to give her the impression she was keeping me from something. I was just her plaything and I stumbled dutifully through the doorway, joined in her laughter, mumbled that I would be back before very long, was perhaps actually a little relieved to postpone this awesome final embrace: I'd never kissed anyone full on the mouth before and wasn't quite sure how it was done. I pounded down the two or three steps and felt uneven grass beneath my feet, heard her say good-night and thanks again for the milk, then there I was on the cart-track among the trees which hid me from view and removed the temptation to turn round, gaze at the two windows, warm and inviting, and at the wondrous creature inside. I hurried on home.

I hadn't kissed her, not properly, but I had at least felt her firm, round breast against my bare arm when she had so charmingly pushed me away, said goodbye and how she'd like me to call again.

10

'*Tum* tum-tum-tum, ti-tum ti-*tum*-tum. . . .'

I swung Jo across the floor of the hut. We were having more success with the tango than we'd had with the waltz. He had kicked off his wellingtons and was following my lead better than he had done in the barn. But there was still a long way to go before he'd be able to try his luck on any dance floor, even though it had probably never even occurred to him that this was on the cards. He wanted to *know how*, at least theoretically know how, to trip the light fantastic with his heart's desire on the plank floor at the summer fête. Something to anchor his fantasies to, for it's fantasies that count for a thirteen-year-old, I thought condescendingly. I was aching to tell him about my visit to Weasel Cottage the evening before, yet loyalty and a completely new feeling of decency held me back. But he was stealing a march over me. We ground to a halt, exhausted. Our joint rendering of the 'Blue Tango' finally broke down in breathless shrieks; our dogged would-be tango had lost all resemblance to the elegant, passionate dance from South America, and we were glad of the chance to let go of one another.

All of a sudden he said: 'I gather it was a Saturday night out for you last night – even if it was only Thursday!' He howled with laughter at this witticism and at me standing there in the middle of the floor, unmasked, bewildered and completely caught off my guard. 'Aha, happen you thought you could sneak up there and get a bit on the quiet, did you? But oh no, it didn't quite come off though, did it? There's not much that escapes me, you can bet your arse on that!' He flicked the home-cut lock of hair away from his eyebrow, looked up at me uncompromisingly: he was the superior one, the aggressive one, even though I stood here with all the aces in my hand. *I* was the one who'd been to Weasel Cottage, a joy he couldn't remotely dream of attaining in his revolting little boy's fantasies. And yet I was on the defensive, groping desperately for something to say.

'And who told you that?'

He laughed. He hated me for this, hated me for the advantage I had over him. 'Gerd,' he said and guffawed even louder when he saw me squirm with embarrassment. 'Gerd was over at Fagerlund last night. She said it was for Mother, but I bet it was you she was looking for. . . .'

So they had told him I was over at Cathrine's. I hated this snooping. I'd gone down to breakfast late on purpose that morning to avoid any questions about my errand the previous evening. I'd done no more than mumble a reply to Aunt Linn's guarded hints, gulped down my breakfast and dashed out again, absorbed in thoughts of Cathrine and our time together the previous evening, of our goodbye (a kiss, it *had* been a kiss, the prelude to a real kiss?), of our next meeting, which was bound to be soon. . . .

'Well come on, then! What did you do? Did you feel her? Was the little slut panting for it?'

Jo was dying to hear what really he didn't want to know.

'Well, we . . . er, we. . . .'

But it was impossible to hold on to any notion of decency with Jo in the vicinity, with Jo's sneering challenge right there under my nose.

'We just snogged a bit,' I said, hoping the gods that watch over the little details in our miserable human lives wouldn't be too hard on me. 'You can't just jump into bed together straight off. . . .' It was meant to sound so experienced, so worldly-wise, but actually it sounded like an excuse. 'We . . . er . . . we really got going nicely in the end. And she wanted me to stay. . . .'

The hint intended to egg him on also fell flat. My cheeks burned with shame and anger at what I had let myself in for, but I couldn't get rid of the wild urge to put one over on him.

'She asked me to stay. I'm sure I could've stayed the night if I'd wanted to . . .'

'You were snogging, and she asked you to stay. . . .' Jo

could barely contain his excitement. 'And you still didn't jump at the chance?'

His reaction to these nauseating half-truths that I forced out of myself was abrupt. He threw himself on to the bunk, smacked himself on the thighs, drummed his heels on the mattress.

'And you still didn't fuck? You raving loony. That's just what she was waiting for! Don't you see? That's just what she wants! Haha!' He rolled around on the bed, howled up at the ceiling, unable to contain his merriment, his envy, his hostility. 'Well, at least you got a feel of her slit, I hope?'

'Er no, not exactly . . .'

'What the hell's up with you? Are you a homo? Didn't even feel her slit! That's the first thing you should do, then they become as willing as lambs!' the thirteen-year-old informed me, sending fresh war-cries up towards the rafters. Then, almost patronizingly, he said: 'So what the blazes *did* you do with her, then?'

'I . . . we . . .'

'Didn't you even get a feel of her tits?'

'Course I did! Well, a bit. Outside.'

'Outside!' He snorted. 'Outside's no good. You have to get at their bare skin. Tickle them in the right places Then they soften up, can't say no!'

He lay there on my bunk, his arms and knees pulled right up under his chin. His hard eyes didn't leave me for a second, scorn and envy positively oozing out of them. But I wasn't going to give in, I had to make one last-ditch attempt.

'But she's fair, not dark like you said. . . .'

His laughter rattled round the cramped hut, cutting through my defences, my keen sense of rivalry, right into my ignoble, unreliable innermost self, where my heart pounded painfully and contritely for my Cathrine. 'You homo!' he yelled. 'You must be a bloody homo! Letting a chance like that slip!'

'She's fair,' I yelled back. 'She has fair, curly hair. Not dark like you said! You've never met her! You've never bloody well clapped eyes on her!'

'Homo!' howled Jo. 'Letting a chance like that slip away! You're out of your tiny little mind.' His voice reverberated even louder than mine. He had even more to hide, even more to be afraid of, prospects even more hopeless than mine. For he was only thirteen and a half.

'By the way, Gerd was up here yesterday asking after you,' said Aunt Linn at the dinner-table. 'She came just after you'd gone to Weasel Cottage. Said she needed you to give her a hand with something or other.' And she looked at me as though she didn't particularly approve of the fact that Gerd Bergshagen had called just for the sake of meeting me.

'Yes, I bet he's charmed the pants off her already,' said Uncle Kristen jokingly.

'Don't be silly, Kristen!' She sounded sharp. She didn't like such talk because he seemed to revel in it.

'Oh, who knows? Peter's grown up a lot since the last time he was at Fagerlund, no mistake about it. For all we know, he might have become a bit of a Don Juan since then,' he chuckled.

But there was no real humour or joy in his laughter. It was my trip to Weasel Cottage last night he had in mind. No, he didn't seem to be in such a good mood today. And after dinner he asked out of the blue: 'Has someone been in Mary Cottage recently?'

The ensuing silence gradually took on a sombre note as Aunt Linn did not say 'Yes, it was me, I was over there yesterday afternoon' as I'd expected her to, as I knew she ought to have said, since I'd seen her with my own eyes unlock the red-painted door and disappear inside, only to emerge a moment later and hurry back over the farmyard like a heavy, mournful bird battling against the wind. And this kindled my curiosity again and brushed aside the touch of shame surrounding the episode of yesterday afternoon, when I'd spied on them and had used her as the object of my fantasies about women, of my adulation. For she just sat there silent, still not answering; placed her dessert spoon beside the plate, folded her hands in her lap as though she hadn't heard his question at all, while he also continued to sit there, his watchful eyes and the lines around his tight-lipped mouth full of seriousness. And I, who knew the name of the guilty party but didn't know the nature of the crime, also remained silent, waiting, thinking that actually there were other things which would have interested me even more in the light of all that had happened since we'd sat here yesterday dinner-time, yet all the same I was on the edge of my seat with suspense.

'No, I haven't been in there,' she said casual and straightforward, as though lies were something totally unheard of, and it came as a shock to realize that she too could turn untruth into truth when it suited her, a knack which all grown-ups seemed to take completely for granted in their dealings with others. 'No, I haven't been in there. Why d'you ask?'

'I've just been in there myself,' said Uncle Kristen curtly. 'And no one's going to tell me that somebody hasn't been messing about in there.'

'But who could that be, then?'

'How should I know? But somebody has, right enough. The dresser drawers were half open, the bureau was topsy-turvy, and it even looked as though someone had been rooting about in her wardrobe.'

He looked at her accusingly, but she remained sitting unperturbed with her hands in her lap, glanced at him, then glanced down. Then she asked in a voice almost devoid of expression: 'What were you doing in there, then?'

'Me? Oh, nothing. Just a couple of things I was looking for. Nothing in particular . . .'

'And did you find what you were looking for?'

They were each trying to get the upper hand. Each knew what the other had been looking for but couldn't admit to being involved. The tension was almost unbearable, for I too was implicated. Something told me I ought to have known what they were going on about, what it was that was so important for them to find out, and all of a sudden I knew: *the letter!* It was the letter they were going on about, the farewell letter Marie had written, the letter I had dreamed up two evenings before in the garden. So they too thought there was a letter, then. So they too presumed she was dead, had taken her own life. I pondered on the word 'dead', the grown-up word 'dead', I whispered it, tried to understand it, but didn't succeed in getting it to mean anything more than 'gone', 'run off' or 'disappeared'. But she was 'dead'. Now it was certain and they must be to blame, or at least partly to blame, the way they behaved. And it was something to do with his being 'young' and her being 'old', I knew it. I felt it so strongly now that the silent conflict between them had finally surfaced. Every time Marie or something connected with her or with her disappearance was mentioned, it was as though a chill emanated from her, directed at him, an animosity towards this cheery husband of hers with his strong, healthy body. And at the same time I sensed in him regret and compassion for her and her mature, placid bulk, her plumpness, which the resignation of middle age had imparted to her. If there was anything in Jo's sordid insinuations, it was this, this which lay at the root of it all, which was the cause and effect of the shabby, sordid little fact which, when it came down to it, meant 'unfaithfulness'.

But there was something else besides, something niggling away at the back of my mind like toothache, a tiny little detail I had overlooked, which was significant in this context; no, not overlooked, but nor had it been properly registered at the time the incident had happened, when Uncle Kristen stood there taking a leak behind the cowshed wall and afterwards disgraced himself like an oversexed schoolboy, when his hand was no longer in his trouser pocket, but was busy with something or other as he stood there, his pee making the steam rise from the manure heap: a piece (several pieces?) of paper which fluttered down into the tangle of dried weeds . . .

'How d'you mean, found? I wasn't looking for anything,' said Uncle Kristen emphatically. 'The roof needs seeing to. I was just taking a look at it, that's all. . . .'

The atmosphere was unbearable. I mumbled a 'thanks for a nice dinner', hurried from the table, had to get out. I had to think over everything by myself. I had wanted to be above all this. My fifteen-year-old's speculations would only have made everything so much more complicated for them and me alike. For me, everything was so simple: either-or, black or white; the art of compromise was unknown to me, everything I experienced appeared to me in its most radical interpretation, and apart from this, I had my independence to think of.

But there was no escaping the fact that I was part of it, all the same. I'd seen them both yesterday afternoon. I was implicated as a witness, and there was no denying that curiosity stirred within me, arousing my senses. I had to see if there were any further clues, if there was any evidence that could be added to the pile of evidence against them which I already had.

A shadow raced over the farmyard. The grass bowed down low against the ground, its white underside turned up by the wind. Was it going to rain? I waded through the beds of nettles which each year grew in abundance between the hen-coop and the old well. The dry stalks from previous years snapped beneath my trainers; but new, bright-green nettles were growing up closer to the ground and brushed against my ankles, stinging me right through my socks. Yet it didn't really hurt; Jo *ate* nettles. I thought about this as I beat a path through and endeavoured, like the outdoor man of nature I yearned to be, to follow Uncle Kristen's tracks of yesterday.

A pungent smell rose from the muck-heap. This must be where he had stood. No, over there! The scene of his disgraceful and embarrassing behaviour, his 'youthful sin', so incredibly compromising for a full-grown man. I felt my feet sink in, felt the bile rising in my throat. The smell had become almost overpowering. I thought of the thin column of steam that rose into the air when you peed on warm manure. Nauseating. I could see his footprints quite plainly here. A piece of crumpled white paper lay close nearby, another a few yards away, a third and a fourth had been blown away on to the actual midden itself and lay there sodden, partly submerged in the muck. I picked up the two I could reach, flattened them out and saw that they were parts of a letter, written in strong man's handwriting, not at all like Uncle Kristen's. There were few words and they weren't hard to read. The message had been a short one: 'Mr Kr . . .' it said on one piece, 'low me to wri. . . .' And on the next line: 'cannot stand by and see such im. . . .' And on the next: '-morality like this'. On the other piece, it said simply: '-tionship with such a yo . . .' and 'for your own good'. The rest of the letter had been swallowed up by manure and urine.

I wasn't quite sure what to make of this. Obviously this letter had nothing to do with Marie's letter of farewell, because if he'd had that letter yesterday afternoon, he clearly wouldn't have needed to look for it today in Mary Cottage, where Aunt Linn had also already looked. I couldn't quite understand what the letter was; it was formal and, from what I could read, almost menacing, was written in blue pencil and looked as though it had been done in a hurry. All the same, it must have been an important letter, otherwise Uncle Kristen wouldn't have wanted to get rid of it in this way.

I stood inhaling the sickly sweet smell of manure, feeling almost faint. Suddenly someone called out. They were calling my name. It was him! Uncle Kristen! I crumpled the bits of paper together and threw them as far away as I could into the tangle of weeds. Then I crouched down and was hidden from view. He called a few more times, then a door banged and silence fell. I waited a little, then began to make my retreat, sneaked bent double through the weeds, then shot round the all-important corner, where he could see me if he was standing at the kitchen window, crept under the ramp leading up to the barn, along the endless barn wall, then looking as though butter wouldn't melt in my mouth, walked straight across the farmyard, up to the front door, into the hall, took a deep breath and marched into the kitchen.

He was standing beside the kitchen worktop gazing out of the window (how long had he been standing there? I wondered, horror-struck). But he looked surprised when I came in; perhaps he'd been lost in thought and hadn't seen me after all? There were only the two of us in the kitchen.

'I heard you calling,' I said, panting.

'Yes . . .' he said, vaguely. Then he suddenly looked at the floor where I was standing. 'Just look at your feet, Peter!'

I had to take a look myself, but already knew what an idiot I'd been: the wet footmarks trailed behind me across the kitchen floor. I'd forgotten the most obvious thing of all – my mucky shoes.

'What've you been up to?'

'Oh that, I was behind the barn. . . .'

I could have wept with shame at having exposed myself in such an obvious way. 'I . . . I wanted to dig some worms,' I lied in desperation. 'I thought I might try my hand at fishing.'

'Yes, not a bad idea.'

So he let it pass, even if his sharp eyes kept on returning to my manure-stained footprints by the door.

'I say,' he said after a while, 'I wonder if you could pop down to the shop for me? You can take the bike.'

Of course I could. Anything whatever to avoid further questions, to avoid being unmasked openly, to 'make amends'.

'I need some nails,' he said. 'I'm going to repair the roof. D'you think you could also get them to order a roll of tarpaulin?' He was staring out of the window again. 'If it'll just stay fine. . . . Can you manage that?'

'Sure,' I said.

'And there's one other little thing. . . .' He fell silent, smiling, looking at me slightly embarrassed. 'I was thinking of some small knick-knack for the little girl at Weasel Cottage, for baby Hanna. A little teddy bear or something like that. You'll find something. . . .' He looked so sheepish, so apologetic; there was something else on his mind which apparently wasn't easy to come out with. 'And don't say anything to Linn, will you? You know what she's like. . . . She doesn't like us having anything to do with those two up at Weasel Cottage. She's so afraid people will gossip. . . . Just put the things in the toolshed when you get back, OK?'

'All right,' I said as matily as I could. There was something about Uncle Kristen that made it difficult to go on thinking the worst about him. At that moment it was somehow impossible for me to associate him with anything shady, despite what he had been up to behind the barn wall yesterday. He was going to repair the roof. He'd maybe had legitimate reasons for going into Mary Cottage. In spite of everything, he was no doubt an honest farming man, Dad's brother, my uncle whom I'd always been so fond of and looked up to so much. At that moment, I'd gladly have lent him my sheath-knife, even though he would almost certainly use it in ways I wouldn't approve of. He was sending me down to the village to buy a teddy bear for little Hanna, but claimed it was Aunt Linn who was so afraid of gossip. Yet somehow I couldn't bring myself to suspect him, not now as he stood there smiling at me so trustingly.

I sped down the road on the old bicycle and thought about what he might have said if he found out that Cathrine had kissed me yesterday, yes *me*, in spite of all his muscular, hairy, youthful manliness. Me!

A rich carpet of green stretched over the fields on either side of the narrow farm-track. The wind buffeted the silvery foliage on the old drooping birches by the gateposts marking the boundary of Uncle Kristen's farmland, at the point where there had once been a gate. Clouds billowed up, filling the afternoon sky. I wobbled about on the unusually high saddle. The chain creaked as I pedalled along. It was a mile to the co-op, but it was downhill nearly all the way. I liked the sound of the gravel crunching beneath the tyres. A gust of wind buffeted me off course. The air whistled through the spokes. It was starting to blow harder, which suited me fine; weather in my face, wind and rain in my hair – just the thing for a man of the forest.

Cathrine. There wasn't a shadow of a doubt that her kiss had really meant something, that she loved me, for I was so head over heels in love with her.

11

Gerd Bergshagen was standing outside the shop when I came out again after my errand. 'Oh, hello Peter,' she said. She was just unhooking her net shopping-bag from the handlebar.

'Hi, Gerd,' I said, a touch embarrassed, but also hugely self-assured today. It was a pleasant kind of nervousness I felt as I stood with my back to her, strapping the cartons of nails to the parcel carrier, together with the bag containing a garish yellow plastic duck for baby Hanna. They didn't have any teddy bears at the co-op.

'If you hang on a tick, we can go back together, OK?'

I waited.

Then we rode home side by side, past the bus-stop, the petrol station and the community centre, at a gentle pace, dismounting at the slighest suggestion of a hill.

'Are you going to the summer fête, Peter?' she asked as we wheeled our bikes past the green field in front of the community centre.

'Er yes, I think so.'

'I bet it'll be fantastic. The Karlsens are going to be playing.'

'Oh?' I hadn't the foggiest who the Karlsens were.

'They're really great. They've made a record as well!'

Then we pedalled along again without speaking.

'I hear you were over at Fagerlund yesterday,' I said, attempting to play the innocent, as if I didn't know perfectly well why she'd been there!

'Yes.' She blushed. 'I was wondering if you could give me a hand with something.'

'Sure I can. No problem.'

'Are you good at English?'

'Well, not bad.'

'In that case, I'm sure you'll be able to help me with a letter to someone in England I'm corresponding with.'

Her boy-friend in England. Her romance of last summer. Perhaps I was a trifle jealous, even if I didn't *care* about Gerd in that particular way.

'Of course. No problem.'

'Thanks a million, Peter.'

She thanked me so profusely, so avidly that it was as though there was much more to her question than met the eye, but just at that moment the wind blew her hair down over her face, so that I couldn't catch her eye and tell what she was getting at.

'Just come over some time when it's convenient. Or maybe I can pop over to your place.'

The white road rose and fell between the sloping fields, and dark clouds tumbled over one another as they swept over the crest of the ridge. We pretended not to notice the change in the weather, the wind which snatched away our words, leaving nothing but formless sounds, and the downpour from which now there was no escaping.

'I was talking to Cathrine this morning,' she said after a pause.

Now it was my turn to blush. I fixed my eyes on the shiny handlebars, so that she wouldn't see how happy I was at what had happened up at Weasel Cottage the previous evening, and at the same time how terrified I was lest Cathrine had let her tongue run away with her and breathed as much as a word about my wonderful secret.

'She said it was nice you called. And she said you'd talked about all kinds of things. She asked me to say hello if I saw you.'

'Oh? Thanks a lot.'

Even if my face managed to conceal my elation, my voice betrayed me by jumping up an octave.

'I think she's a bit sweet on you, Peter. . . .'

Her laughter was strangely excited and strident. Perhaps the look on my face betrayed me after all.

'Oh, come off it. . . .'

My cheeks were aflame. I locked my gaze on to the handlebars. 'A bit sweet on you' – how strange and old-fashioned it sounded, but it was just what I needed, the confirmation I hankered for.

After a moment, she said: 'I say, don't you think Cathrine's pretty?'

'Er, yes. . . . Fairly. Yes, she's not bad.'

I could have sung hymns in praise of Cathrine, but couldn't put all my cards on the table like that.

'I think she's the prettiest girl I've ever met,' sighed Gerd, pushing back the ash-blonde hair from her face.

We'd reached Coombehills, dismounted, and were walking side by side, kicking small pebbles, each pushing our bikes, our footsteps sending up clouds of dust from the gravel and taking good care to look straight ahead and not at one another.

'What are you going to do when you've finished school?' she asked, when neither of us had said anything for a good while and my whole head seemed to reverberate with the sound of the wind and our footsteps on the gravel.

'Dunno. . . . Go to university maybe. I've no idea.'

I hadn't the faintest idea what I wanted to do. I had no special interests, no special gifts so far as I was aware, and the very thought of having to plan ten to fifteen years, if not a whole lifetime ahead, seemed totally depressing to me, who could hardly tell what person I wanted to be from one day to the next.

'Oh, I bet you'll go to university and become a doctor or something like that.'

I agreed with her. I also thought I was destined for something big, despite my acute inadequacy. But naturally one didn't voice such thoughts.

'And what about you?' I asked instead, for I could tell that this was what she really wanted to talk about.

'I want to be an air hostess,' said Gerd Bergshagen without a moment's hesitation. 'I'm going to try and get on the training course this autumn.'

'What a great idea,' I said, taken aback, not having expected such initiative from her, even though she had been to domestic science college the year before. 'Isn't it hard to get in, though?'

'Yes, it is, but I've got good marks and a great testimonial from the Tourist Hotel. . . .'

Where she had met up with the English bloke. It was starting to get on my wick, this business with the English bloke.

'But Jo doesn't think I'll get in . . .'

'Why not?'

'He says I'm too flat. He says that all air hostesses have to be at least thirty-six across here.' She traced a horizontal line in the air at about the level of her bust.

'Too *flat*?' I asked, open-mouthed. 'Well, I'll be blowed . . .'

'Do you think I'm too flat, Peter?'

She was wearing a skirt today, with a blouse and a cardigan on top; on her bare calves, fine white hairs bristled against the wind. Now she was holding her cardigan open so I could determine how 'flat' she was. And I stared at her as though I'd never set eyes on her before, and in fact I hadn't really. I realized that I'd always looked upon her as slightly off-putting because of Jo's unsavoury accounts. But this was about to change now: her freckles, her snub nose, her hair which had grown long and looked much better than before, her large eyes (cow eyes, was Jo's scornful term), asking me for a positive assessment of her prospects as an air hostess, even her mouth with its small, rather pointed teeth, had somehow become precisely what made her attractive in a modest way. Indeed, she was almost beautiful when she looked at me as she did now, provocative yet so vulnerable, since a flimsy summer blouse was all that stood between her pluckiness and blushing embarrassment.

'*Am* I too flat d'you think?'

'No, I, er. . . .'

I had to force my eyes to assess the bulges under her blouse. How could anyone ask *me* about something like this? Me, in whom the slightest hint of feminine curves, on statues, in pictures or on the women I chanced to see in the street, triggered off the lewdest fantasies. I couldn't help thinking of Cathrine's slim figure and her breath against my hot ear and the pressure of her firm breast against my thin – oh so thin! – arm (and that had happened yesterday, only yesterday evening!); it hardly showed at all through her dress. No, Gerd's breasts were anything but small, as far as I could judge.

'Er, no, I can't say I do. . . .'

I found it impossible to say this to her in plain words; yet I was somehow still hypnotized by the rising and falling of her blouse, and in answer to her invitation stared unabashedly, failing to notice that I had let go of the wobbly bicycle, which crashed to the ground behind me.

'Damnation!' I tore my eyes away and, reaching out for the bicycle, clutched at emptiness, for it already lay there in the road, one wheel revolving gently, the handlebars entangled in the spokes of her bicycle. 'Hell and damnation!'

Together we struggled to get the bicycles and our unruly feelings on to an even keel again.

We reached the place where our ways should have parted, where she had to turn off the main road, along which I still had to continue for a while. Then she said: 'I can just as well go home via Fagerlund, actually. It's just as quick.'

It wasn't hard to see through her: by no stretch of the imagination was it as quick for her to go home via Fagerlund, for she had to trundle her bicycle along the path the last bit, yet she wanted my company and I was proud, grateful and not a little flattered by her manoeuvre. We cycled slowly and lazily, laughing and chattering into the wind, even though it was gusting so strong that it was hard to hold a steady course. And above us the sky was a helter-skelter dance of wan summer smiles and leaden clouds.

The first shower hit us as we swung into the farmyard. I dashed straight for the toolshed, closely pursued by her. We took shelter together as the rain teemed down around us, me with the cartons of nails and the duck under my arm, and her clutching her net shopping-bag in her hand. Once inside, we stood looking out at the tumultuous downpour, laughing and shivering, trying to get our breath back. Our bikes lay where we'd thrown them, against a pile of wood. She was standing right behind me, close, close enough for me to feel the warmth of her body, hear her breathing, which made me uneasy yet elated, since I felt as though we were on a desert island here in the cramped toolshed for as long as the cloudburst lasted, cut off by an impenetrable wall of white, wet rain stretching from the sky right down to the grass. Here I was, a prisoner, together with the intrepid Gerd Bergshagen, who had been to the domestic science college, who had a boy-friend in England and had shown me her breast for my professional opinion. My timorous heart beat faster, quickened by my anguished hopes, my lack of experience, my helplessness, in time to the incessant drumming of the rain on the roof.

I'd put down my three parcels on the battered work-bench. She was still clutching her shopping-bag. One of the parcels had burst and two or three bottles of women's toiletries and a little jar had spilled out. 'They're for Cathrine,' she said, when she saw what I was staring at. I looked quickly away, as though something highly personal or even unseemly had been revealed. 'She asked me to buy her some cosmetic items. I'm going up to her place this evening. We're going to make ourselves up!' She said this as though confiding something risqué, something secret, intimate. At least, that's how I construed it. The thought of the two of them plastered with make-up up in Weasel Cottage, unrecognizable, 'grown-up', made me quite inexplicably ill at ease, excited and anxious all at once. 'Cathrine's so good at it. She's promised to teach me how to make myself up like Ava Gardner. And she's going to make herself up to look like Marilyn. . . .'

I cringed. Activities like these took them at one fell swoop light years beyond my reach. Where did I, a mere fifteen-year-old, fit in with two grown-up girls who got up to all sorts of dubious hanky-panky with cosmetics? Went in for make-up orgies? I thought of the ridiculous toy duck I had bought and felt I had a hand in, Uncle Kristen's present. Now the mere thought of it was an embarrassment, the generosity I had felt, devalued, scorned. I would have given my right arm to find out what the two of them got up to when they were alone, what they talked about, told one another about themselves. But how, how on earth could I find out? Asking was quite out of the question. . . .

The drumming of the rain continued unabated. We stood there in the toolshed like two people shipwrecked, close together, close enough to hear our breathing, slipping in and out of phase, in and out, perhaps standing as Uncle Kristen and Marie had stood in the porch at Bergshagen, if what Jo had said was true. And it was Gerd who had seen them.

On a sudden impulse, I burst out: 'I say, is it true you saw Uncle Kristen and Marie . . . er, necking at Jo's confirmation party?'

She looked at me. 'Is that what Jo told you?'

'Yes.'

'Oh, he always has to go and exaggerate,' she said, irritated.

'So it's not true, then?'

'Well yes, they *did* have their arms round one another . . .'

'Oh?'

'But what everybody round here says about him just isn't true. I mean, that he made a beeline for her. If anything, it was the other way round, but of course no one wants to hear about that. I'd known about it for ages. She told me about it one day last winter. She was really down in the dumps and said he was the only one in the world who meant anything to her, but that obviously it was out of the question, and that she had such a guilty conscience. . . . I *knew* that something would happen!'

'Oh, how d'you mean?'

'Because of the way she was talking. It was so odd. She said it would be best if she disappeared, so that she didn't bring bad luck on others. She said she knew someone might get into deep water for her sake. I didn't realize what she meant. She surely had no reason to be so down in the dumps. She had admirers galore. She said Aage Brenden had proposed to her at a party one Saturday night, though she knew jolly well what *he* was after. . . . She was so kind and friendly. I can't see why everything seemed so difficult for her. . . .'

Gerd had large, shining eyes, cow eyes as Jo had called them, and I had agreed with him. I would never refer to any girl's eyes as cowlike ever again; never ever. She had moved closer, I could feel her cardigan touching my shirt-sleeve. This contact, however slight, somehow seemed comforting and protective.

'And when she disappeared,' Gerd went on, lowering her voice, 'I wasn't the least bit surprised, because in a way I'd half expected it, after what she'd said. . . . She could be very moody, they say it's in the family. . . . Oh, I'm sure she's gone and drowned herself in a bog, Peter, what do you think? It's so horrible to think of. . . .'

What had happened to Marie made it so much easier for us

to draw closer together in the shed. Our own modest doings paled into insignificance when compared with the heavy, sombre thoughts of sorrow and enigmatic, unanswered questions that were inextricably linked with the events here on the farm. The misfortunes of others could thus be exploited to one's own advantage. Now it was easy for me to press my arm against her side so that I could feel her warmth from my shoulder right down to the back of my hand, a human warmth, damp from the rain. Then it was her turn: she took my other hand and pressed it firmly against her breast. In the midst of the sudden shock, the joyful panic, I became aware of the incredibly firm softness, a strange independent weight like a warm living and moving thing in there under her blouse. Then I took hold of it gratefully.

'Oh Peter,' she whispered. 'Go ahead. It's all right. Am I as flat as Jo said I was?'

I'd placed my free arm around her waist. Our breathing was rapid and heavy, not in time, reluctant almost, afraid lest any distraction brought our thoughts back to humdrum matters, to our normal existences, in which we scarcely knew one another: Jo's sister and a gawky nephew from the city, a tottering daddy-long-legs and a modest cabbage butterfly. I held her as tight as I could, feeling at her breast, haltingly offering her my tenderest feelings, only hoping she was able to receive them.

But something seemed to be missing. I'd felt it at the back of my mind, but hadn't dared to act upon it. I didn't know how to go about it, how to get the other person to join in, what exactly to do in technical terms, without putting both feet in it. Of course I'd witnessed it often enough in films, in magazines, and on rare occasions in the park, in the timid, lacklustre reality of everyday life. I could have had a shot at it, imitated it, yet when it came down to it, I lacked the courage and so had to leave it to her. She placed her hand behind my neck, pulled my face down close to hers, and I barely had time to feel her breath on my face before she placed her mouth around my tightly pursed lips, pressed hard and emitted a sigh, as though indescribably relieved. As for me, I returned this moan with a passionate intonation of my own, that much I did know at least. And her tongue probed about on the outside of my lips, which I clamped tightly together, as though terrified. She was attempting to soften them, to soothe

the anxiety that welled up through my reticence in stabs of fury, to melt the iceberg of inexperience with her slimy sweet saliva. But I was rigid and unbending.

It seemed to clear up for a moment, for the sun swept across the door-frame where my eyes were glued, and smiled upon me, brightening up my thoughts a little. But immediately after, it was pouring down again.

12

I was setting snares, attaching fine strands of horsehair with slip-knots to branches which were likely haunts of wood-grouse, adding pieces of bread as bait. Of course, to do it properly, it should really have been berries, which the birds were fond of, but it was too early, everything had only just flowered, and even the bilberry bushes were still covered in tiny pale-blue flowers out here in the shade. Bread would just have to do. It wasn't the season for setting snares, but I was a hunter, wanted to be a hunter, to be free and alone, to lead an independent existence out here in the forest, to live off my wits and whatever nature provided, or at least wanted to know this was feasible.

I tried out the slip-knot on my forefinger: it tightened smoothly, soundlessly, mercilessly; a hungry capercaillie was doomed to die. I'd found the horsehair in the stable. Dad had once told me that they used to catch thrushes like this as kids. Horsehair and rowan berries. Thrushes were also fair game, but I was more ambitious: I would live like a lord on fish and grouse. They could jolly well keep their meatballs down at the farm.

It was the crack of dawn. I'd woken up after a disturbing dream about Gerd, about her thick, warm tongue. I'd got up and studied my spotty, adolescent face in the cracked mirror above the washing-bowl, could still hear her voice saying: 'You've got such long eyelashes, Peter. I've never seen a boy with such long eyelashes. . . .' The inadequacy of what had happened in the toolshed. A few days had already passed since then, yet I was still fearful that I'd cut a very poor figure. And I'd betrayed my Cathrine. Though – well, no, I hadn't, not *really*; she'd been in my thoughts the whole time, even when Gerd had clamped her lips to me like a limpet. ('Isn't Cathrine pretty, Peter? She's the prettiest girl I know.') I had no alternative but to withdraw into my own isolation, yet with a slight feeling of triumph, of satisfaction all the same: I really had charmed the pants off her and no mistake about it; she must have been quite carried away to do what she'd done, say what she'd said. In the mirror I'd tried to size up my irresistible charm. . . .

Then a brisk run. You had to build up your muscles, keep in shape. The no longer new trainers were soaking wet. The forest steamed after the rain of the past few days, though the sun was warm again today. The air was full of fragrance. I felt so free, so strong out here in the forest. Who was there who could enjoy the richness of this magnificent natural setting more deeply and profoundly than I? Who had better cause? Who had more right?

I attached the snare carefully to the juniper bush, scattered some pieces of bread at a suitable distance. Certain death for a greedy capercaillie. Sheer delight for the hunter. I was lord of the forest.

Along the stream with my fishing-rod later that day. Today, in weather like this, everything had to be given a try. I knew there were fish in the stream, even though I'd never succeeded in catching one in all the long hours I'd spent wandering up and down the banks every summer I'd been here. But not until today had catching something been so important. Today I'd be lucky, today of all days, since kindly girl's eyes looked down benevolently upon me in everything I did, watching my every movement and adding a golden glow to the sunshine that warmed my neck and shoulders, shimmered in the foliage, and transformed young birches into taut sails. I couldn't fail to catch a fish today! What, just one fish? No, lots of them, more than I could eat, so I could dry and salt them and hang them up in the time-honoured fashion of hunters, keep them until later, perhaps even give some to Aunt Linn and Uncle Kristen so they would see how clever and self-sufficient I'd become. . . .

For it was my lucky day.

I cast hook and sinker out into the current. In most places the stream wasn't so deep as to prevent me from following the earthworm's helpless dance over the smooth, white stones on the bottom. It was swept away at quite a pace out of sight, and further away still, until Uncle Kristen's fishing-line was fully extended, whereupon I wound it in and inspected the bait before casting again, against the current, following the pale pirouettes of the earthworm over the stones until I could no longer make it out.

I'd found myself a nice spot on a large, flat rock which jutted right out into the water. The stream was only about five or six yards across at this point. On the opposite bank alder bushes grew right down to the water's edge. From the bushes there issued the sound of small creatures scurrying about, rapid wing-beats, spooks, which were perhaps no more than the warm breeze, for I was day-dreaming. And some footsteps that I heard further in among the trees were not distinct enough, specific enough to be anything other than part of my day-dream.

The surface of the babbling stream shimmered. The blue and white earthworm slid helplessly from stone to stone on the bottom, its purpose to coax out fish on a still, warm day in July, the month of plenty, which had already shown me some of its bounty.

Thoughts came and went in a constant flow, too fleeting to hold on to, vague day-dreams about falling in love, about Gerd, the strange Gerd Bergshagen, who was anything but plump and plain as I'd originally believed, who had invited me to feel her breasts, no doubt because she thought I was experienced, was able to compare, able to assess whether she was too 'flat' to become an air hostess, who had whispered 'Go ahead. It's all right' while still clutching the shopping-bag. What a feeling of power it gave to think of the breathless goings on there in the shed – even though she'd had to take the initiative. And Cathrine, my lovely Cathrine, whom I'd not seen since my visit to Weasel Cottage despite my firm intention to go up there again. I'd been invited, after all. She'd kissed me on the cheek, asked me to come. . . . But I was the one who'd found excuses not to go. And *he* had been up there with some milk again. . . .

A hot, almost sultry July morning when the fish wouldn't bite. One could suddenly be overcome by an inexplicable bout of faintness, all of a sudden feel the sweat trickle down over one's chest and back, be tempted to sit down, if not lie down, under a shower of gentle sunlight pouring down through the foliage. Sharp splinters ricocheted from the countless dimples on the surface of the stream. How close, how overpowering everything felt this morning. A dragonfly shot out over the water, hovering there, allowing its metallic hues to glitter for a second, then another, and flew off. How beautiful! Oh to be a dragonfly, with such self-assuredness, such elegance!

But still there was no bite. I walked down beside the stream, cast and made a wish as I followed the worm with my gaze, ever hopeful. I wanted to catch a fish, just one, to prove that luck was still on my side, that exercising my charm on girls, feeling their breasts in the toolshed, wasn't the only thing I could do – there were greater things in store – to prove that what I treasured in my breast as I strolled along was the truth, not imagination, wishful thinking, almost as though something had already been promised to me. So I cast the line and with my eyes followed the worm longingly until it disappeared from view.

But the fish still refused to bite, forcing me to change my spot, to walk downstream, pursuing my hope as it gleamed seductively in every smile of the sun upon the clear water. The going became harder. I clambered over boulders, struggled through dense scrub and undergrowth, snagged my fishing-rod on branches and jerked it free, sending showers of leaves raining down on me, floating on to the surface of the water, then sailing out of sight. It was warm. I gazed longingly at the stream as it babbled along clear and refreshing, lazy beneath the treacherous, swaying turf, which hung green and tempting out over the edge of the water. I was getting close to the bathing place by the old mill now. The stream was already wider, and only a hundred yards further down it widened out to form the Mill Dam, a miniature lake a good forty yards across at the widest point. I could strip off and jump in. This was all the more tempting because I recalled the summer evening two years before when I had stolen away here without permission and bathed naked in the tepid water, turned brown by the iron in the peat.

I carried on casting, though I'd virtually abandoned all hope of catching anything. I went off to seek out a sheltered spot where it might be possible to get undressed. It was broad daylight and there might therefore be people at the Mill Dam itself, or at any rate somebody might turn up at any moment. I had to find a spot where I could be completely alone, yet where the stream was also wide and deep enough for me to be able to swim. There must be a good many such places, I thought, as I laboriously cut a path through the undergrowth which at this point was denser than usual. I also seemed to remember having seen a place once, a little bend, a flat place, only I wasn't quite sure where it was. . . . But when I eventually spotted a suitable place, a little grassy bank which then ran out into a flat rock falling gently into the inviting water, it was unfortunately on the opposite bank. The stream was too wide and deep for me to wade over at this point and, furthermore, something else, something totally unexpected, totally disconcerting, caused me to gasp for breath, as, quick as lightning, I bobbed down among the bushes. A body was stretched flat out on the grass, a girl's body, a slim, white figure, her gracious curves from outstretched arm to ankle interrupted only by the lower half of a bikini and a mass of sun-bleached, curly hair: Cathrine! It was my Cathrine lying there sunbathing in a sheltered spot, so undressed that her hair was all I recognized; her arms and shoulders, the narrow back and long legs were like décor borrowed from a dream, full of promise, a revelation – such an expanse of naked flesh. . . .

She hadn't heard me. She lay still, so utterly still that I was almost a little alarmed. Was this, after all, an apparition, an elfin vision here beside the stream? I felt faint in the sultry heat, amid all the overpowering scents down here amongst the squat bushes. Was there nothing to link this reposing, nymphlike figure, this outstretched body of a girl, with the happy, hospitable, welcoming creature, who of her own volition and quite unabashed and sincere had sat and told me, a fifteen-year-old, about her life and experiences, about how she felt lonely out here in the country in a cottage in the middle of nowhere, how fond she was of company, and had kissed me goodbye, asking me to come back soon?

Cathrine. I had to whisper her name into the mellow haze floating through the undergrowth, filling my head, making it swim: Cathrine. There she lay, face down, with no more than a little patch of cloth over her round, curvacious behind, resting or asleep, perhaps slumbering like Sleeping Beauty herself? At any rate I could scarcely believe that there she was, only twenty to thirty yards from where I was hiding, a distance turned to light years by her nakedness. I was annihilated, completely brought to naught by lovely Cathrine's bare shoulders, her back and thighs and her tiny polka-dot bikini. Naturally it didn't occur to me to reveal my presence; indeed, the mere thought of doing so caused my hands to go clammy with embarrassment. The narrow strip of pale skin in the grass stole every last jot of the impetuous self-confidence I'd felt a moment ago.

I crouched there in the bushes, staring at this prostrate girl's body, so white in the sun and completely at the mercy of my covert scrutiny. Ants crawled into my shoes and flies regaled themselves on my sweat-drenched neck and in my ears and the sun scorched my cheeks. Then all of a sudden I froze inwardly, for there was something else that had finally caught my attention: I saw the little carry-cot which had been placed in the shade, where a tiny hand had momentarily shown itself, had thrown out a toy which its owner had lost patience with; a yellow duck, a plastic duck with a garish orange beak now lay pathetically in the grass. My duck! When had Uncle Kristen been able to give her the present I had bought on his behalf? When I had gone down to the toolshed to fetch my fishing-rod early this morning, the parcel had still been there on the work-bench. And I saw something else besides: two empty bottles discarded in the grass. *Two* bottles. Lemonade? Coca-Cola? What difference did it make, there were *two* of them. Could both of them be hers? I saw two cups as well, paper cups of the sort people use on trains.

It also occurred to me that I'd heard a noise a little while before, footsteps, higher up the stream. At least it might well have been footsteps, though I hadn't paid any particular attention to them. It might have been him! He might have been here just now! The thought made me gasp for breath. The awkward position I found myself in was pulling my bones out of joint. Sweat poured off me.

I became aware of a garment she was resting her head on, a dark-blue garment with white stripes; the sleeve, the buttons. It was a working shirt, a familiar working shirt, the one I'd seen

Uncle Kristen wearing early this morning when I'd asked him if I could borrow the fishing-rod. Now it lay there on the green grass supporting her head. Him! He *had* been here! He had seen Cathrine like this, talked to her, drunk lemonade with her, given her presents. He might even have stripped off too, to sunbathe and show her his scar. Perhaps even. . . .

I had to get away. I could no longer bear sitting here looking at the spectacle of her with thoughts such as these on my mind. I had to get away. I slowly began to make my retreat, step by step, my eyes meanwhile riveted to her body as it lay there so slim and small, at once unattainable and provocative, innocent and inviolate, yet none the less suspect, polluted by the presence of Uncle Kristen. But it was hard to manoeuvre the fishing-rod through the undergrowth. I mustn't make a sound. Impenetrable bushes forced me out towards the stream again, something gave way beneath my foot, moss slipped on stone. I lost my footing and fell, using my hands to break my fall, but had not let go of the fishing-rod, which struck the water with a joyous splash, and like as not I would have followed it, clumsy as I was, and still desperately anxious that she shouldn't see or hear me, but saved myself in the nick of time by grabbing hold of some branches. And there I lay spreadeagled on the open bank of the stream, still clutching the fishing-rod, which now bobbed up and down trying to wriggle out of my grasp into the current and with the other hand smarting and full of leaves and broken twigs, my eyes still glued to the naked figure which now, at this excruciating moment, suddenly burst into life, raised itself up on one elbow and turned in my direction, treating me to an amazing full frontal and putting the finishing touches to the disaster. Astonished, two eyes and two large dark nipples stared at me from the opposite bank.

I looked down, looked away, struggled to my feet, or at least attempted to, yanking the miserable fishing-rod out on to dry land, too sheepish to look across at her, hardly able to move, scarcely able to breathe from despair, from shame at being caught red-handed as a Peeping Tom, and by her of all people, in such a ridiculous and undignified way. My face burned. I had to hide. The only thought in my head was to get away. Far away! Away from it all! But of course I remained glued to the spot, racked with unspeakable self-recrimination, my gaze following the ripples smiling on the sunlit water, as I numbly wondered whether this was my final hour. Was this the end? Eternal darkness and damnation?

'Hey there, Peter!'

Her voice rang out like a bell over the stream, carefree and happy. It was impossible not to surrender to its charm, so I took my courage in both hands and looked up. She was covering her breasts with one hand, smiling, waving with the other hand, apparently not the least bit upset.

'I didn't see you. Are you fishing?'

'Er . . . yes, I lost my footing.' (Idiot! As though she didn't know full well!)

'Yes, they're terrible, those rocks, aren't they? Did you hurt yourself?'

'No – I don't think so really.'

With my free hand I brushed the bits off my clothes to show her that I was perfectly all right, meanwhile continuing to clutch the fishing-rod as though it was my last hope of salvation.

'That's lucky. Have you caught anything?'

'No, not yet. It's . . . er, it's maybe a bit too warm today.'

'You ought to come over here and sunbathe instead.' She beamed at me from the grassy bank, quite unperturbed by her nakedness and my stuttering confusion. 'It's so lovely over here!'

I could have fainted with relief. It began to dawn on me that there wasn't the slightest hint of reproach or suspicion in her voice. What a miracle! Could it possibly be that she thought I'd only just come down here and hadn't seen her before she saw me? That I'd lost my footing in all innocence, as it were? Or was it simply that she didn't care two hoots? Was it possible that being half naked in the presence of men was just as natural for her as discussing her love affairs without turning a hair? The way she made all my fears and inhibitions vanish into thin air was a complete enigma to me. She was in a class of her own, so invulnerable, so far above the blinkered propriety that I and all the rest of them up here stood for. She was an elf, an ethereal being. . . .

I could sense the feeling of relief fanning out through my whole body, turning it to jelly. I could scarcely grasp that I was saved, was in all humility willing to do any kind of penance in honour of the gentle power that had rescued me from my dilemma. There was naturally no question of exploiting the situation still further by accepting the invitation to sunbathe with her. That would have been tempting fate. Besides, the naked presence on the grass on the other side of the stream was far too disturbing. What the dickens would I say or do if I suddenly found myself there beside her? Who on earth was I to meet the challenge of this unique opportunity? Jo's gross remark rang again in my ears: 'And you *still* didn't fuck? Are you a homo?'

'You can get across higher up, I think. Isn't it shallower there?'

'Er, yes, maybe. . . .' But I shook my head evasively. My eyes were glued to her hand which only just covered the breasts I had got a clear look at a minute before. The first breasts I'd ever had a proper look at in my life. 'Oh, I think I'll carry on fishing for a bit. . . .'

I announced my retreat to her over the water in a barely audible mumble. The sun beat down red hot. The stream flowed by so serene and inviting. The thought of lying there on the grass right beside her, perhaps with the added bonus of stealing a peep at her breasts now and then. . . . Who could hope to catch any fish in broad daylight and in weather like this? I had to pull myself together: men were single-minded, and decisiveness and strength of will always made a good impression. Besides, I'd made up my mind to spend the whole day fishing in penance for the crime I'd just committed. I was already fiddling with the entangled fishing-line, trying to loosen the knots, discarding the pathetic remnants of the bait, threading a new worm on to the hook and, just to show her, I cast the hook and sinker with all the professionalism I could muster. She couldn't help but see that I meant business. And what is more, this gave me a pretext for standing here near her, yet at a safe distance, for a little while longer.

'You said yourself it was too hot,' she laughed.

'There are some better spots higher up.'

The line stretched out but there wasn't the faintest hint of life down in the murky depths. No further postponement was possible. I reeled in the line. She had lain down again, head resting on her elbow, and lay there looking at me. I waved indecisively.

'See you, then!'

'Come back if the fish don't change their minds, won't you?'

'OK.'

I took two or three decisive steps, but couldn't help turning round again one last time: 'I . . . er . . . may pop up to the cottage one of these days!'

'Fine!' she shouted back with a wave, giving me another glimpse of her breasts with their rings round the nipples. Then suddenly I spotted something else: she'd altered her hair, which was now gathered up away from her face and held in place by a ribbon, which I got a clear look at, a woven rust-red and yellow ribbon, just like the one Uncle Kristen had tried to hide from me up in the hut – he'd whipped it down from the nail where it had been hanging and hidden it in his pocket. Of course I couldn't swear it was the same ribbon, but it was similar. And it might be more than a mere coincidence.

I hurried on my way, out of sight, my head hot and my knee aching after the fall, haunted by doubt and by her nipples, two hard rings on the white skin. Because of the baby and the breast-feeding obviously. I'd read about it in a reference work at the library, my solitary source of information in matters of practical sex: nipples changed colour. Pictures. Erection. It pained me to think of the inexorable physical processes bound up with Cathrine's slim body. She was an experienced woman, had been a married man's mistress, had given birth to a daughter, suckled her, been to bed with goodness knows how many other men. . . . Everything had somehow passed *through* her body, it had been 'used', more 'used' than that of portly Aunt Linn, who'd had no children. All the same, Cathrine was so young, so slim and graceful, unblemished, that we could have been the same age. Her body was 'young' and 'used' all at once, full of promise and yet beyond reach. . . . Could Uncle Kristen really have been there just before me?

I paused, well out of sight, still smarting with embarrassment, doubt and self-recrimination, found a spot and cast the line more out of a sense of duty than conviction, for it was shallower again up here. I followed the worm's melancholy progress over the slippery stones. He'd no doubt been there with Cathrine just before I'd arrived, with his strong, manly yet youthful body, his thick black hair and strong forearms. But all the same. . . . I gave my fervent desires free rein, allowing them to float along with the gentle current. I conjured up the magic of being in love: she'd smiled and laughed and waved, invited me over, so easy-going, not even remotely embarrassed by her nakedness. Didn't that mean something? Didn't that mean I was special? That everyone else had to be excluded? The thought filled me with a feeling of warmth. The helplessness I'd felt a moment before was already being spirited away by my indomitable fifteen-year-old's vanity. Now I could see nothing but her smiling eyes and her breasts with their dark-brown tops, also smiling in their way.

The line had run right out and quivered gently in the current. I wound it in. I'd completely forgotten about the fishing and about my recent resolutions; I'd have to pack it in soon. But something was holding the line back. The rod was tugging slightly; there was something alive at the other end. In a kind of ecstasy, I experienced the fisherman's most wonderful moment: I'd got a bite! I forgot all I'd ever learned about fishing, whipped the rod up into the air with a massive jerk, sending showers of droplets off the line, glimpsed the silver of a fish's belly shoot over my head before the line and rod crashed into the undergrowth behind me. I'd caught a fish and it was safely on dry land!

I was ecstatic with happiness as I crawled around searching for my catch. So it was my lucky day after all!

It was a perch, a tiny little perch, which in my carelessness I'd shaken free of the hook and which now lay gaping and writhing in the heather, the hot sun playing on its lovely colours. My fish. How lovely it was! I tried to pick it up, but it slipped from my grasp. Its scales were covered in pine needles and other bits and pieces. I would have to kill it, I knew that. It mustn't lie here being tormented, but I couldn't bring myself to do it. Neither it nor I wanted this. It was so beautiful with red pectoral fins and a greenish-grey back with dark-coloured stripes. It jumped and flipped about, lying there gasping for a moment before curling up on itself again. Then I got hold of it, held it firmly in my hand, knowing what I had to do, but unable to do it. Not for anything in the world could I have inserted my fingers under its gills and broken its neck. Instead, I ran down to the water's edge. I'd spotted something which might come in handy here: a tin can. I swilled it out, filled it with water and dropped the fish in. It swam round two or three times before lying quite still at the very bottom of the can. That meant it was perfectly all right, otherwise it would have floated on the surface; that much I did know.

Carefully, I placed my catch on the bank and disentangled my fishing-line from the twigs and leaves caught in it. Then I set out for home with my fishing-rod slung over my shoulder and the tin clutched securely in my hand. I was so happy! I felt I had to be kind and nice towards everyone. I had been richly rewarded today and had to do my own bit in return, protect life, even the life of this little perch which I had caught quite legitimately. All life, even flies. . . . Because Cathrine's lovely breasts had looked upon me and smiled.

Back up in the hut it was hot. The flies sat on the window-panes bloated to bursting-point. The heat caused the creosoted timber walls to creak. I filled the jam jar with water and dropped the fish in, scattering a few breadcrumbs on the surface, though it wasn't tempted. Then I lay on the bunk watching a spider's aerial acrobatics up under the beams, feeling drowsier and drowsier until I nodded off. I slept till I felt the sun upon my face through the open door. It was then that I became aware of them, all the flies, masses more than usual here in the hut. They crawled and buzzed all over the place, flying in and out of the shafts of sunlight, colliding with the window-panes, jostling for a place on the jam jar. And there in the jam jar lay the little fish floating belly up on the surface and enveloped in a thin film of yellowish slime.

13

Some days later, I received a visit from Jo. He had things to tell.

'They play strip poker!' His voice fairly quavered with malicious pleasure.

'Who does? Where?'

'Gerd and that townie lass. Up at Weasel Cottage. I wormed it out of her. I knew they were up to some blinking hanky-panky up there!'

'Oh?'

'Yes, it was clear as day. She's up there practically every evening in the week, most evenings at any rate. She takes make-up and hair lacquer and all sorts with her . . . I *knew* it!'

He was triumphant, laughing and grinning, showing his yellow teeth. He'd scraped his knees, wasn't wearing any socks and his ankles were covered in grime. He was the most unsavoury lad I'd ever come across, but he was my summer pal all the same, and there were more things that united us than kept us apart. Now, at any rate.

He had something else on his chest, though.

'Gerd told me they'd run about in the nick afterwards on the grass. Two girls . . . filthy buggers! Happen they're "les"!'

'Bloody hell. . . .'

I wasn't quite sure what to make of it. He might have added the last bit off the top of his head, invented it just to cap his story with yet another juicy titbit. Actually, he was fully capable of having invented the whole caboodle, but I remembered Cathrine asking me whether I could play poker. Could *this* have been what she was getting at? The thought of it sent the blood rushing to my head: I couldn't even *play* poker!

Jo was in great form: 'You'd better grab your chance now, while she's on heat! They don't wait for ever, you know . . .'

'No, you're telling me.' I had to say something in reply, even though it was far beneath my dignity and broke all the commandments I'd set myself to live by. 'I grab all the chances that come my way.'

He came back quick as a flash: 'Oh yes? Have you been back up there, then?'

'No, but I ran into her down by the stream when she was sunbathing one day.'

'Oh?'

'She was starkers. Abso-bloody-lutely starkers!'

'Flipping heck!' he gasped. 'So what did you do, then?'

'Me . . .? It was rotten bloody luck, you see, because she had the nipper with her and I was on my way down to give Uncle Kristen a hand with the haymaking.'

We'd just started the haymaking, so it could easily have been true.

'Rotten luck!'

'Yeah, bloody rotten. Still, I got a dekko. . . .'

I cringed, I grovelled in filth and slime, unable for the life of me to comprehend how I could bring myself to betray her, my Cathrine, so shabbily to this little squirt, yet, there again, I *had* to get the upper hand over him. And over her too, Gerd's partner at strip poker. And I'd succeeded. . . .

'Holy bleeding Moses. What was she *like*?'

'Not bad,' I said, casually. 'Tits a bit on the small side though . . .'

'Told you so, didn't I?' said Jo, who had still not so much as set eyes on Cathrine Stang. 'I told you so,' he said, revelling in my tall stories.

It was afternoon. Quiet. Hot. We didn't say a word for a while, perhaps both too excited by the barefaced lies we had been swopping. The thought of the two of them making themselves up and playing strip poker was a nightmare, but it excited me as well. I placed myself in their shoes, first one and then the other, for I had rights over both of them and an investment too, in a way.

Suddenly Jo asked: 'Hey, I say, Peter, how d'you reckon boys "do it"?'

So this was what he'd been ruminating about as he sat there.

'Damned if I know.'

I'd heard all kinds of far-fetched speculations but could never bring myself to believe that any of them could possibly have a place in real life.

'D'you reckon they "fence"? That's what I think. But Soeren Skaug says they do it from behind.'

'From behind?'

'Yes, from behind. Just like dogs do.'

'Oh, it must hurt.'

'Too bloody right. Mucky buggers!'

We applied our minds to this technical problem for a while until at long last he came out with what had been on his mind.

'Hey I say, how about a quick one now?'

'Now? Here, you mean?'

'Yes, now. Right now. D'you feel like it?'

I did in fact. It must have been the thought of those blasted girls.

'OK, then.'

'OK.'

It was about a week since I'd met Cathrine. Even the best of resolutions weaken in time. So a little reluctantly, though with a wonderful feeling of relief, I returned to childhood in the company of Jo.

The snares. I'd clean forgotten the snares! I'd had so much else on my mind. . . .

I went to inspect them after Jo had gone. I no longer had any desire to kill birds. I couldn't comprehend what on earth had made me set such traps for tiny living creatures. It was so easy to forget things one had grown out of. Now I hoped the snares were empty, or, if I'd actually caught something, that my prey would still be alive at least. A thrush, a crow perhaps, or maybe even – and that would be best of all – a raven, barely injured, so I could take it home with me, care for it and tame it. That's what I hoped now.

But the snares seemed to be empty. The first three I looked

at hung there just as I'd left them, even the bait still intact. The fourth had disappeared without trace – that is, if my memory was right about where I'd placed it. There hardly seemed any point in looking for more of them; I'd set five, thinking that would do. There was probably nothing in the fifth one either, though something told me to make the detour all the same. After all, it wasn't far.

And in the fifth snare there was a little bird. It was a robin and it was dead. It had been caught by one of its wings and hung there strangely contorted, head down and beak agape and its delicate claws curled up as though round a twig. On the wing that had become snagged in the horsehair noose, the transparent feathers formed a beautiful fan, but the other wing hung there, small and grey and lifeless, pointing towards the ground. Long, pale blades of grass reached aloft like sentinels guarding the lifeless body.

I disentangled it carefully, unable to bring myself just to throw it away, so stood there with it in my hand. It was completely stiff and weighed practically nothing.

Dejected, I made my way home, carefully carrying the bird close to my body as a token of the remorse I felt. In the hut, I laid it on a piece of newspaper and examined it. It was so beautiful, so perfect and the red feathers on its breast trembled faintly each time I breathed. The beak and claws were of the finest filigree. The feathers on the broken wing rested weightless one upon the other forming the shape of a fan. I looked at it so long that it became a cherished possession, a treasure I would save, taking it out only when I wanted to look at something beautiful. I was pleased with myself.

But the flies also wanted their bit. They crept and crawled all over the bird, despite my attempts to waft them away. I would have to hide it from the flies. I folded the paper carefully around it, knelt down and shoved the little parcel as far as I could under the bunk. It would be safe there. I might bury it later, if only I could find a suitable place.

When I came down for the evening meal, there was a great commotion at the farm. The cows had broken through a fence and were on the loose trampling down the barley field. Uncle

Kristen had just dashed off to drive them back. I hurried hot on his heels.

When I got there, he'd already got most of them back into the pasture, but two or three stubborn ones were running about with their tails in the air. He loped after them with heavy strides, up to his knees in the stiff ears of the barley, shouting, wielding a switch. The cows' ungainly gallop and Uncle Kristen's lumbering efforts to catch up with them and head them off was like a grotesque ballet. I stared, spellbound, making no attempt to help him, knowing he'd manage anyway.

And manage he did. He was familiar with their capricious ways, drove them towards a gap in the fence waving his arms about wildly, shouting and lashing at them with the switch. He was seething. I'd never seen him strike the animals like this before. It wasn't much fun to watch any more. I could hear him cursing them and the whoosh of the switch through the air. Now they had reached the gap in the fence. He drove them through. The last of them received a hefty kick on the hocks. Silly bloody critter!

I'd no desire to walk back with him, not when he was in such a foul temper, so I ran ahead. I couldn't fathom what had got into him, even though obviously it was damned annoying to find the whole herd down among the crops. It was so unlike him to behave like this.

I reached the farm with the blood pounding in my throat, sprinted over the farmyard, in to Aunt Linn in the kitchen. There was a sweet smell. She'd been making jam. Jars of strawberry jam stood in a row on the worktop. Wasps were buzzing away under the ceiling, crawling against the window-panes.

'He's got them back in!'

She was sitting at the table set for the evening meal. Slices of bread had been buttered, side-plates and glasses had been put out. She neither spoke nor moved when I came in. She sat at her place as though she had not been expecting anyone, head resting heavily on her hand, her eyes hidden. A tear fell on to the table. I saw there was a letter at Uncle Kristen's place. The postman must have been late today. The address on the envelope had been written in blue pencil. And on the kitchen worktop near the door stood the smallest of the milk cans, shiny, right at the edge, as though impatient to be taken to its destination.

14

During the warm days that followed, we carted hay into the barn. Uncle Kristen handed the hay up to me from the heavy racks, and I trampled it down. It was hot, the sweat poured off us, but he never let up. I didn't sit up there on the hay on the way back to the barn as I'd always done in previous years; I was too old for that sort of thing now. I trudged along behind the hay wagon up the road leading back to the farm, feeling my feet swell in my sweat-soaked shoes and longing for some shade and a glass of water to quench my thirst. But he never seemed to need a rest, just went on handing bundle after bundle of hay up to me there on the wagon, driving the hay wagon back to the farm and dumping loads of bone-dry hay into the storage space below. High up there in the hayloft I felt almost faint. As I watched him at work, so utterly absorbed in what he was doing, my suspicions seemed to fade. It was hard to believe that someone who worked like Uncle Kristen did, day after day, could at the same time be chasing after a young girl who lived all on her own in a cottage nearby. It didn't make sense. As he swung the pitchfork, tirelessly lifting the hay up to me on the wagon, Uncle Kristen became once more just good old Uncle Kristen.

Yet one day I did catch a glimpse of his scar. He'd been bitten by a horse-fly, rolled up his trouser-leg, and kept on scratching himself. There, half-way round the calf like the crescent of the new moon, was a furrow, about the width of a finger, where the hair refused to grow. This was it then, the scar he'd no doubt been boasting about to Cathrine. And in the evening I took out my sheath-knife and made a long and painful cut on my arm so that the blood oozed out; he wasn't the only one who could stand pain. . . .

'What've you done to yourself there?'

We were repairing the fence. There had been a bit of rain during the night, so we'd had to stop carting the hay into the barn. It was almost overcast, but warm. We toiled away with the stakes and the sledge-hammer. The boards for the fencing lay in a sweet-smelling pile where they'd been tipped. The resin seemed to be melting out of the oily wood because of the heat, even though the sun came out only now and then.

'Where did you get that scratch from? Not the girls, is it? Heh, heh, heh. . . .'

He was looking at the long mark on my arm and his laughter rang false. His 'matey' tone made me doubly embarrassed. What was he driving at? Who was he suggesting I was involved with? Was he jealous? When he talked like this, he was no longer the trusty farmer I could rely on; he was a grown man trying to make himself look 'young' and therefore suspect, capable of anything, of flirting with young girls – such as Cathrine. I'd gone back over the time we'd spent in one another's company word by word, minute by minute, gesture by gesture. Was it possible that she could show the same generosity towards others as she had towards me? Surely not. No way! Yet as recently as two evenings before, he had gone up there with the milk can again, and what about his moodiness and fidgetiness? And when he talked like he was doing now. . . .

I held the stakes and Uncle Kristen hammered them in. Sweat ran off us and we didn't say much. The old fence leaned at an angle and in some places had actually rotted away completely. I had to test him out, calm the unease that had invaded me again.

'I say, Uncle Kristen, can you play poker?'

He was in the process of plunging the crowbar into the hole for the stake, twisting and turning it from one side to the other.

'Poker? Well, not really. I did play a bit when I was doing my national service, but that wasn't exactly yesterday, you know. . . .'

A slight easing of the concrete suspicion.

A beetle crawled out from under a stone and hurried on its way, busy yet ineffectual, almost touching in its earth-bound panic. Its wing sheaths glinted as it moved along. It was easy to forget that some beetles could fly; it was such a rare sight. They were at home on the ground, rushing hither and thither among small pebbles and pine needles, scurrying along the furrows.

Uncle Kristen was stooped forward, struggling with the crowbar, plunging it into the ground, twisting and turning it this way and that. The way he was standing he seemed squat and broad, his shoes heavy with thick clods of ochre-coloured earth, and when he took a few steps he bent at the knees as farmers do. This was the gait of someone accustomed to walking over uneven ground, over unploughed land, resolute, vigorous, but slow to the observer. It was the beetle's cumbersome gait, close to the basic essentials of life. Uncle Kristen was the toiling beetle in person, vigorous and reliable, utterly oblivious to the fact that he had wings. . . . The thought of it comforted me.

It was getting on for the midday meal. We had been hard at it for hours. The fence stood straight as a die behind us. Every now and then the sun burst forth; it was baking hot. He straightened up.

'Come on, let's go for a swim!'

'A swim?'

'Yes, down in the dam.'

'OK, why not. . . .'

But I was scared stiff. Did he mean straight away? What about my trunks, which I hadn't even unpacked? Did he really mean that we. . . .

We had worked our way down to the bottom corner of the field. The Mill Dam was just near here, over on the far side of the pasture, only five or ten minutes away at the most. He didn't have his costume with him either. Did he really mean. . . .

'Just a quick dip before dinner.'

The very thought of it seemed to cheer him up. There was no getting out of it; I'd have to go along with whatever he suggested.

We laid our tools down and set off. He walked ahead and I followed behind, fearing the worst. Nothing could save me now.

The Mill Dam lay calm as a mirror, a patch of sky reflected between the shadows under the narrow banks. Not a breath of wind ruffled its surface. Not a sound disturbed the distant hum, the pulse of nature, emanating from the forest. Nothing could deter him from the plan he was set on, and protect my panic-stricken modesty.

We stood in the middle of the grassy bank getting our breath back after the walk. He set about unbuttoning his shirt, while a thrush commented disinterestedly on the spectacle from the top of a fir tree. I stood there like a statue, rigid with embarrassment. The dam lay there unfathomable as a mirror. It must surely be very deep at the deepest point. And what of the currents. . . . It had been a quagmire before the dam was built and both man and beast had gone missing in it, so it was said. But then people said all sorts of things. . . . The tempting water lay there still and menacing.

'You've nothing against a dip in the altogether have you, Peter?' He'd taken off his shirt and laid it on the grass. 'No, young folk don't bother their heads about that sort of thing, I'm sure. . . .' He answered his own question, sitting on the ground, busy untying his shoelaces. 'Young folk today have got rid of all those complexes our generation always allowed to spoil its fun. . . .'

And glancing at me as he said this, he saw that I was still standing there as though spellbound, unable even to contemplate starting to undress. He saw, yet did not notice, looking straight past me up towards where the stream widened out to form the beginning of the dam, where a couple of hundred yards up on the other bank, a clearing, a little patch of green surrounded by trees and bushes, could just be made out – Cathrine's sunbathing spot. . . . Was this really what he was looking at?

'Oh, young folk,' he went on with obvious relish, stretching his white feet out in front of him, his crooked man's toes playing with the grass. There was a smell of sweat. 'Young folk nowadays are grand. It's us grown-ups who cause all the bother. It's our fault that things are the way they are, not theirs. They could teach us a thing or two, teach us to see the world through their eyes, to be truthful and honest.'

He had unbuckled his belt, started to undo his trouser buttons. It was Cathrine he was talking about as he stood there undressing, quite unperturbed. I trembled with rebellious indignation.

'No, you're lucky Peter, you've got so much youth ahead of you still. I only hope you know how to take proper advantage of it. When you're old, it's too late.'

He had stood up and dropped his trousers. His scar glinted like the blade of a scythe, stretching from the shin round the calf. The scar he'd used to charm Cathrine with. The scar I'd told her about. Then he pulled down his underpants. His body was snow-white in the sun. I looked away, pretending to fumble with my own buttons, and suddenly heard him call from down at the water's edge: 'Get a move on!'

'OK. Just a minute. . . .'

I'd undone a couple of shirt buttons just for appearance' sake. Now, hesitantly, I pulled my shirt over my head. The sun was baking on my narrow shoulders. My nose was red and about to peel. I sat down to take my shoes off, to gain a little time.

'It's not cold at all!'

I risked another look in his direction. He was standing near the bank, water up to his knees. It shelved down steeply there. He was waving and calling to me. His chest was white, with a triangular mass of hair; his belly was white, his shoulders white, but his forearms ridiculously brown. Yet what I was looking at was his manhood, dangling between the strong hairy thighs, dark, heavy, almost menacing. What did a man have to go through for his poor thing to end up looking like that? I'd rather die than show him my spindly little thing, expose my precarious dream to such awesome experience. His body had the strength of youth, yet at the same time it was tainted. And Cathrine's small girlish breasts had dark rings round them from suckling her child. It all 'fitted in'. Almost too well. I was powerless against such an alliance.

'Hey!'

He plunged in, splashing and kicking, turning the water around him to foam.

'Yoohoo!' In a falsetto. 'Come on, then! It's lovely!'

But I stayed put where I sat on the dry ground, like a girl

having a period, just looking at him, at this physical abandon, this youthfulness in a grown man's body. Now he was swimming out with long, powerful strokes.

'Watch this!'

He dived and disappeared from view, then resurfaced, laughing, blowing out water and clearing his nose. He dived again. The last I saw of him was his white, hairy rump and his heels disappearing down into the black water. He was gone. And he stayed under a long time. I didn't count the seconds, but it struck me that he'd been under longer than it was humanly possible to hold one's breath. But then he reappeared, spitting and thrashing about with his arms, waving to me with one arm and shouting something I couldn't catch. I ran down to the water's edge. He swam over to me, panting and coughing and spitting out dark brown water. 'Give me your knife!' he shouted, gasping for breath. 'Your knife!'

I was carrying my knife in my belt, couldn't figure out what he wanted it for, but drew it out of its sheath all the same and waded three or four steps into the water, reaching out to hand it to him, up to my knees in the ice-cold water and still wearing my trousers. He waded over to me. There was a look of horror, even terror, in his face. Without saying a word, he took the knife from me with numb, inhuman fingers. At the same time, he threw something he was holding in his other hand up on to the bank. Then he turned and swam away from me.

On the grassy bank lay a piece of cloth. I picked it up, looked at it, realized I was trembling, even though I didn't understand what was going on, what he was doing out there. Yet it was as though something within me had grasped it at a deeper level than my reason: Marie. In my hand I held a piece of thin white cloth with a flower border, the colours almost completely washed out. The flowers had been red and yellow.

Out there in the water, Uncle Kristen dived time and time again, disappeared from view, came back up gasping, then dived again. I stood at the water's edge, not moving, not thinking, at least trying not to think. He dived over and over again, as though in a frenzy, straining and struggling with something on the bottom. Then he seemed to have got hold of it at last, for he began to swim back in, slowly, with heavy strokes, dragging something behind him under the water. And now I knew what it was, even though my mind refused to register a fact so gruesome.

He came right in to where it was shallow, white-faced, his teeth chattering with cold and fatigue. Behind him he was dragging a longish, shapeless bundle, a bloated white form with human limbs, a train of white cloth, an excrescence which had been a head, and around it a mass of blonde hair. . . . I stared and stared as though transfixed, until he seized me by the arm.

'Don't look at it, Peter.'

His voice was small and gasping. He pulled me away against my will. His hand on my shoulder was trembling and I knew he was more shaken than I, who had still not yet really taken it all in. He led me away up over the grassy slope to where we'd left our clothes. With his ice-cold hand on my arm, I dared not turn round and look.

'She'd got entangled in a root,' he said, as though talking to himself. 'Hopelessly entangled. I had to cut her loose. Cut her dress. . . .'

He started to get dressed. I pushed my feet into my shoes, picked up my shirt. Wet from the knees down, my trousers clung dripping wet to my legs.

'But I lost your knife, Peter,' he said after a while. 'I lost my grip on it and it sank to the bottom. Sorry about that . . .'

'Oh, the knife . . .' I said. It no longer interested me. It was the lifeless bundle down there on the grass that interested me. I felt a strange urge to go down and take a closer look at it, as though to convince myself it was not what I thought it was, 'dead', that awesome 'grown-up' word, yet my body threatened at any moment to ignore what I told it to do. I struggled desperately to fasten my buttons.

He had already got dressed and stood there waiting for me.

'We'd better fetch the bailiff, I suppose.'

'Yes.'

I was ready. Ready to go. I took great care not to look in that direction. He glanced at me.

'I'm really sorry about the knife, Peter. Such a good one too. Solingen steel.'

His hair stuck to his temples and forehead. The colour had

drained from his lips; his eyes were strangely gentle and friendly.

'Oh that,' I answered. 'That's nothing.'

We hurried back home through the forest. He walked ahead and I followed thankfully a little way behind. Sunshine and flowers all around. I stepped on silvery trails left by snails on the path. No one must see I was crying.

THREE

The Go-Between

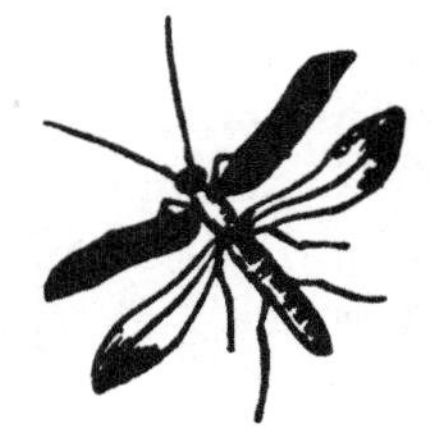

15

Of all insects, spiders are the most fascinating.

I would observe them up in the hut. At all times of day and night, they would surprise me by turning up where I least expected them, hurrying unperturbed and purposeful towards their secret and exclusive lairs. My fingers got caught in their webs everywhere, on the kitchen worktop, in the low-set, peeling window-frame, even suspended between the covers of the book I was reading in the evenings. Each morning there was a fresh, intricate, silken web suspended between the half-rotten overhang of the roof and the door-frame.

We had learned about spiders at school, and I vaguely recalled many details which now took on new and fascinating significance. I remembered that they were called *Araneae* in Latin, after the virgin Arachne, whom Athene turned into a spider. They are more numerous than any other form of insect, with at least twenty thousand species. Even though most species are cannibalistic, they are also capable of living together in 'families' and 'societies'. In some species, the mother carries her offspring on her back until they are big enough to fend for themselves. When the young spider wishes to leave the nest, it climbs up to the highest, most exposed place it can find, turns its spinnerets towards the wind, which teases out a thread eventually so long that it can carry the spider away. By this method, it is able to cover several miles with a favourable wind.

The young male spins his web, kills his prey with poison, devours it and grows until the old skin becomes so tight that it has to be shed. He sheds his skin in a suspended position, pressing his legs together beneath him until the skin splits across his back. Then the laborious process of discarding the skin begins. Up to six hundred movements are required before all the limbs have been disentangled. Then he can start to use his new skin, though to begin with he is usually soft and vulnerable. When fully grown, the male ceases spinning webs and goes off in search of a mate. When he has found one, fertilization is achieved by the male transferring drops of his semen with his forelegs on to the female's sex organs. It is not true that the female always devours the male after copulation.

The spider is invincible; weightless, frugal and untiring. It can live for months on two or three flies and spins a fresh web every day. With its unique silk, it painstakingly constructs a predetermined number of delicate radii, weaving cross-threads in and out to link them together. Thereupon, stock still, it awaits its prey. With four pairs of eyes, it watches over the four corners of its world. Nothing can escape its sensors, which are so finely tuned that the delicate hairs on its legs can detect even sound-waves. In the window-frame hung abandoned husks of flies in torn webs, testifying to its deadly efficiency.

No, I never tired of observing the spiders. They crawled forth in their hundreds from all the cracks in the old woodwork, imperturbably absorbed in their own doings. So unwavering. So efficient. So certain of eventually accomplishing their task, achieving their purpose with their fearless endeavours. I often longed for the spider's qualities, in fact I would actually rather have been a spider than a dragonfly, despite the fact that the dragonfly was a thing of beauty, causing all to stop and admire the colours and elegance it possessed in such abundance. When people saw spiders, they shuddered and trod on them – if they dared, that is.

Perhaps that was why.

16

I didn't see Cathrine again until the summer fête.

The time since Marie's body had been found was filled with activities of all kinds. Nothing on the farm was the same, even though the days still appeared to pass as before. We had already assumed she was dead, but now all of a sudden we *knew* it; now there was no soothing doubt to shelter behind any more.

When Aunt Linn heard the news, she broke down and shut herself in the bedroom, refusing to speak to a soul, or to come out. Uncle Kristen and I ate our evening meal in the kitchen on our own, facing one another across the broad table, not saying much, neither of us wanting to bother the other with humdrum matters, to disturb the funereal atmosphere with comments on what we had all tacitly understood must have happened and which had now been brought out into the open so brutally and inescapably. The bailiff had called that afternoon. The corpse was brought to the farm by horse and driven from there to the railway station by ambulance. For a time, the farmyard had fairly crawled with people. The news spread fast and neighbours called to pry and add their two pennyworth. From the kitchen window, I saw Jo and his father talking to some other people. I didn't go out. But Uncle Kristen went out and talked to the men, nodding gravely and shaking hands, friendly and dignified towards those who talked behind his back.

But in the evening, he ate very little and didn't say much, and when we'd finished and I was about to go, he walked over to the worktop and picked up the little milk can. 'Come on, we can walk together part of the way,' he said. 'I was going up to Weasel Cottage with the milk anyway.'

There wasn't a sound to be heard from the bedroom.

A post-mortem was held and it was established that the cause of death had been drowning. It was also ascertained that Marie had been four months pregnant when the accident had occurred. The body showed no traces of physical violence and there was nothing to suggest that poor Marie had been the victim of a criminal offence. The fact that she had been clad only in her nightdress when she was found suggested that she had taken fate into her own hands. But, publicly, suicide was not mentioned. I read the reports in the local paper, listened to what was said by the grown-ups.

Aunt Linn stayed in bed for two days with a temperature. Afterwards, she got better quickly, and soon everything appeared outwardly the same as before, but silence reigned in the house. I knew she was turning over and over in her mind the inescapable fact that Marie really had been pregnant, that the rumours had been right. And I knew that Uncle Kristen was going about knowing he was a marked man.

'What did I tell you?' whispered Jo, who had come up to the hut with the sole purpose of stirring things up again. 'So he'd been having it off with her, hadn't he? But *you* wouldn't believe it, *you* thought it was just talk, didn't you? Four months gone. Holy smoke! They're bound to take a blood test. They can do that, you know, to see who the father is. It's cast-iron *proof*. They're bound to do it!'

Jo was sitting on the bunk and had the effrontery to fiddle with an erection. I loathed both him and that miserable worm-like member of his, declined his offer of onanistic fraternization, invented an excuse, said I'd just done it and got rid of him at long last. I was too old for Boy Scout games now.

Three evenings that week, the milk can for Weasel Cottage had stood on the worktop and Uncle Kristen and I had walked together to where the path forked. By the third evening, I could bear it no longer, and, one with the shadows, crept soundlessly after him up over the heath. After all, I knew the path like the back of my hand; I'd walked along it often enough in the evenings, getting as far as the cart-track, where, bewitched by a glimpse of light from magical windows, my courage and determination had failed me. What if I stumbled upon an orgy of face painting and strip poker? And even worse, what if I was invited to join in?

I crept along behind a shirt, a lighter shadow, a movement I could only just make out in the twilight ahead. He didn't hesitate. His steps crunched cheerful and confident on the gravel. I crept along behind him with baited breath, worn out by my wild imaginings, by jealousy, weighed down with self-contempt, sick with envy. He knocked on the door, a quick, confident knock. It opened. I lay in the ditch and peered so hard that my eyes began to water. He went in. That was all, but it spoke volumes to my tormented imagination.

I waited, deciding to go through with the whole thing, right to the bitter end (of course he might just be making polite conversation in there), but after half an hour (was it as long as that? I wasn't wearing a watch) huddled in the ditch, I couldn't take any more and staggered back, exhausted, annihilated, racked by sobs brought on by my impossible dreams, my helplessness and by intense arousal. Found consolation in a soothing, helping hand when I got home.

The funeral was to be a very private affair. Marie was brought home in her coffin after the post-mortem and placed in the hayloft that night. All the thresholds had been decked out with sprigs of pine, as was the custom. The preparations for the funeral gave Aunt Linn an opportunity to shake off the cocoon of sluggish remoteness that had enveloped her like a bad dream since the body had been found. She cleaned and polished the entire house till everything shone and smelled fresh. Even in the hut she insisted that a thorough going-over was needed, and I stood watching as she swept the body of a small bird from under the bunk, and shared her utter disgust at the little white maggots crawling amongst the feathers. There was no stopping her. She whizzed all over with cloths and rags, as though the sorrow and the shame that had totally overwhelmed her during the first few days now gave her exasperating energy. But luckily she didn't find Jo's girlie magazine, despite changing the sheets.

After the burial, Mr and Mrs Bergshagen and Mr and Mrs Johannesen, the closest neighbours, were invited over for coffee.

Jo and Gerd were also there, Jo unrecognizable, his hair plastered down with water as it was, wearing a freshly ironed small-check shirt, polished shoes and three-quarter-length socks, which refused to stay up. Gerd with her hair rolled up in the shape of a pretzel, in a forlorn attempt to make herself look grown-up. After coffee, we sat talking about this and that, steering clear of the one thing on everybody's mind. Then it was time for them to go. Mrs Bergshagen dragged a reluctant Jo home with her. Sjur Bergshagen stayed behind to give Uncle Kristen a hand with something in the barn. Gerd offered to help with the washing-up. I felt out of it. For a while, I lounged about in my usual place on the bench, watching the two of them wash up in total silence. Then my restlessness drove me out into the farmyard. I could hear the men in the barn. The afternoon was cloudless, just as warm as all the others had been. It would be a summer to break all records if it went on like this. And it was dry as well. Things didn't look too promising for the corn.

I was waiting for Gerd, keeping an eye out to see when she'd finished the washing-up and would be setting off home. I had to speak to someone. She was the only one who could be approached on that sad day. While we'd been drinking coffee, she had twice glanced in my direction, looking down again with a conspiratorial smile, her breasts neat bulges beneath her demure Sunday dress. So there I sat on the fence, plucking up courage while I waited.

When she came, I was nevertheless lost for words, said hello, but was suddenly unable to think of anything to talk about on a day such as this. Then I had a brainwave; the words came right out of the blue:

'Fancy coming up to have a dekko at my place?'

'Ooh yes, I'd love to!'

Her reply was so quick and enthusiastic that I realized the idea had already occurred to her. Perhaps she'd even volunteered to help with the washing-up so that the others would get on with their own business and an opportunity might present itself?

I walked ahead up over the path, the clip-clip of her Sunday shoes behind me. I wasn't just nervous, I was paralysed with fear, yet my desire to become a full and complete human being was even stronger. Uncle Kristen made such a song and dance about youth but was just deluding himself. I had realized what was needed: experience, that was the thing, a scarred and hairy body, a penis like Uncle Kristen's, a crotch like a gathering storm; even his murky sin against Marie ultimately counted in his favour. All of this I wanted for myself. It was with a feeling of portent, of meeting fate half-way, that I led Gerd up along the path towards the hut.

'But it's lovely up here!'

'Yeah, not bad, is it.'

I closed the door and stood close beside her. This time we were quicker off the mark. She clamped herself to my lips and sighed. I panted with as much abandon as I could muster through my nose and groped my way towards a hospitable breast, which lay within easy reach. We vied with one another in our panting and remained standing there like that for what seemed like an eternity.

I'd planned to take the initiative, to try and get 'inside', but it was a highly complicated matter when the dress was buttoned behind the neck. It riled me, and I squeezed as greedily as I could to exact my pound of flesh in revenge for such a badly designed dress.

'Come on, let's sit down,' she whispered.

Till this prompting, I'd hardly dared stir from the spot where we stood, scared as I was of breaking the spell our embraces had cast over us, and of revealing an embarrassingly prominent erection.

Then we sat side by side on the bunk, trying to repeat the same manoeuvre, with the result that we both tumbled backwards and found ourselves in a topsy-turvy jumble of limbs, smothered in giggles. We were helpless with laughter. But we were horizontal! Things were going swimmingly and far quicker than the lad who sat next to me in the physics lab had led me to believe was possible. My heart raced flat-out with terror, suspense and bafflement. I knew what came next, even though films usually ended at this point, so I freed my hand and fumbled my way to a leg, a soft, warm thigh, a hitherto unattainable dream above the knee. There was no protest, but her breathing grew quicker, more laboured, as though my timorous groping was somehow painful, something almost beyond the threshold of what she could bear. Then it was my turn to press my lips on hers, as I advanced my hand a little higher. Still no objection. Emboldened, my hand moved still further, perhaps too fast and too much at one go ('You have to go at it bit by bit,' the lad in the physics lab had said, 'you have to pull the wool over their eyes, so they practically don't notice what's going on . . .'), since she gave a sudden start and wriggled free.

'No, no, Peter.'

Already I regretted it, knowing it had all gone too fast, that it was far too much to expect that . . .

'It's the curse, you see.'

Curse, what was she talking about?

'Curse?'

'Yes, curse. You know.'

Yes of course I knew, as soon as I'd had a moment to collect myself a bit. I felt completely shattered and disgusted with myself. I was an obnoxious, uncouth slob . . .

'Oh, I'm sorry. I . . . I didn't realize . . .'

'It'll be over in a day or two.'

So she wasn't cross. She was apologizing. She referred to it in a natural, matter-of-fact way. I was the one who was shocked and upset, beside myself.

I had more or less released my grasp of her. I leaned on my elbow, looked into her honest face, placed my hand carefully on her breast again. It was incredible how quickly you became 'acclimatized' in these latitudes!

'You said you had a letter you wanted a hand with. . . .'

We had to talk about something else now, perhaps recapture some of the earlier magic.

'Oh, it's not important any more. I managed it myself. It wasn't all that hard anyway. I've finished with him.'

'You've finished with him?'

'Yes, it was someone I met at the hotel last year. He's been writing to me, but I wasn't ever all that keen on him. I wrote back to tell him there was someone else now.'

'Oh?'

I knew what she was driving at, and my chest swelled with pride and delight.

'It's you, you see.' She giggled and buried her face in the hollow of my neck. 'It's been you all along!' Then, after a pause: 'But I'd better be off soon.'

We clamped our lips to one another and rolled backwards and forwards on the narrow bunk.

'I say, aren't we awful doing this on a day like this . . .'

'Yes, disgusting, isn't it!'

I was beside myself with joy, with triumphant pride. It felt as though I'd become a man already.

But at the evening meal I was again reduced to the role of onlooker in the drama between the two of them. A milk can had been placed on the worktop. It sat there like a warning signal, imposing silence on the meal table. Till she could bear it no longer.

'D'you have to go up there tonight as well?'

'Look, you know she needs milk for the baby.' His voice sounded tired and irritable.

'I don't suppose you'd consider sparing a thought for other people just for once. When all's said and done, we've only just . . .' – she gave a sudden shudder, as though the windows had been blown open and the snug kitchen had suddenly been filled with cold air – ' . . . laid Marie to rest today.'

'Who do you mean spare a thought for? Those flibbertigibbets down in the village?'

'Oh no, spare a thought for anyone else, *you*?' she murmured almost inaudibly, on the verge of tears. I recognized the symptoms by now, but she pulled herself together again. 'Look,' she shouted all of a sudden, causing us both to jump out of our skins. 'Don't you think you've caused enough trouble as it is?'

At long last, the accusation was open and unequivocal. What a relief! Now the walls must surely split asunder and the roof fall in and crush us all to death! But he didn't bat an eyelid.

'Oh, I don't think there's much to choose between us when it comes to causing trouble in this house,' he spat between clenched teeth, scowling at her, so full of recrimination that she lurched from the table and, with a groan, rushed for the door.

So now it was just him and me. There was nothing about *him* to suggest that he'd just sent his wife packing in floods of tears. He had self-control. Control, the most important thing in the whole world. I had been in control that afternoon when I'd squeezed Gerd's soft breast and coaxed her into saying what she'd said. I'd been in control then. And I'd been intoxicated by it. But that was child's play compared with this.

At long last he glanced at me: '*You* surely don't believe what they say, do you Peter?'

He was trying to drag me into it again, get me on his side. But I wasn't having any of it: 'No, er, well who d'you mean exactly?'

As a fifteen-year-old it was my privilege not to know. I could take refuge behind my age, using it as a pretext, take refuge under my veneer of innocence, my childishness, my lack of understanding, of percipience, of interest in the affairs of grown-ups, all of which added up to an unassailable bastion founded upon a complete dearth of information. Case dismissed for lack of evidence!

'Yes, well who *do* I mean. . . .'

He suddenly looked crestfallen, worn out, older, if anything more like my father. . . . Yet I'd fallen straight into his trap, and now I felt pity like a quagmire beneath my feet. *My* pity for *him*, the grown man, the scarred and hairy man, with a scrotum and a penis like a bunch of overripe fruit, the man who shamelessly exploited his manhood in order to turn young girls' heads and seduce them, the man who was a Judas to his wife and desecrated his marriage, *he* was gaining my sympathy!

'But why should I drag you into it?' This was no doubt largely addressed to himself; he looked so dismal as he sat there opposite me at the table, where the plate of sandwiches still sat barely touched and rings of cream disfigured the glasses of milk. 'But promise me you won't believe a word of it when you hear rumours about us, rumours of any kind. You know what incorrigible gossips people are, and there's no limit to what they manage to concoct. You won't believe them, will you, Peter?'

'N-no, course not,' I stammered, my self-defences crumbling.

His voice sounded so bitter, and he had a look of my father as he sat there. He was asking for my support. He was my uncle, who had always been kind and straight with me. He was a beetle with honest hands and earth on his boots, and I couldn't really bring myself to believe he was capable of doing any wrong. But there had been a strong element of truth in the rumours. Marie had been expecting, and he must have been the culprit, he must have been the father, because that's what they were saying down in the village, because there had been anonymous letters and even Aunt Linn accused him in her every gesture. And although Gerd had said Marie had been just as much to blame, that didn't alter anything.

And then there was him and Cathrine. . . . Even if I didn't *believe* it, couldn't bring myself to believe it. Admittedly I hadn't a scrap of evidence, just my own entrancement and his behaviour, which was a sort of reflection of the restlessness I felt myself. But what kind of proof was that? Wasn't there on the other hand a great deal to indicate that actually it was me she was keen on? Hadn't my personal magnetism, my power over women been proved once and for all that afternoon? Hadn't it been *me* she'd confided in? Hadn't it been *me* she'd waved to so trustingly?

I rose hurriedly from the table, saying I was tired and wanted to go. He said good-night and remained sitting where he was. Outside, the sky hung suspended, white over the tree-tops.

When I was almost up at the hut, I heard the farmhouse door close behind him. Sound carries a long way in the evening. The gate was opened and closed. Once or twice I heard his footsteps on the path. He was on his way up over the heath with the milk: at dusk, even a beetle can take to the wing, ungainly, heavy, making a humming sound and thus a sitting duck for its many enemies. I'd killed one myself once, squashing it with a bat. It was one afternoon when we were playing in the park. It had been my shot. The beetle had made straight for me, large and blue and shiny, visible from a long way off. It had flown straight at me, steady, relentless, humming. I'd taken aim and swiped at it with the bat – crack! – splattering myself with whitish liquid. The empty husk fell to the ground some way off. I'd been showing off; a real ace of a shot. I'd been hugely pleased with myself. Insects were just insects in those days.

I lit a lamp and lay down on the bunk, trying to think of something to take my mind off the ache in my chest, trying to laugh at myself, tell myself what a conceited fool I was to believe I'd any chance with Cathrine, trying to think of more cheerful things, of Gerd's body, of her breasts, so warm and willing under her dress, of her thighs, of the softness above the knee – I'd managed to get quite a long way up . . . of her hairs and her slit, impossible to imagine in any detail, yet all the same it was just a matter of time ('It'll be over in a day or two'). She'd virtually promised me. . . .

I fumbled for Jo's girlie magazine under the mattress; I had to have something to look at in my misery. My hand came into contact with some paper, but it wasn't the magazine. All the same, I pulled it out. It was a letter written in an open, scrawly girl's handwriting. I smoothed it out: 'Dearest Kristen. . . .'

It was a letter, a letter to Uncle Kristen. Then the penny dropped. This was it! The letter! The mysterious letter I'd conjured up in my imagination; the letter they'd been looking for, the letter which perhaps held the answer to what had actually happened at Fagerlund that spring. Here it was, at long last! My eyes darted over the page, I was too excited, too flustered to read the words properly, in consecutive order, just snatched a word here and a sentence there, at random, yet I still got an impression, a picture of poor dead Marie, of him, and of the relationship between them. In the flickering glow from the lamp, I read:

> Dearest Kristen. I know I shouldn't be writing this to you, I've done you enough harm as it is . . . I've got myself into a situation I can't . . . best I disappear for good and so I won't be a burden to others any more . . . decided to do this . . . *know* that it's for the best, don't ask how I know . . . and you've always been so good to me, you'd no doubt have taken care of the baby like your own, I know you want . . . wouldn't have worked . . . would only make trouble for other people. . . . So you must forgive me for . . . they say down in the village, I can't help that. I did what I did because I loved you, you know that . . . deeply, deeply in love with you. But now everything's ruined . . . but you mustn't blame . . . even if you don't like him. He was good to me . . . whatever people say about him. . . . I'll have to say goodbye now, Kristen. Don't be angry

with me for what I'm doing. It's for the best. Your ever loving Marie.

I didn't sleep a wink. I lay awake the whole night, staring through the window out into the darkness. I watched the darkness fall and watched it disperse. Slowly various outlines started to appear like shadows on a frieze of homespun cloth, then between them newly carded wool and vertical tree-trunks with light-grey bark, then branches and leaves and a pale strip of sky. I'd left the door open. It was so warm, and I had to keep my ears cocked. I lay there listening for the sound of the gate, of the outside door down on the farm. For at night sound travels far in the forest. But I hadn't heard a thing and I'd wept.

I had wept for Marie, for the love which is never reciprocated, the hope which is never fulfilled, and I'd wept for him too, my innocent Uncle Kristen, whom all had wronged, but who was not really completely blameless, not any more. I would have heard him if he'd walked past on the path and opened the gate. I hadn't slept, not a wink. I'd lain there listening and weeping, listening and peering out into the darkness, which slowly turned into ragged homespun cloth, then ash, then smoke from a chimney, then ghosts, apparitions shown up by the light. I had thought about how the power now lay in my hands. I had found the paper that cleared his name. But ought I to clear it? Did he deserve to have his name cleared, the way he had behaved? I thought of my Cathrine, of her eyes, her mouth, her voice, her curly hair, of her small breasts with the dark nipples, and also of him, of how he had sinned against all this during the night (and how many other nights?). It was as though *I* was his victim, as though his hands, his lips, his desires desecrated *my* body and my hopelessly vulnerable dreams of love and mutual trust, and all the freedom that radiated from her whole being! No, it was more than I could stand. I broke down and wept. He was a criminal, a brute, an out-and-out savage. I hated him.

I didn't fall asleep until a thrush had broadcast its shrill notes from the top of a pine tree outside my window, as the sun was just casting aside its veils, before they caught fire, before they fell in flames all over the forest. It grew light. It was morning.

17

But I didn't see Cathrine again until the summer fête, when she was standing among a group of youths, laughing, allowing herself to be hauled on to the dance floor by one after another of them. Jo and I, slightly tipsy, leaned on the low barrier surrounding the newly laid dance floor on the field beside the community centre, watching the dance band up on the dais that served as a podium, and also the crowd of young and old shuffling around in time to the waltz.

It was a light evening, still early. The air was mild, with a vestige of lingering heat, an echo of the tinder-dry afternoon, and the heady scents of high summer mingled with the sounds, the movements dictated by the dance. People coming and going, forming groups here and there. Voices, some loud, some soft, from person to person, carried clearly through the dusk.

The huge bonfire of wooden boxes was to be lit at midnight. The rhythmical swaying of the dance (and *her* on the dance floor, just now with the chap from Westmoor, whirling with such grace and nimbleness, so much smaller than her partner, when what she needed was my support, my loving protection! 'There she is,' whispered Jo. 'Well, I'll be. . . .' He followed my gaze, could see from my eyes, and knew all the others here anyway.). The hypnotic shimmer of cymbals and drums up on the dais, the bloated face of the saxophonist, the saccharine chords of the accordion, which could bring out goose-pimples on the strongest of arms. The summer fête. We filled our lungs, breathed in deep its atmosphere as we leaned on the low barrier.

But she still hadn't seen me.

We stood elbow to elbow, eyes on the dancing, admiring the

musicians, their hair slicked down, and breathing in the smell of trampled grass and freshly sawn planks. We looked with fear and longing at the group of youths standing on the grass, a dense wall of male backs surrounding the three or four most popular girls (and *she* was one of them, my lovely little Cathrine, my sophisticated, refined young Miss, in the midst of these rough-hewn peasant upstarts . . .). Shouts and laughter could be heard from the solid, impregnable mass out there. We longed to be part of it, but the distance between us and the age of eighteen or nineteen seemed incredibly, insurmountably great. But this didn't stop us from tittering away and having a good time all the same, watching older, determined couples who, in the effort, lost the beat, then we giggled again and enjoyed ourselves, thinking we were slightly tipsy.

Jo had turned up at the hut that afternoon with two bottles of Bock beer he'd pinched from the cellar. He had smartened himself up, putting on a freshly ironed shirt (the one from the funeral), with a small check pattern, sporting long trousers and with his hair plastered down with water. You had to have a drop to give you Dutch courage to go down to the fête. He was about to see Cathrine, the girl he'd fantasized so much about, for the first time.

We'd drained the two bottles of beer and the sought-after slight tipsiness had not been long in coming. Now we were raring to go: California, here we come! On top of the world, and taking great pains to appear wobbly, we had bicycled down to the community centre, where the wind was taken out of our sails by the crush of people already present, who had obviously agreed among themselves beforehand to ignore us. So we lost no time in finding our way to the barrier next to the band.

Gradually more people turned up. The evening somehow seemed to be closing in around us, even though it was still quite light. Voices sounded louder. A number of people sat together on rugs and jackets with shiny linings, dotted about here and there on the grass. Thermos flasks were offered round and small, flat bottles went the rounds from one eager hand to another. New groups gathered around the dance floor. The hip-flasks glinted. Laughter rang out. The orchestra took a break. Abandoned instruments shone forgotten on the podium. Crowds of people streamed into the community hall where refreshments were being served. All of a sudden, Jo was gone. I'd been so busy keeping an eye on *her* that I hadn't noticed him go. She had danced the last dance before the break with another boy from the village. Now they were threading their way over to their little knot of friends. He had placed his hand on the small of her back. It cut me to the quick. It was as though the lad's coarse hand lay on her naked flesh.

I felt so utterly helpless as I stood rooted to the spot beside the dance floor. Would she see me? Would I manage to catch her eye? Get the confirmation I longed for? Would there be a chance to dance with her? I realized that I was standing there expecting her to come and ask me to dance. How could anyone be so damned conceited! It was ridiculous! Obviously it was the male partner who had to do the asking. But where would I find the courage to walk up to that rowdy group over there and ask one of the girls, a twenty-one-year-old, to dance, when I was only fifteen? And then have the guts to dance. . . . For this wasn't like the formalized politeness of the dancing school, this was a challenge, an affectionate duel to music, pursuit and flight round the dance floor, cobbled together for the occasion from rough pine boards smelling of resin. It was a battle. The man held his partner round the waist, while she defended herself with both hands, placing them on his shoulders, on his chest or round his neck. From primness to total surrender.

I realized I wasn't the least bit drunk any longer, and had hardly been so either. The new nylon shirt I'd been so proud of felt sticky and uncomfortable against my skin. What I really wanted was simply to leave, but that was out of the question, since I had to be here to see what happened. More and more people kept coming and the various groups were starting to get rowdy and boisterous. It was as though the tension had slowly been accumulating, as though the warm evening, the dance, all the people there had generated a pool of energy, which had to be discharged between individual couples. I looked round anxiously for Jo and caught sight of Gerd in the middle of a group of young girls. She wasn't looking in my direction just then. I felt sure she hadn't seen me, or perhaps she too found me contemptible, childish, insignificant in these hectic surroundings? Now she was standing with her back to me, so I couldn't see much of her: a flowery blouse, a plain full skirt and a broad, tight-fitting elastic belt round her waist. This was what most of the girls were wearing; it was modern, or at least it had been not long since. And her shoulder-length dark-blonde hair looked almost black now as the dusk came stealing in. I wondered nervously whether she had called upon her skills as a beautician this evening. . . . A titter ran through the group of girls and made me turn away.

Jo reappeared as suddenly as he had left, resourceful as ever. 'I ran into a mate of mine. He's got some booze! Come on, d'you fancy a drop?'

There was a sickly sweet smell on his breath. Fair enough then: in for a penny, in for a pound.

'OK.'

He led the way. There were people all over the place, talking in loud voices and laughing. A short distance away, there was a little mound surrounded by some birch trees. There was a bench there. Side by side, three or four lads were sitting on it looking rather down in the dumps. I'd seen one or two of them before but didn't really know any of them. They had combed their hair painstakingly and seemed to have grown out of their Sunday best. All of them were my age and no doubt felt just as awkward as I did.

'Want a fag?'

One of them held out a pack of cigarettes. Jo seized one eagerly. I declined, having no desire to flaunt my ignorance. Jo lit up, took a drag and exhaled, spat, grinned, and was in great spirits. He was exactly like me, but even younger and dafter.

A horse-faced lad called Christopher eventually produced his bottle after being prompted several times. We took a swig. It tasted sweet and not at all as strong as I'd feared. We took another swig. Jo laughed and spun round on his heels. The music had started up again. It was getting crowded round the dance floor. We emptied the bottle and Christopher slung it disdainfully into the bushes. A slow, warm feeling of well-being slowly invaded me. Was this being drunk, which I had been so afraid of but all the same longed to experience? No, I could stand up straight, so it couldn't be. I looked at Jo guffawing at a joke somebody had told. I felt a bit merry myself. Now he was turning towards the least likeable of the lads, and in a loud whisper, his malicious eye on me, said: 'Peter says he's charmed the pants off that townie lass!'

'Oh, put a sock in it!' I shouted, growing hot under the collar and bitterly regretting ever having divulged my day-dream to this unreliable little squirt.

'So you haven't been snogging with her, I suppose?'

He wasn't to be stopped; he winked down at his pals, who stared at me disbelievingly.

'Well yes, I have. . . . But it wasn't anything to write home about . . .'

'And the two of you weren't swimming in the nick down at Mill Dam the other day, I suppose?'

'No, we weren't exactly swimming . . .'

'You still got an eyeful of her in the altogether, though, didn't you?' He was squeezing every last drop out of his advantage, and there were no depths to which he wouldn't stoop.

'Well yes, I did . . .'

'The bloody tart!' Christopher exclaimed, wiping wet lips with the back of his flabby hand.

'And you still say you got nowhere with her? Pull the other one!'

The others laughed too, lewd and expectant. Jo was basking in the limelight. Filled with spite and envy, his flinty look pierced mine. Now he'd got me where he wanted me. The mild exaggerations I'd fed him with largely for fun now sat like arrows in my breast. He had exposed me with his unerring boy's instinct, now he could finish me off whenever he chose to. A gradual dizziness in my head met the queasiness welling up from my stomach like columns of smoke, ending up as a tickle at the back of my throat.

'And he still hasn't danced with her! And he said he would too!' Jo's eyes were glossy with triumph and also perhaps with Christopher's sickly liquor. And this was the boy who had practised the Viennese waltz in the sweat of his brow on the barn floor! The others nodded in scornful agreement. Well, what the heck was I waiting for, then? I who had such fantastic luck with the much sought-after Cathrine . . .?

I was so befuddled and worn down that I saw their scornful

goading as a way out of this tight corner. Nothing could be worse than standing here glued to the spot being got at by these peasant yobbos.

'Well, I'll go and have a spin with her, if that's what you all want. . . .'

Jo's cocksure superiority faltered slightly. The others sat there, elbows on their knees, smirking at me in disbelief. The stale smell of drink hung like an almost visible barrier between me and them, a woolliness, a devil-may-care indifference in my head: there was nothing I would shrink from. I turned on my heels and made my way – a trifle unsteady, I thought, and mightily pleased about it I was too – towards the dance floor. I had the impression they were following me, but at a distance.

It was really crowded now, with people everywhere. It was no longer very easy to get through. I kept on having to manoeuvre to avoid the people in their Sunday best, swarming towards the music, the dancing, the glare from the large floodlights which had just been turned on. I couldn't see Cathrine anywhere. Where she had stood surrounded by her nauseating partners, there was now a dense and completely impassable knot of people. The orchestra was playing a foxtrot and I staggered on in an arc round the brightly lit dance floor. There wasn't a trace of her. I would have to get right up to the barrier; she might be dancing. I pushed and shoved my way through the onlookers, bumped into someone, mumbled 'sorry' without taking my eyes off the dance floor and the dancing couples. The taste of the liquor lay like a blurred torpor behind my eyes, making concentration easier. I stared straight ahead, paying no attention to what was happening on either side of me, bumped into someone else, a girl this time, a hoarse, sheepish apology being all I could manage, and was about to walk on . . .

'Peter!'

It was Gerd. It was Gerd I'd run smack into. I couldn't see her friends anywhere near. So I was saved.

'Peter, you've been drinking!'

'Does it show?' Surprisingly, pride, relief and laughter caused my voice to falter.

'Does it show! You're as white as a sheet and you're staggering about like a drunkard!'

'You don't say,' I giggled, delighted. Just imagine, you could see I'd been drinking. I felt on top of the world. 'Fancy a dance, Gerd?'

'Are you sure? Do you think you're capable of it?' She couldn't help laughing too now, or at least smiling at me as I stood there holding back waves of absurd merriment.

'Course I can. Come on, then!'

She was dead keen, that was obvious. I noticed that her mouth was red and that her eyebrows and eyelashes were painted black, but that didn't bother me. Tonight was no time to be intimidated by female wiles.

'Well, come on, then!'

'My goodness, you're a fine one. . . .' But she'd already agreed, I took her hand, which was permissible, since we were going to dance, and we pushed and shoved our way through to the illuminated dance floor fraught with danger. Then, barely before we'd had time to take a deep breath, there we were, in the middle of the circle of light, struggling to get hold of one another properly. The band was playing 'Smoke Gets in Your Eyes'. I placed a hand round her waist and began blindly to propel her in the direction most people seemed to be moving in. It wasn't at all difficult, even though we did keep bumping into other couples. But so did the others, and in fact it seemed as though most people on the dance floor weren't quite steady on their feet. I held her warm hand in mine, my other hand resting on her broad elastic belt. She wouldn't look at me, but looked to one side (perhaps she was looking for her friends in all the throng?), but she danced quite close and easily followed the hesitant little improvisations I attempted, to conceal the fact that I'd suddenly drawn a complete blank as far as dance steps were concerned. But I still felt on top of the world, and it had turned out that I wasn't a complete dead loss on the dance floor after all: I, a fifteen-year-old, dancing cheek to cheek with eighteen-year-old Gerd, who was 'in love' with me, at a public do. A heroic deed of this order was not spoilt by a bit of dizziness and a few side-steps to keep me upright. To my surprise, I noticed that one was just as well hidden here in the crush of dancing couples as down there in the crowd of onlookers, that actually it came down to the same thing, that it was just a matter of having the courage to stride up on to the boards and grasp the girl in front of you round the waist. . . .

The music stopped. Immediately there was more room on the dance floor. We stood there, slightly unsure of ourselves beside one another, not knowing exactly what to say or where to go.

'Fancy another dance?'

I had the courage to ask because I could still taste the sickly liquor on my tongue, was still buoyed up by the courage generated by the hint of sickly dizziness, and because it seemed safest to stay put. The idea of having to move didn't appeal to me, and I wasn't really sure what you did after a dance at a public function. It somehow seemed to take so much more guts to twirl round on this plank floor than to dance the tango at a private party in a flat in town.

'How about another one? Shall we?'

'OK, if you want to. . . .'

Her eyes were still searching in all directions, as though she was looking for someone, but was still close enough for her hand to come into contact with my shirt-sleeve now and then.

'Cathrine's here too. I got Mother to look after the baby for her.'

Cathrine, oh yes. I had to laugh, I'd almost forgotten Cathrine and my rash decision to dance with her. It didn't seem all that important just at this moment, but all the same I began to scrutinize the couples around us to see whether she was among them. But she wasn't.

The next number was a Viennese waltz, and just as I was stretching out my hand to Gerd, to invite her to dance in my meticulous but alas so incorrect way, at the same time longing to get my arm round her again to give us an excuse for remaining there, I caught sight of Jo's face. He was leaning over the low wooden rail some way off, where we had both been standing a little while before, peering eagerly in amongst the dancing couples. He still hadn't caught sight of us. Gerd stood waiting, looking unfamiliar in her lipstick and eye-shadow, but compliant and full of expectation all the same. Around us people started to move, throwing themselves with gusto into the swirling movements of the waltz, stamping and whooping. I had a sudden crazy idea: I seized her round the waist with both hands and swung her round. I *knew* how to waltz. She drew back a little, then smiled and placed one hand behind my neck and one on my shoulder. Then we danced. I steered her out towards the rail where Jo was standing, knowing exactly what to do to shut him up. As we drew nearer, I carefully pulled Gerd as close to me as I dared, felt her legs tight against mine, and lowered my head, bringing my cheek close to her scented, lacquered hair. At that precise moment, he caught sight of us and his insolent mug was one white mask of surprise. With a feeling of vindictive triumph, I realized that she had placed both arms around my neck and gently pulled me closer, just as we whirled past right under his nose. His pals were also there. I was delighted. Let them all see me rubbing his nose in it! We danced clamped together, my cheek against her hair. We continued to dance like this even after we'd left the gawping lads behind, even when they could no longer pick us out in the throng of eagerly waltzing couples; even then we continued to hold each other tight, and I could feel her legs pressing against mine in a way I couldn't put words to. No one had clung to me like this at the dancing school. Feeling every movement in her body from the waist down just as distinctly as though it had been my own, here, surrounded by all these strangers, gave me an uncertain but at the same time blissful feeling of being on the threshold of something unknown, something longed for and fantastic. Never before had I understood the opportunity dancing afforded for pressing bodies together from the hips down. You would almost have thought that the steps we took in unison had been invented to promote a subtle massage of this highly strategic area – anatomically speaking – and with only one possible result: I felt a twinge of embarrassment at the thought of what she couldn't *fail* to notice pressing against her belly, but the slight queasiness which was such a helpful companion in tight corners succeeded in dispelling the fear that it was perhaps brazen of me to reveal so flagrantly that my mind was elsewhere. And indeed, there was no denying that I enjoyed this little insolence of mine, plumb in the middle of the discipline of the Viennese waltz. And as for her, she held a warm hand on my neck just below the hair-line, and her hair smelled of lacquer and setting lotion and her hips followed mine as inseparably as though we'd been Siamese twins. Perhaps she *liked* being exposed to such provocative behaviour. Was Gerd 'experienced' when it actually came down to it? Did she too have a 'past'? What had she got up to with her previous boy-friend from England? Thoughts such as these filled me with unease. The 'public' way of making overtures to someone was quite unlike holding a young girl tight and giving her a feel, allowing oneself to be kissed by her in the toolshed. It was a mating ritual we had embarked on. She with her make-up and her compliance, I with my clumsy invitation to dance, with my anticipation sticking up like a flagpole in my trousers, as futile as it was involuntary. I could have achieved the same result by pressing my belly against a tree-trunk in the forest. Make-up, hair lacquer, my newly pressed trousers: we went on dancing, I went on dancing with Gerd in blissful dizziness, and she, she danced with her warm hand on my neck, the other one now resting on my chest, as though at any moment it might decide to undo the shirt buttons of its own accord. And above our heads furry night insects flew frantically at the floodlights and were burned to ashes. . . .

Jo's face, white and distorted again: we'd danced right round, and here we were at the vantage-point of childishness once more. He was standing alone now, had perhaps dismissed his pals, to avoid having them around him as he stared defeat in the face a second time. His sister and his pal who were dancing – and how! – the Viennese waltz, which he himself had practised with the most secret hopes and desires concealed beneath his usual depraved exterior. In every single triumphant fibre of my body, I felt how this humiliated him, much more in fact than if I'd been dancing with Cathrine, Cathrine who was beyond the reach of both of us, who was more dream than tangible (for him, at any rate, but perhaps not for me), Cathrine who was like an arena in which we fought it out with wild, boyish exaggerations. No, it was this that was the reality, it was Gerd, in all her make-up, who in all innocence had taken her weekly bath in the wash-house, observed and scornfully commented on by Jo, now dolled up in her Sunday best, with kind, honest protruding eyes, grateful Gerd, who had whispered: 'It's been you all along'; it was she who really represented the female of the species for both of us.

'Oh,' she said – or had I imagined it perhaps? – when the

music had stopped and we were once again standing up straight, and I pretended not to notice that I was still holding her warm hand.

The orchestra really seemed to have got into its stride, for the pianist launched straight into a frantic boogie-woogie, driving most people from the dance floor.

'Come on, Peter,' she whispered, 'look, everyone's going . . . I'm not much cop at jiving.'

She pulled me away towards the gap in the barrier. All the white faces in the crowd seemed to be turned towards us. I kept one hand in my pocket to conceal the spectacle of my shame. There was such a crush by the exit that we had to stand there for a while, waiting for a chance to move out on to the grass, and when I quite by chance glanced back over my shoulder, there she was.

She was jiving with Aage Brenden, the famous Aage Brenden, the chap with the motor bike, the chap who'd got Marie in the family way (though I was the only one to know this; everybody else thought it was Uncle Kristen), Aage, the lady-killer from Nordmo, with drainpipe trousers, gold lamé threads in his jacket, Brylcreem in his long hair and the manners of a waiter. Aage was dancing with Cathrine to the hectic boogie-woogie rhythm, sending her spinning from him so that her thin skirt billowed up around her narrow thighs, pulling her in again and pressing her close to his gold lamé jacket, throwing himself and her first to one side then to the other. His shiny hair flopped down over his cheek, while hers was like a golden aura round her pale face. She laughed beneath the harsh glare from the floodlights, showing her teeth, and delighting in the uninhibited dance, the pace, the rhythm, the whirling movement. . . .

'There she is!' whispered Gerd at my side. Both of us gazed as though spellbound at the two of them dancing. By now they were the only couple on the dance floor; it was as though their frenzied dancing in time to the gymnastics of the musicians up on the podium had made everyone else take refuge in abstinence: there was just no competing with them. Aage Brenden's shoe soles clattered frantically over the plank floor, his long legs gyrating in his skin-tight trousers, the gold buttons on his jacket flashing and his hair flopping down over his eyes one moment, only to be flicked back again the next in that macho way of his. Narrow as a shoelace, his yellow tie flicked wildly over his shoulder. All we could see of her was her curls and, now and then, her broad mouth and white teeth, and her eyes that laughed and shone with excitement, with mischief and defiance. (But why though? I asked myself, as I stood numbly observing this spectacle.) It looked as if both of them wanted to tear themselves and each other to pieces to the riotous accompaniment of the boogie-woogie. A kind of sigh ran through the crowd each time Aage Brenden's strong arms threw her out into a breakneck spin, now forward, now to one side, now to the other, her skirt billowing out, revealing a liberal expanse of her white thighs. Each time that slicked-down hair of his was flicked back into place and hastily patted down by a much-practised hand, all of it in carefully calculated time to the jazz rhythms. Aage had been to sea, had a broken nose, tattooed arms (according to Jo), and my Cathrine was dancing, spinning and fluttering around him as though this was where she really belonged, as though this was the sort of thing she sat up there in the cottage longing for: boogie-woogieing for all she was worth, with a notorious local dance-hall heart-throb as her partner. For she was radiant; she was in her element, turning her dance into an exhibitionistic spectacle for all to see: my Cathrine.

'Just look at her!'

Gerd was just as fascinated as I was. Cathrine's slave, she lacked all the qualities that were precisely what made her mistress so irresistible. It wasn't that she was plain or lacked charm, but there was something too dependable and submissive about her attractiveness. I called to mind a lukewarm kiss in the rain compared with a hot electric charge on my cheek, for one incredible second one evening at Weasel Cottage. How was it that one girl gave an impression of cosiness and smuttiness when she at long last made up her mind to reveal something confidential about herself, while another got the tiniest little gesture to look like an incomparable token of favour, a symbolical promise, privileges that drove one wild . . .? Gerd must also know that this was so; that was what made her so loyal, so unselfish, so subservient in her strange friendship with Cathrine.

We had let go of one another. Everyone around us seemed to have stopped in their tracks and stood there watching Aage Brenden and Cathrine. The boogie-woogie was drawing to a close. The pianist was bouncing up and down on his chair, rocking the whole podium. The saxophone bellowed to a climax. The drummer was playing as though the end of the world was nigh.

'Heavens, just look at them!'

She sounded on the verge of tears.

All of a sudden I felt slightly sick. The dizziness had shifted. I felt a prickling sensation behind my nose, towards the back of my throat. Now I hadn't even a brazen erection to comfort me; I wished I was miles away, back in a nice place where things were what they appeared to be, where grown-up girls of twenty-one did not kiss me on the cheek or wave to me when sunbathing by the stream. Back to a situation where I could be sure of the meaning of everything around me. Moths swarmed out of the darkness, collided with the hot floodlights and fluttered dying to the ground.

At long last the number was over. Aage stood legs apart in the middle of the dance floor, a champion, fished his comb out of his pocket and combed his hair back into place. She appeared out of breath, though radiant, as if her batteries had been recharged, and leaned heavily on his arm, straightening her skirt, adjusting a stocking. I felt the queasiness fill my head and simultaneously well up in my gullet. Away! I turned and took two or three steps towards the exit, where everyone was crowding together. Gerd followed me, but by now I had ceased to pay any further attention to her. The nausea was threatening to overcome me. I thought I was having hallucinations. Uncle Kristen's face suddenly stared out at me from the crowd, so vivid, so grave, so tense. I closed my eyes and pushed my way forward.

Just then it happened. A voice shouted loud and clear over the dance floor: 'Bloody tart!'

Several others joined in: 'Townie slut! Get back to your bastard brat! Clear off!'

It came from the far end of the dance floor, causing a stir, stopping most people in their tracks, causing them to exchange glances, eager for more, looking for cheap thrills. A wave of hostility, of hatred, suddenly swept over the large crowd. At the same time a kind of hilarity burst out. A woman right next to me suddenly went into a paroxysm of loud, unrestrained laughter. Her friend joined in with a piercing, hysterical cackle, covering her face with her hands. From all quarters came whoops, whistles, heckling. The malice penetrated even my befuddled preoccupation with myself and my own concerns. I turned and saw a small group which had formed at the far end of the dance floor. One of them, clearly the ringleader, made threatening gestures to Aage Brenden. They were joined by others, who leapt over the rail. The shouts and laughter grew louder. The stream of people, which a moment before had been moving away from the dance floor, now swarmed back in an unruly mass. Desire, excitement and malicious pleasure were in their faces and voices, their laughter and shouts as they cried: 'Clear off!' and 'Shame!' Suddenly I realized that what was happening was dangerous. Of course I had seen all along through a kind of haze of confusion, surprise and bewilderment that *she* was what it was all about, Cathrine. It was she whom rumours in the village were about, the townie lass with the illegitimate brat, who kept a shady household up at Weasel Cottage. Now she'd gone too far, the moment of truth had come: the townie slut had danced right under their noses and had not only tarted herself up and made a thorough exhibition of herself, but had won the attentions of Aage Brenden, hero of the dance floor, the chap with the worst reputation, whom every little boy strove to emulate and every girl dreamed of going out with.

More and more people gathered at the far end of the dance floor. Onlookers pressed against the barrier. Aage Brenden stood there having a shouting-match with someone in the other group, had let go of Cathrine's hand and was clenching his fists. Although he was big and tall, there were a lot of them. She stood alone, a pace or two behind him, fragile, pale in the harsh glare. Laughter, whoops, shouts and whistles cut through the air like knives. She was utterly helpless. It was *now* she needed a man to defend her. It was *now* she needed the protection I had lavished upon her in my thoughts so many times, now, when two or three hundred people stood packed tight round a poor country dance floor made of planks, threatening her, mocking her, simply waiting for something terrible to happen to her at any minute. It was now that help was needed, now that her saviour should appear like a knight in shining armour. . . .

I stood transfixed, completely paralysed by a fear akin to panic, fear for Cathrine's safety and for my own, more for mine than hers. I too was an outsider here; at any moment there was a chance someone might link me with her. What if the excited crowd took it into their heads to have a go at both of us? I shrank down, making myself as insignificant as possible, simultaneously cursing my insignificance and my cowardice. I heard Aage Brenden shout something, saw him tear his jacket off, throw it on to the floor by the low podium, where the musicians stood helplessly following the spectacle. Then he grabbed one of his opponents by the shoulder and gave him a shove, propelling him backwards. The man gave as good as he got, lashed out, tore Aage Brenden's shirt. Then others joined in. Soon five or six of them were involved in an angry brawl. They panted, stamped, groaned out curses. One man was knocked to the ground. Aage Brenden had two of them at him, one of his shirt-sleeves hung loose about his wrist. He butted one of them with his elbow and struggled to shake the second one off; there was blood between his teeth. His bare forearm was blue with tattoos. A young lad clambered over the barrier, rushed up and gave Cathrine a shove so that she screamed and fell to the ground. In a flash he had melted back into the crowd which had gathered around the fight.

The little coward! I felt sobs welling up in my throat, cursed these thin arms which protruded like matchsticks from my shirt-sleeves. Oh, why was I not a grown-up? Why wasn't I strong? I'd have massacred the lot of them! And at the same time I trembled with an insane fear of physical violence.

Then Aage Brenden crashed down with someone on top of him, another chap landed him an almighty kick, which caught him in his side, causing him to draw up his knees and groan. Some people laughed, others cheered. Cathrine was half sitting, half lying on the planks, trembling, covering her face with her hands. Seven or eight chaps had formed a ring round her and the helpless Aage Brenden.

'Bash them in!' 'Give the tart a bit of what for!' 'Go on, give her one!' came the shouts.

Now Cathrine was completely at their mercy. As for me, I fought with all my might against the tears, the fear, the boundless humiliation. I'd have given anything for the courage and strength to go to her assistance, but at the same time I crouched like a dog behind the backs of the people who were shouting, prepared to undergo any humiliation, to resort to lies and deceit to save my own skin from their awesome rage. I scarcely had the strength to watch any more, so terrible was what had broken out around me. The bailiff, I thought in desperation. Where's the bailiff?

Then something else happened, completely out of the blue. A man dashed out on to the dance floor, rushed straight at the group as though he would knock down anyone who got in his way. His voice rang out over the din of the excited crowd: '*Have you gone clean out of your minds, then?*'

The nausea welled up in me again; I thought I was seeing things. The man had wiry black hair, a broad, square-set body, and his legs buckled slightly as he walked, even when he ran, as he was doing now. It looked like . . . yes, it could almost be . . . but it surely wasn't possible. . . .

'*Leave the lass alone!*'

His sharp tone struck all the onlookers dumb; something had curbed the ill wind they had almost allowed themselves to be swept along by, which had almost carried them away. A voice was all that it took, just a voice. . . .

But one of the young lads over there had a scornful grin on his face and took a threatening step towards the newcomer, who responded by seizing his arm and, with a heave, threw him across the floor, sending him crashing into the podium. An old fighter was swinging into action. Before the lout had had time to collect himself, his mate went tumbling after him. In the crowd, people had started to move again, someone spoke, someone laughed, someone else jeered, though most of them remained riveted to the spot, myself more stunned than any of them, for I'd caught a glimpse of the face of the fighter who had suddenly erupted on the scene: It was *him*. There could be no doubt. Uncle Kristen!

The strong, slightly stooping figure was unmistakable, the wiry mop of hair, the narrow eyes beneath bushy eyebrows. . . . Now he threw out an arm to grab the third one, seized the hair at the nape of his neck and forced him to his knees: 'Will . . . you . . . just . . . leave . . . decent . . . folk . . . in . . . peace?'

He spat out the words into the face of the lout, who squirmed beneath his grip. A shove, and he too went tumbling towards the other two, still coming to their senses after being caught off their guard.

Then it was all over.

Uncle Kristen knelt down beside the tearful Cathrine. The crowd fell so silent that you could hear what he was saying to her, even though he spoke in a soft, comforting voice, almost in a whisper: 'Have they been giving you a hard time . . .?'

Imagine being able to muster so much tenderness, so much self-control, even at such a dramatic moment as this!

'Come along now. . . .'

Carefully he helped her up. She was still sobbing beneath the hand she held in front of her face. What a coward I'd been to let her down! I could hardly bear to think how spineless I was. He led her slowly towards the exit. His firm arm lay round her fragile shoulders, her arm round his waist. They walked away like this, like two people in love, for all to see. The crowd parted to let them through. Then they were gone, lost among the heads and bodies that thronged together below the floodlit dance floor, grey and shadowy in the twilight. The old truck started up in the car-park, and I saw the headlamps sweep across the fields on the other side of the road.

All of a sudden, Gerd was at my side. 'Heavens, Peter, wasn't it absolutely terrible? Did you *see* him? Did you see how he dealt with them? Wasn't he fantastic . . .?' Her hand grasped my arm as though she wanted to be protected just like Cathrine had been by Uncle Kristen. Then I couldn't hold it back any longer. I felt the sickness coming on, water gathering in my throat. My stomach started to heave.

I tore myself loose and ran away from her, pushing and shoving my way through the crowd of curious onlookers, who still stood staring at the two or three of them who had been involved in the scuffle, and who were now busy brushing the dust off their knees, or holding their handkerchiefs against cuts and bruises which were still bleeding a bit. The accordionist played a few tentative bars of an old-time waltz and the drummer rattled out a call to order on the cymbals. Just one more knot of people I had to manoeuvre past, my teeth clenched, then I would be free, then all of them would be behind me. Almost choking, I half ran, half stumbled towards the clump of trees I glimpsed through the night-blue sky, my eyes watering, the vomit smarting and burning in my throat. I'd made it! With no further thought for anything around me, I crouched on my knees and elbows and spewed my guts out into the undergrowth.

Eventually it passed. I managed to control the spasms that racked my body like sobs. I wiped my nose, dried my eyes and felt deeply and utterly ashamed of my wretchedness. The dark grass felt cool against my bare arms. My palms were sweating. My throat burned. I wanted to go home. I would sneak past the bestial mob, find my bicycle and pedal home as fast as I could, home to Aunt Linn. . . .

Then I heard a movement immediately behind me. The panic of a few moments before was still with me, and I turned to ice, wanting to run away, but meeting a strong blow to my right ear before I'd managed to turn round or get to my feet. The blow sang in my head. Behind eyes screwed tight shut, I saw stars slowly explode. Someone jumped on me from behind, got me in a grip and pulled me down. With both arms pinned to my body I was helpless. Then others jumped on top of me, pushing me to the ground. They seemed to come rushing out of the darkness itself, from all directions. A voice hissed close to my ear: 'We'll teach you a lesson, townie wimp!'

Someone sniggered.

Boys' voices. Boys' laughter. I opened my eyes and caught sight of the lad who'd had the liquor: yes, it was Christopher. No doubt about it! So it was Jo's pals who'd ambushed me. The wide-eyed fear that had first paralysed me gave way to uncontrollable rage. I twisted like an eel to free myself from the hold from behind me, which pinned my arms in a vice-like grip. Something hit me smack in the face, making me warm and numb, though without hurting all that much. I threw my head back and felt it clash with another head. The grip on me loosened and I could move again. I seized a hand and sank my teeth into it as hard as I could. A howl indicated that I'd achieved my objective. I received a further blow to the face, but this time scarcely noticed it. I raised myself on to my knees, lashed out wildly around me, got hold of some hair and pulled so hard it felt as though the whole scalp would come off, the victim howling with pain. I waded in with both hands, knocking him down, slamming his head as hard as I could into the ground, putting my knee on it, wildly aiming my fists anywhere I could reach on the flabby body. Someone jumped on top of me again, trying to push me off his pal, but his aim was poor and his blow struck me only on the shoulder. Putting both hands on his face, I scratched for all I was worth. My body was performing feats I'd never known it was capable of. My head felt like an ocean in which I drifted helplessly, without control or direction. My will, the wild energy that powered my limbs with such unerring precision, such an urge to destroy, was functioning independently of my paralysed consciousness.

At last I got to my feet. The lad I'd scratched flew at me, but I met him with an outstretched fist, catching him slap on the nose. A sharp kick on his thigh from my pointed dancing shoe put him out of action for good. Again, someone came at me from behind, but I was ready for it, so it was no hard task to free myself from this hold. A hefty shove sent my assailant crashing backwards into the undergrowth. I caught a glimpse of him and saw who it was: he'd offered me a cigarette on the bench. To the right of me, someone took to his heels, disappearing behind the trees. The boy I'd scratched had already gone. The one I'd hit and whose hair I'd pulled lay moaning where I'd left him: Christopher, the one with the long horse mug.

The fight was over. My head was swollen and aching. My nose hurt. I could hardly see out of my right eye, but I'd won. I adjusted my clothes a bit. The buttons had been ripped off my shirt, the nylon shirt that was almost new, my trousers were stained with earth and grass. But I'd won. I'd beaten them, sent them packing. I was trembling like a leaf, but I couldn't help it. Something was hurting in my chest. I wondered vaguely whether Jo had had a hand in this. Whether he had been the one who'd run off first, or whether he'd merely talked the others into ambushing me. I'd beaten them, given them all a thrashing. It was my first real fight and I'd beaten the whole damn lot of them! But I was in a sorry state, trembling in every limb and something was hurting in my chest.

The dance was in full swing again, with stamps and shouts. I sneaked right round the far edge, in the shadows, trying to get my legs to do my bidding, but my knees were knocking and blood was dripping from my sore nose down on to my shirt, though I made no attempt to stop it. I almost tripped over couples locked in embraces on the tall grass here in the darkness, a little way away from the crowd and the din, but I paid no attention to them. I just wanted to get home. Home to Aunt Linn.

The bike stood where I'd left it. Jo's was nowhere to be seen. I pedalled unsteadily up over the long gentle slopes. The dynamo whirred away monotonously, the lamp casting a wavering beam on to the gravel. At the farm all was quiet, the kitchen windows in darkness. It must be after eleven. She's already gone up to bed, I thought.

I put the bike in the shed, opened the garage door a crack: the truck wasn't there. There was a light in the bedroom. So she was still awake. I dampened my handkerchief in the dew and wiped my face as best I could. It stung and smarted. She was bound to comfort me.

I went in. No one locked the door out here in the country. I stood in the kitchen for a moment before switching the light on. All of a sudden I felt miserable, stiff and sore all over. I must have looked quite a sight, but that was partly the point. I stood in the darkness of the kitchen for a moment just to breathe in the smells, the warm, clean smells of all the summers I'd spent here, all the meals I'd eaten, all the strawberries threaded on to stems of grass and carried home to beg for milk and sugar to eat them with, all the fleeting joys and sorrows of summer. I stood in the darkness of the kitchen to find the way back to my innocence, the innocence I needed to set my plan in motion, the innocence I needed to be sure that what I intended to say and do was harmless and had no real consequences for the people who deep down I was fond of, while part of me had long since calculated what the consequences would be.

I turned on the light and walked over to have a look at myself in the mirror. Yes, I really was a sight. One swollen cheek glowed beneath an eye which had closed, the eyelids gummed together; there was a ring of dark dried blood round my nose. With the handkerchief I rubbed a bit more at the scratches. Then I heard the gentle call I'd been waiting for.

'Is that you, Kristen?'

From the bedroom.

Without hesitating, I walked straight up and opened the bedroom door. There she sat in her rocking-chair with a book in her lap. The double bed stood in the corner as it always had, but it was turned down at one side only. So Uncle Kristen didn't sleep here any more. Just as I'd thought.

'No, it's only me, Aunt Linn,' I said, as she looked up at me.

She started, her eyes first filled with fear, replaced almost immediately by deep shadows of worry as her brow furrowed.

'What on earth have you been up to, Peter?'

Suddenly there she was beside me, her arm around my shoulder, speaking to me in comforting tones as to a child: 'But what's happened, Peter? Have you been drinking? Are you hurt? Come on, let's get you cleaned up a bit.'

She was trying to drag me out into the kitchen, but there was something I had to get off my chest first, and it turned out not to be difficult, since the care lavished on me caused my knees to tremble, my lips to quiver and my eyes to fill with tears of exhaustion, surrender and childishness. Into her dress I sobbed: 'It was a fight. . . . Somebody was trying to have a go at Cathrine. . . . And. . . .'

At this point I gave in completely, since it was the truth after all, even though I wanted to assign myself a place in the heroic battle for Cathrine's safety. The fight I'd been in had been about the same thing; in the final analysis it had been the same fight, only fought by different people. My whole body ached, my nose was still bleeding, so I could surely steal a little of the limelight from the almighty Uncle Kristen.

'There were seven or eight of them. They were getting at Cathrine . . .'

'Heavens, Peter, did you go and get mixed up in that?'

'Yes, a bit,' I said with a loud sniff. 'Then Uncle Kristen turned up . . .'

'*Kristen!?*'

'Yes. . . .'

I noticed her stiffen. I didn't dare look at her. I'd said it. There was no turning back now. I was a bit of a kid looking for comfort, weeping at my own helplessness, spontaneously reporting on what had happened, with neither responsibility nor concern for what this information might entail for my aunt, who sat up late at night waiting for her husband.

'Yes, he dealt with the lot of them. None of them stood an earthly against him. . . .'

Oh, I felt the tears salty and bitter. Even my heroic deed in the fight with Jo and his pals paled into insignificance when compared with the horror I'd felt before Uncle Kristen's intervention on the dance floor: the knight in shining armour, who always appeared in the nick of time and saved his princess.

'And what then?' It was as though she was reluctant to ask.

'Dunno.'

'How d'you mean?'

She was still holding me close to her for comfort, but her voice sounded as though it came from a distance.

'No, I dunno, really. . . .'

Something within me held me back. I knew very well I was blameless as regards the conflict between them, that I'd come here for Aunt Linn's comfort and for no other reason, that no one could hold me to account for my – completely truthful – version of what had happened down at the dance, but at the same time I somehow suddenly grasped the full significance of the havoc I could wreak.

'But you were there, Peter. You must know what happened afterwards.'

She held me tightly by both arms, she was imploring me, *had* to find out, had to seek confirmation of her worst suspicions. She was simply asking me to be a Judas because she thought I didn't understand what was going on, because she couldn't possibly suspect that part of my confused consciousness registered and understood every single nuance in the silent battle between them, that, by my involuntary insights and the innocence which they both, and I myself, believed in, I in fact somehow controlled what was happening and what was going to happen.

She looked into my eyes and implored me. I was only fifteen

years old and I had to give in, and against my will I did give in, but with a feeling of victorious pride, betraying him exactly as I had planned to, except that everything was so much easier, because she was actually asking me to do it.

'I think he gave her a lift home in the truck.'

I didn't regret it. It was done and I was calm and collected now. After all, I was the one who'd spied on them. I'd found the letter. I knew more about what was going on than any of them. I was in control of this game now. Everything would be explained. They would be shown the fateful letter all right – but when it suited me. It was my lead now.

'Oh surely not, Peter,' Aunt Linn whispered in my ear. 'Oh no, surely that can't be true, Peter?' And her tormented voice was so full of sorrow that for a moment I once more resorted to tears, out of sympathy, out of commiseration with them both and with myself, because we were each imprisoned in our own worlds and were strangers to one another.

'It's at least an hour since they left. I thought Uncle Kristen would be home by now,' I said, snuggling up close to her.

I don't think I did what I did out of pure malice or vindictiveness. I wasn't being evil any more than I am now; one is not always evil because one sometimes does malicious things and harms other people. When one is almost sixteen and has placed oneself outside and above people's dealings with one another, it is easy to make a wrong choice. A fifteen-year-old is a changeling in a setting too large and at the same time too small for him. There is no place in the world of humans large and also small enough for the fifteen-year-old's mad hopes and cruel limitations. He therefore chooses to make the wrong choice in his melancholy, graceless and inadequate way. So it was not only spite or malice that caused me to betray Uncle Kristen; it was the hope that I could not abandon of rooting out the lies, of ironing out the ambiguities. I gave him away so that, at long last, there would be justice in the world.

We stood there on the floor, she with her arms around me and I with my face buried deep into the soft hollow of her neck, where so many tender dreams had begun. My big, plump Aunt Linn stood in the middle of the bedroom floor, hugging me tight in her arms and weeping, weeping silently down on to my head, which sought comfort where comfort was always to be found.

'Oh no, Peter,' she whispered. 'Oh no, Peter. . . .'

I felt the power at my command as I stood there snivelling; this time, I'd taken control. Victory was mine! But at the same time the ineradicable childishness within me wondered whether the bonfire had been lit down at the fête. The year before last they'd set off fireworks as well!

18

Uncle Kristen had asked me to help him weed the turnips. We each walked along a furrow weeding, him ahead, me a little behind, each with our long-shafted hoe. Calm and silent, he strode between the furrows, bending slightly at the knees, his boots heavy with black earth. Once again he was the beetle, the toiler, the dutiful farmer and husband. The betrayal I was guilty of changed nothing, outwardly at any rate. And his faithlessness, which was now clear for all to see. . . . I couldn't comprehend how anyone could contain within him such contradictions without any outward sign of it, without simply exploding with boundless triumph, or burning up and crumbling away with shame and self-recrimination. And as for her, I felt sure she wouldn't have breathed even a word about it, simply allowing it to sit there smouldering between them so rancorously, so destructively. This is how it was when a married couple no longer shared the same bedroom. All of it flew in the face of my reason, offended me, making my paltry defences even more vulnerable and ridiculous. A small bluish shadow under my right eye was the only proof that anything out of the ordinary had happened at the summer fête.

It was the Saturday after the fête, and we stopped work early, strolling back up with the hoes slung over our shoulders beneath the lofty sky, which drifted towards the horizon on wispy clouds.

'Tomorrow we're going to have chicken,' he said out of the blue. 'D'you want to be in on the killing?'

And of course I did want to, but felt anxious all the same.

'You usually chop their heads off, you know,' he said almost cheerily, after he'd caught one in the hen-run, running around in there with arms waving like a big black scarecrow among the terrified, cackling hens. The one he'd caught he held casually by the wings, as if lifting a puppy by the scruff of the neck. The hen was already prepared to meet its doom, its neck sticking stiffly straight out from its body. Its beady eye looked at me, blinked, blinked and looked at me again; from the open beak there issued only an occasional barely audible squawk.

'In the old days they used to do it another way. . . . You're man enough to see a bit of blood, aren't you?'

I nodded. It was only four days till my sixteenth birthday – Wednesday, 4th August.

He stopped outside the low woodshed door and crouched down on his haunches, the hen between his legs, one foot on each wing, pinning it to the ground. With one hand he held the thin neck just below the head, and in the other there was suddenly a small knife, sharpened to a shine.

'Watch this now,' he said, quite calm. 'The point is to let it bleed to death, then the meat tastes better.'

Without further comment, and with a carefully calculated movement of his hand, not quick, but not slow either, he made a deep incision in the hen's neck at the point where it met the body. Immediately blood spurted out on to the white feathers. The bird let out a discordant screech and attempted vainly to beat its wings, its pathetic efforts causing the brown blood to trickle on to the ground, where a little puddle formed. A further screech, hoarser this time, then further writhing and twisting of body and wings caused more blood to drip on to the rotting sawdust by the woodshed door. I shuddered. The blood-curdling performance turned my stomach. Why on earth had he wanted to make me witness this slaughter?

'I think you're getting a bit pale about the gills, aren't you!' He glanced up at me as the prey writhed beneath his hands. 'You young 'uns aren't as tough as they were in my day.' He said this cheerfully, he who had cowed the fighting cocks on the dance floor, who was 'grown-up', manly and unshakeable and yet 'youthful' and full of vitality. Who demanded – and got – everything.

The wretched chicken's death throes were soon over. Uncle Kristen carried it up to the house by the feet. It was going to be plucked, cleaned and placed on a dish in the fridge overnight.

After the evening meal, the smallest milk can once again stood ready on the worktop. It was the first time since the summer fête. Uncle Kristen paced restlessly up and down.

Then out of the blue she said: 'Tonight *I'm* going to take the milk up!'

'You?!' He was almost shouting.

'Yes, me, yes. Why not? Is there any reason why I *shouldn't* go?'

'No. . . . Reason? No, none whatever . . .'

'In that case then. . . .'

That decided it. She would brook no argument.

But he wasn't going to give in so easily, was obviously acutely embarrassed by this move of hers.

'Come on now, Linn. Surely there's no reason for you . . .'

'Whyever not?' She bridled. 'I think it's high time I too had a chance to meet this Miss Cathrine Stang who seems to be on everybody's lips. Perhaps I might be able to give her a hand with something as well.'

'Oh, don't go and make such a fool of yourself!' said Uncle Kristen, cutting her short. He was angry now.

'Oh, you can rest assured I won't do that!' she said in a sharp tone I'd never heard before. 'I think others have beaten me to it where that's concerned!'

And off she went.

Before we'd had time to collect ourselves, the door banged behind her. Uncle Kristen raised and dropped his arms in a gesture of helpless amazement. Through the window we saw her hurrying up over the narrow path, her dark head bowed, a hand in front of her mouth, as though to stifle a scream.

We'd talked about having a party to celebrate my birthday. She wanted to bake a cake ('You're not too big and grown-up now for a bit of cream cake, are you Peter?'). I could invite anyone I wanted to. Gerd and Jo were obvious choices. She wanted to ask Mr and Mrs Bergshagen over for a cup of coffee a bit later in the evening. She'd appeared cheerful, the idea of having company seemed to have brightened her up. But the whole time, the milk can had stood on the worktop under the kitchen window.

The next morning, a Sunday, I received yet more confirmation that capricious manhood was about to take possession of my body. In the mirror that hung on its nail above the stand bearing the wash-bowl and the mug, I saw clearly that a growth of hair had appeared under my nose, and there were three or four, no, even more, dozens of long, light, downy whiskers on my chin.

A beard!

Not before time. Most boys in my class shaved, or said they did. I had longed for this day. I pulled my shirt off, lifted my arms and carefully inspected my armpits. Yes, more hairs had appeared, and they were longer and darker than when I'd last taken a look. Well well!

And just at that moment there was a knock at the door. I thought it must be Uncle Kristen, or Jo perhaps (I had a bone to pick with Jo!) and called out 'Come in' as I nonchalantly started to put my shirt back on.

But it was Cathrine. Suddenly she was there in the room, with a hint of a question in her eyes.

'Hello, Peter.'

'Oh Cathrine, hello. . . .'

I must have looked utterly nonplussed, for she smiled, despite the serious look on her kindly face today.

'Goodness, look how brown you are!'

I blushed, fumbling frantically with the last shirt buttons.

'Oh yes, I've been working in the fields.'

I'd finally plucked up courage, baring my torso, my shoulders, my thin chest and my belly, which I'd always thought looked rather effeminate with its flabby folds. After the first days of sunburn, a golden, rather attractive tan remained, which to my eyes made my arms, shoulders, chest and belly look more or less acceptable, or at least somewhat less misshapen than hitherto.

'You haven't been swimming, then? I've looked for you once or twice.'

'No.'

I'd sworn never set to foot near the ominous Mill Dam

again, ever.

'Oh, isn't that where they found that poor girl? You were there at the time, weren't you?'

'Yes, that's right.'

I was grateful to her for remembering.

'It must have been terrible.'

'Yes, it was. It was no joke, I can tell you.'

There was nothing more to be said and my torso was fully protected by the bright summer shirt. I wondered what she would say next.

'I say, Peter,' she said, as though suddenly remembering why she'd come, 'er, d'you think you could do me a favour?'

'Yes, sure I can. . . .'

She shook her head irritably, almost as though not satisfied with my answer. Then she gave a sad little smile.

'Oh no, this is ridiculous. I've never been a good liar. I'd better just tell you it exactly as it is. I seem to have gone and put my foot in it again, you see. You must know I had a visit from your aunt yesterday . . .'

'Yes, I do.'

'And she . . . she . . . well, she was friendliness and niceness itself, but I had the feeling she was threatening me!'

'*Threatening* you?'

'Yes, I don't mean directly, but she started talking about how hard it must be for a girl in my situation, and then she said that you had to look after your reputation round here, because not long ago a girl had been hounded out of the village because she'd lived an immoral life. Apparently she'd run after married men. . . .' She shook her fair curls incredulously. 'So more or less directly, she was saying that she'd get me hounded out of the village if I went on letting Kristen visit me.'

I was flabbergasted. I'd never thought Aunt Linn was capable of threatening anybody. 'My God!' was all I could find to say.

'And later, at about midnight, *he* came and said we'd have to be more careful. . . . And I suppose it's true that he's been up quite a lot recently, he's been so fantastic with Hanna, and you know. . . . You know how it is, it's been lonely living on my own, I've been so glad of the company.' She looked at me and gave a charming, helpless smile. 'It seems I can't help getting mixed up with married men, Peter. Do you think it's awful?'

'Awful? How d'you mean?'

Nothing Cathrine did could be absolutely wrong – so long as she told me about it in that sincere and natural way of hers. Something radiating out from her whole being seemed to dispel my sombre thoughts about the corrupt and immoral aspect of her relationship with Uncle Kristen.

'Because it's been just as much his fault as mine. I certainly haven't run after him. . . . I only wish it'd never happened. He may be sweet and good and likeable, but round here everybody knows everybody else's business. . . . It could never work.'

She paced up and down the room as she talked, catching the sunbeams by the window, touching the spiders' webs in the window-frame, and finally sitting down on the bunk, thus emphasizing the fact that she really was there, her realness filtering through my half-believed visions of an elfin princess, an improbable visitor from the land of dreams. I stood like a pillar of salt transfixed to the spot, elated and jubilant. I had thought it was all over with her, with all girls, after the summer fête, but here she was, small, trim and beyond compare, her hair an aura round her head, here with me in the hut, sitting on my bunk, and about to tell me all about her and Uncle Kristen. My only worry was lest something here in the room, something about the unmade bed, the clothes thrown over the chair, the suitcase and rucksack in the corner, the things on the table, should betray my secret world of self-abuse, the contemptible universe of the fifteen-year-old. But even if for me everything bore the hallmarks of puberty and painful inadequacy, it didn't appear to awaken such suspicions in her, for she continued to talk as she looked at me, sincere, fair-skinned and blonde, but sad as well.

'D'you think somebody might have said something to her, to make her suspect us? Well, I suppose we haven't been all that careful.'

My heart sank. 'Oh, I don't know,' I said. 'People talk . . .'

'Of course, of course they do – I know that. And I expected it, after the summer fête. Come to think of it, why weren't you there?'

'I *was* there.'

'Were you, Peter? Heavens, I didn't see you. Did you see me?'

I nodded.

'Why didn't you come and say hello, then we could have had a dance. I'm sure you're a better dancer than those clods up here. All they can think of is dancing you into the ground just so they can show off.'

My chest swelled with pride.

'Did you see the fight?'

'You bet.'

'Heavens, wasn't it terrible? What a load of yobs. My knee still hurts a bit even now.' She showed me a bruise on her knee. 'Goodness knows what would have happened if Kristen hadn't come to the rescue. . . . Oh, Peter!'

She looked so helpless, young and unprotected all of a sudden. I wasn't going to let her down now. I would agree to anything she asked, anything at all.

'Peter, I know it's silly of me to drag you into this, but like I said, he came yesterday, in the middle of the night, I was already in bed, but he went on knocking at the door till he woke me. He was worried, saying she knew about it all and that from now on we'd have to watch our step. We'd have to meet somewhere else, he said. He thought that we could meet here. It would be easier for him to get away. Yes, I know it's awful of me, but the thing is, he asked me to ask you a "favour", to think up something you could do, once or twice a week, so we could meet here. . . . Oh, Peter, I shouldn't have put it like that, what will you think of me now? I feel so ashamed. . . . I agreed to go along with it just this once, because I wanted to put an end to it, you see. I don't want to be involved with a married man again. Everything gets so serious and tragic. I don't want to be mixed up in marital quarrels. I know it's a bit late in the day to say this, but it somehow seemed quite different this time – to begin with at least. Out here in the country everything seems so different, sort of more natural. . . . It 's just that he's been so fantastic to me. But after yesterday, after what she said. . . . I can't stand scenes, not any longer! So if you could co-operate just this once, so that I could get a chance to put an end to it, make him understand that it's just no use. . . . Will you do it, Peter? Oh, Peter. . . .' Suddenly there were tears in her eyes. 'Peter, you must believe me when I say that it wasn't my intention to get mixed up in anything this time. But I suppose I must have been a bit in love with him, though I never intended it to get serious. I would never destroy a marriage. I so easily get involved in things like this, even against my will. If only I'd had a loyal friend I could trust, someone decent, someone who could love me. . . .'

Then she came over to me. While she'd been getting all this off her chest, I'd been trembling like a leaf. First out of jealousy, then out of relief and now out of pure arousal, out of love, for it was me she meant, there was no doubt about it. A good, loyal friend who could love her, it was me!

She placed a hand on my arm, and her head reached no higher than my chin, which bristled with a profusion of ridiculous blond whiskers. 'Peter,' she said, 'you're the only friend I've got up here, you're the only one I can rely on, even Gerd has behaved so strangely of late. . . . (That too! As though I didn't know full well why!) Will you help me? Just this once, so that I can break it off with him? I've made up my mind. Really and truly. Will you look after Hanna for me, let's say on Thursday afternoon, for a couple of hours while I deal with this?'

I felt her arms, the slender honey-coloured arms around me.

'Yes,' I said, 'of course I'll look after Hanna. But on one condition . . .'

'Oh thanks, Peter,' she said. 'I knew you'd help me.'

'On one condition, I said . . .'

'And what's that?'

'I want you to come to my birthday party on Wednesday,' I said pointedly. I had seen a solution, a solution which would be to the benefit of all of us, meeting the needs of decency and justice. It was up to me so to order it that everything went off smoothly, all snags were ironed out and everyone got his due, for I was the only one who knew all the threads and knew where they met, and what lay in store for all of us, at least where Cathrine and myself were concerned. There could be no doubt now as we stood embracing one another. She said she wanted a friend; she was going to break it off with Uncle Kristen. . . . I grew in my own eyes; she helped me to overcome my pettiness and jealousy, my childish puritanism. Without losing a moment, I set about implementing the plan, for it was a plan, or the rudiments of one at any rate.

'You will come on Wednesday then, won't you?'

'But do you think it'll be OK though, Peter? Now that she's been up to my place and . . .'

'Of course it'll be OK! I can invite who I want. It would be a wonderful alibi for the two of you. And you're going to break it off on Thursday in any case . . .'

'Well, yes, I suppose so. . . .' She didn't seem quite certain.

'Then I'll look after Hanna for you.'

'But Peter, think how awkward it could be.'

'Oh no – if you come, it shows you're innocent. And it might make him realize that it won't work with the two of you any longer.'

'Well . . .'

'And besides, I *want* you to come – you're the only person I really want to invite to my birthday party.'

'You're so sweet, Peter.'

We stood there close together, and I felt so important, as though it was I who had saved her from the brawl on the dance floor; and I couldn't resist letting her feel my optimism, my confidence that suddenly began to swell. I pulled her close to me and held her exactly as I'd clasped Gerd when we'd been dancing at the summer fête.

'But Peter, what *are* you doing. . . .' She was breathing heavily against my neck and was sighing almost in spite of herself. 'Oh, Peter. . . .'

I couldn't let her go now.

'I've heard a thing or two about you,' she whispered close up against my skin. 'Gerd's told me that you're such a good. . . . I think she's jealous of us, what do you think, Peter? Are you fond of her?'

'Fond of *her*. . . .'

My voice had totally vanished. I shook my fevered head vigorously, the only way of saying no that was left. Gerd – what was Gerd's half-baked love compared with this?

She smothered my neck with loud smacking kisses. I stood holding her, a big clumsy bear, oblivious to everything else in the world, but holding her tight, tight against me, allowing her without any restraint to feel my love press against her where our bodies met so ineffably hard and warm.

'I think I know what you want, Peter,' she whispered, sweet and sincere. 'But it wouldn't be right, not yet, not now after everything I've told you. Just give me a bit of time. . . .'

Not yet. Just give me a bit of time. . . . Every single word she murmured sparked off wild ambition in my mind.

Then she shifted her position slightly and slipped a slender hand under my shirt, on to my skin, beneath my belt, groping for a position under my clothes which would be pleasurable as well as serving its purpose. And I started, I stiffened, going hot and cold, for nobody, but nobody had touched me like this before. I had never thought it remotely possible that a girl, that Cathrine. . . . But now not only was it possible, it was true. She was so forthright and so tender – shame and degradation were entirely absent from what she was doing. She was above laws, she could do what she wanted and it would simply be grand and wonderful. She led me, she coaxed me to the peak of my adulation. I was like a skittish little foal, while she was calm, persuasive, experienced: a few light finger strokes, a tender hand, a measured fondling, a word, a little laughter in my ear. I sank into a state of bliss, the most exquisite of pleasures, the most ineffable well-being, and almost failed to notice that I'd spurted semen over my clothes and her arm, almost up to the elbow.

'I had a visitor today,' I announced at the dinner-table. The chicken Uncle Kristen had murdered lay carved up and oven-brown on a serving plate surrounded by dishes of cabbage, potatoes, rich gravy. 'It was Cathrine. I invited her to my party. She doesn't know many people here. She said she'd love to come. . . .'

The rapid exchange of glances I'd expected followed. I could read people's thoughts now; I knew everything that went on in their heads. There was still a warm, tingling feeling in my groin after the sublime experience of the morning. The memory of her was like fireflies flashing through my mind. Had dream become reality? Was all this true? I could scarcely believe it, though a slight sensation of warm fatigue in my groin whispered that it had happened just the same.

I had invited her. I knew they would have to accept it,

would have to play the charade and keep up appearances; everything was developing according to rules I suddenly understood. I'd suddenly understood a great deal, so much in fact that I could almost forgive Uncle Kristen his deceit, his faithlessness, his skill as a seducer. I was an accomplice; we were on an equal footing, man to man. It was all because of her and the charm she radiated. He'd fallen for her just as I had. He'd fought hard to win her favour. But I had won.

'Yes, Cathrine seemed a pleasant girl to me. And the little baby's an absolute cutiepie,' said Aunt Linn accommodatingly. 'But perhaps we'd better not invite Bergshagen and his wife for coffee after all, then.'

A glance at Uncle Kristen.

He didn't utter a word and I helped myself from the plate of chicken as though I'd brought down this succulent piece of game single-handed.

19

On Monday I went to find Jo in the fields. He was standing with his back bent over the potato furrows, banking the earth up. His dungarees were bleached white by the sun. From a distance, you might have taken him for a man.

I hadn't seen him since the summer fête and made a point of positioning myself so he couldn't avoid seeing the faint bruise under my right eye which had remained after the hullabaloo that evening.

'Hi.'

'Hi,' he said and grinned shiftily.

I was sure he'd been behind the shameful ambush that evening, but hadn't actually seen him, had nothing on him, so as far as that went he was on safe ground. In any case, that wasn't the reason I'd come. My superiority today was of another order and I intended to exploit it to the hilt and put one over on him he wouldn't forget.

'I'm having a birthday party on Wednesday.'

'Oh?'

As though he didn't know. I'd celebrated my birthday with a party, admittedly only cakes and pop, every single holiday I'd spent here.

'I thought you all ought to be there. Cathrine as well.'

'Oh?'

Nothing more was needed. Now I had him. His eyes flashed inquisitively under the sandy mop of hair.

'Is it definite she's coming?'

'Sure. I've asked her. She popped down to see me yesterday.'

'What? Did she?'

He was doubtless a bit impressed but couldn't let on. Our friendship had always been founded on rivalry in matters both large and small. Now there wasn't much of the friendship left and the rivalry had escalated into bitter warfare.

'We had quite a good time. . . . If you see what I mean.'

'You don't say?' His grin was full of bitter sarcasm. 'You're sure she's not coming just to see your uncle, then?'

I'd been prepared for this.

'Uncle Kristen? Why should she?'

'They looked like bosom pals at the fête.'

'Oh well – somebody had to protect her against those village yobs. Or are you pissed off because he wiped the floor with them? Maybe they were mates of yours?'

Of course he couldn't answer this directly, so confined himself to mumbling.

'That's not what I've heard . . .'

'And I suppose you won't believe me when I say we were fucking yesterday morning, Cathrine and I?'

'Too bloody right I won't!'

'You'll see on Wednesday.'

'How come?'

'I'll prove it to you.'

'Oh yes?'

'If you'll do me a little favour . . .'

'What kind of favour?'

'Your rubber johnny.'

'What about it?'

'I need it for Wednesday. I daren't do it any more without.'

'Like bloody hell!'

'Oh go on, Jo.'

I had him completely in my power. His greedy little mug lit up with curiosity as to what I'd dreamed up, with impatience to be let in on my secret plans.

'Get your own!'

'But Jo, you don't need it just at the moment, do you? I'm off home in a couple of weeks anyway, I'll send you a new one, a whole dozen if you like! In town there are special machines for them.' (I'd heard that they existed, though never seen one. I assumed they were to be found in the finest hotels, at airports and such places.) 'All right then, but if I don't get it, I'll have to call the whole thing off . . .'

'How d'you mean?'

'I'll show you on Wednesday. If you're coming, that is . . .'

'OK, then. You can have it.'

'Great!'

I'd known all along that this was how it would turn out. What could possibly stop me today, a mere twenty-four hours after Cathrine's utterly astounding intimacy, her fondling affection, the like of which I'd never dreamed existed anywhere in the universe, the promises she'd whispered: 'Just give me time. . . .' And just imagine, she was twenty-one (at least!) and a mother and had had admirers galore, whereas I was only sixteen, or as good as, and now it was me she'd chosen, now it was she and I who belonged together. Nothing in the world could cause me to doubt it now.

'It'll be a really great birthday present, that will, Jo,' I said, laughing and getting him to join in the joke, not begrudging him a laugh now that he'd capitulated. Even in his dungarees he looked so boyish and green that I almost felt sorry for him.

On the Tuesday morning, the day before the big day, I took Marie's letter out from under the mattress, reread it and placed it in an envelope. I addressed the envelope to Aunt Linn in large, camouflaged handwriting. I placed the anonymous letter inside my shirt when I went down to the farm to collect the bicycle.

At the shop I bought a stamp and posted the letter. It would be collected that afternoon, taken to the post office near the railway station, sorted and delivered the following day. It would reach its destination tomorrow afternoon, when the party was in full swing, exactly as I had planned.

I pedalled effortlessly up the long Coombehills slopes. The warm weather, the fields, the dark forest below the crest of the ridge and the thought that tomorrow was my birthday, glossed over all the upsetting events of the past few weeks. Afterwards, everything would be better. I noticed that I could take pleasure in the summer again as I'd hoped to be able to, watching the scudding clouds, inhaling the smell of yarrow, of other plants and dust from the grassy verges. I could enjoy myself as I'd been able to so long ago. I could enjoy myself like a little boy on holiday in the country, and I could do so because Cathrine had met me half-way, given me a taste of the happiness it was to be grown-up. Complete.

20

They were expected for three o'clock.

I'd taken the bull by the horns and asked Uncle Kristen whether he could lend me his razor. It was time to start shaving when you were sixteen, besides which the light, downy whiskers on my face weren't exactly a thing of beauty. Trembling with impatience, I endeavoured to guide the blade round the tell-tale lumps and bumps, the spots, all the marks of puberty on my chin.

The table in the dining-room was already laid. On the stove stood a pan full of frankfurters and a tureen containing consommé. The cream cake had been put in the fridge for the moment. Everything was spick and span; she'd put out the finest crockery and now walked about the kitchen, smoothing down her hair and her dress, flushed in the cheeks. Was she really so nervous? As for me, I was in seventh heaven, continually looking at the clock which seemed to have stuck at a quarter to. Uncle Kristen had gone up to put on his 'glad rags', as he referred to them ironically. My newly shaved chin smarted and burned, and I scarcely knew who I most wanted to come, the guests or the postman. He should have been here by now with the message from me to her. To both of them. My birthday present to them. At breakfast the parcel containing a fine new spirit compass from them had lain beside my plate.

But where had Cathrine and the others got to? And what was keeping the blinking postman?

Then I caught sight of Jo's sandy-coloured head through the kitchen window. At last they were here! I shot out to meet them. But it was only Jo and Gerd. There was no sign of Cathrine. She might have been delayed. It was obviously difficult to get down here with the little one in a carry-cot.

But while we were still standing in the kitchen and Gerd and Jo were shaking hands politely with Aunt Linn and Uncle Kristen, having wished me many happy returns and, acutely self-conscious, handed over a parcel through which the familiar shape of a flashlight could clearly be discerned beneath the wrapping paper, there was a knock at the door. Once again I had to go into action – to tacit glances exchanged between the grown-ups – even though I would willingly have delegated the honour to someone else, since at precisely that moment a wave of hot embarrassment surged over me, marring the elation that had borne me along the whole morning. And there she was, warm, a little out of breath, the afternoon sun in her face, in her hair, on her slender shoulder, in a dress like a summer cloud of flimsy, light-coloured material and wearing sandals on her bare, sun-tanned feet; like a personification of my most immodest fantasies, so much so that the thought of having to exhibit her to the whole group of them was almost painful.

'Hello, Peter,' she said. 'Sorry I'm a bit late. It was a real struggle carrying her.'

The carry-cot stood on the front steps between us. Beneath the quilt I glimpsed a tiny head covered in black hair. She was probably asleep. It was the first time I'd seen Hanna. I felt moved, almost in awe, at the same time struggling with a feeling of inadequacy, of jealousy. There was so much, so very much that I couldn't dream of attaining to yet, and I was so impatient, wanting to take the whole lot in one mouthful, already believing I could taste 'real life' on my tongue.

'Many happy returns, Peter. This is for you.'

She handed me a parcel. As soon as I took hold of it, I could feel it was a book.

'Go on, open it!' she said eagerly.

And I deftly pushed aside the red ribbon and unfolded the wrapping paper. On the cover there were butterflies. The title was: *The Hundred Best Poems on Love*. I'd never got as far as the end of a poem in my whole life, yet never had any gift made such an impression on me: poems on love – so straightforward, so beautiful. My voice yodelled as I mumbled out a thank you.

Then from behind me I heard: 'Aren't you going to ask

Cathrine in then, Peter?'

It was Aunt Linn, standing in the hall, red-cheeked and in high spirits herself.

A tray bearing slender wineglasses sat on the sideboard. Uncle Kristen was filling them from the bottle he'd fetched from the cellar. Redcurrant wine four years old. I recalled his mentioning it, boasting to Dad about it once. Now we would all have a chance to taste it.

'Cheers then, and happy birthday, Peter!'

He was unrecognizable in collar and tie and with his hair combed. Only the hand holding the wineglass was broad and coarse, revealing the beetle he was beneath his suit. The postman should be here any moment.

'Cheers!'

'Many happy returns!'

Everyone raised their glasses. The home-made wine had a sweet and authentic taste. Gerd looked at me with large, protruding eyes. I hadn't seen her since we'd danced – so infatuated with one another – at the summer fête. Nor had she forgotten it either, that was clear. She was mine for the taking, all I had to do was reach out my hand. But what did Gerd mean to me today? Today, when I was sixteen and was about to test the extent of my new, limitless potential? Today, when blonde, sun-tanned Cathrine stood no more than two steps from me with her white smile, with raised glass (even if I was almost afraid to look in her direction), radiating the fact that she was mine and mine only?

'Cheers, then, everyone. Nice to see you all!'

Uncle Kristen topped up the glasses. Jo looked at me and grinned an 'everything OK'. He looked as pleased as punch; no pop and cakes party this! The hot afternoon sunshine streamed in through the window-panes. Aunt Linn looked even more flushed and embarrassed with her wineglass in her hand.

'Well, well, well, just think that you're sixteen,' said Uncle Kristen, smiling. He was as happy as a lark. His Sunday best neatness, his polished courtesy as he poured out the wine and led the round of 'Cheers' was a little disconcerting. 'Well, I'll be blessed, it doesn't seem two minutes since you were running about in short trousers, playing cops and robbers with Jo there.' All of us couldn't help laughing at this, the girls especially. 'Yes, sixteen years old, it's a dangerous age to be. When I was sixteen, I was pining to go to sea . . .'

'Were you?'

'To sea?'

His hand was trembling slightly. He had caught Cathrine's eye, held on to it, exploiting his advantage. I felt a bit hot under the collar; after all, it was the first time I'd seen them together and it made the obscene relationship that had blossomed between them even more improbable, not to say outright unbearable to contemplate. His coarse labourer's hand on her graceful, honey-coloured body, his lips. . . . And most improbable of all, his naked man's body with his brown neck and brown forearms where his shirt-sleeves had been rolled up, and his weapon as it hung there swinging heavy and ominous like an overripe bunch of grapes, or perhaps even big, erect and distended. Goodness knows what it must look like then! All this repugnant manhood in close, disgusting contact with her elflike limbs, her pointed breasts, which had shone so white, so vulnerable towards me in the sunshine that day down by the edge of the stream, which I could clearly visualize just by closing my eyes. . . . But I mustn't forget that everything was over between them, even if *he* was still in the dark about it. I vaguely overheard him continuing with his story about when he was sixteen, principally directed at the girls. Jo signalled to me to go over to him, but it wasn't possible just at that moment. Aunt Linn suddenly announced in a loud voice: 'The meal will be ready in a moment. Everybody to the table please!' Then she put down her wineglass on the tray so quickly that a drop of the wine she hadn't finished spilled over and ran down on to the crochet doily. She almost ran out into the kitchen.

'. . . And I had to hoof it all the seventy miles back,' said Uncle Kristen, concluding his tale.

'Seventy miles, good heavens!' said my Cathrine, enraptured. She probably also noticed how distinguished he looked in his Sunday best, his hair combed. But we had our secret plan. She'd given her word, and I still clutched the book containing the hundred best poems on love firmly in my hand.

'I think we ought to go over to the table now,' I said. I

hadn't dared discuss anything to do with the seating arrangements with Aunt Linn for fear of giving myself away. Now it was as though my life depended on grabbing a seat next to Cathrine, making it look completely 'accidental'.

'Well then, I'll sit here at the head of the table,' said Uncle Kristen, 'and Jo and Gerd over there perhaps – and the man of the moment and Cathrine here on this side. . . .'

It didn't dawn on me right away that, in so doing, he had fulfilled my innermost wishes – at least, those relating to the immediate present – at one fell swoop, for Jo was just then squeezing past me, tugged at my jacket sleeve, and pushed something wrapped in a crumpled, sweaty piece of paper into my hand. I felt myself turn scarlet but managed to cram Jo's 'present' into my trouser pocket, unnoticed by the others.

So there I sat, flushed, happy as a sandboy, with an elbow close to her elbow, my knee next to her knee. Jo and Gerd sat opposite, looking at me, he with malicious complicity written all over his face, she with a look, a smile which seemed to hum 'We two, we two. . . .' Uncle Kristen kept Cathrine amused with yet another story about when he'd been sixteen. Her foot bobbed up and down on her heel under the table-cloth.

Aunt Linn came in with a steaming bowl of consommé. She ladled it out. We began to eat. Uncle Kristen was in great form, guffawing, telling further stories, things he'd experienced, which I'd never heard about before. He almost seemed taken by surprise himself at all these memories and by the unexpected outcome the stories took. He roared, pulling faces like a boy. No one ever talked like this here normally; the everyday tone was quite different, repetitively programmed in advance, the same things being mentioned time and time again, for that was how things were at Fagerlund, the unchanging stability one always remembered and could never imagine any different. But now he was telling a story that made us all laugh. She laughed most perhaps, turning away from me towards him seated at the end of the table and laughing in acknowledgement of a point, a funny joke, as we ate our frankfurters and mashed potatoes (my choice) and I observed every single movement she made with her slim leg which I sensed beneath the table, next to mine.

'Come on now, do dig in!' exclaimed Aunt Linn from her

seat at the far end of the table. 'There's more food in the kitchen!'

Plates were passed round. Jo heaped one frankfurter after another in a pile on his plate. But I was full and could only think: You little shit!

'No thanks, I've had enough,' said Gerd. 'But it was delicious, thank you.'

'Well, I may as well have another one,' said Uncle Kristen.

'No thanks very much.' Cathrine smiled politely down the table. 'I really can't eat another mouthful.'

'Oh go on, have one or two more, you hardly eat a thing!' It was both a plea and an order.

'You need it when you're. . . . Just look how thin you are!'

There was such a strange note of urgency in Aunt Linn's voice, as though it had suddenly become all-important to get everybody to eat as much as possible, especially Cathrine.

'Look, I'll go and fetch some more mashed potatoes from the kitchen . . .'

'No thanks very much all the same, I'm full to bursting.'

But Aunt Linn was already standing up, had picked up the dish and was on her way.

'But it was lovely, really it was . . .'

'Nice that you all liked it. . . . Now I'll go and get some more from the kitchen!'

I didn't notice that she was weeping until she said the word 'kitchen' the second before she slammed the dining-room door after her.

That was when the incident with the spider occurred.

All of a sudden, Cathrine gave a scream and shot back in her chair, almost tipping it over. I just had time to see a spider, a perfectly normal spider, about the size of a small coin, which had lowered itself down and hung there on an invisible thread at exactly the point where her head had been a second before, before she had screamed and a panic-stricken sweep of her arm had caused it to fall straight down into her lap. A further scream, further wild waving of arms as it ran down over her dress towards the bare skin on her honey-coloured thigh. Then Uncle

Kristen's large hand swept over her dress, her thigh, swept the spider down on to the floor where he immediately trod on it.

The self-assured gesture, the masculine hand on the soft, round thigh brought back the scene between him and Aunt Linn in the garden that time a few weeks ago so forcefully that I almost had to gasp for breath.

'Oh!' Cathrine laughed and gasped, gasped and laughed. 'Good grief, I can't *abide* spiders, they drive me crackers! I'm awfully sorry.'

A laugh of relief went round the table, but my heart sank, because I remembered her telling me, the evening I'd visited her, that, far from being frightened, she was fascinated by insects. Why did she react like this now? And as for him, he laughed loudest of all perhaps, still leaning against her, his hand resting on the back of her chair as though ready to perform further heroic feats if called upon to do so, ready at any moment to massacre insects for her sake. His expression was indulgent and paternal, with at the same time a hint of subservience, of meekness almost, in his strong eyes when he looked at her. Cowed, sheepish, that was how he looked, he who was so strong, so clever, a match for anything and everybody, now sat there playing the fool with Cathrine, one hand on the back of her chair, sunning himself in his presence of mind, his ability to squash spiders, as though any Tom, Dick or Harry wouldn't have been able to do exactly the same, as though *I*, who sat closest. . . .

'Heavens, it frightened me out of my wits, thanks a lot. . . .' She beamed at him, and as she thanked him yet again, I noticed that she placed her hand on his, resting on the back of her chair, squeezing it as though it was the most natural thing to do at a birthday party, *my* birthday party.

Gerd said: 'Ugh, aren't spiders horrible?'

Jo's mouth was crammed full of sausages.

'Oh come off it, spiders are nothing to get into a tizz about,' I said, feeling I had to intervene, contribute, be strong and courageous myself. 'They're totally harmless. They only catch insects. There are no spiders anywhere in northern Europe which are dangerous to humans.'

But no one seemed particularly impressed by this declaration of solidarity.

'I think they're *repulsive*,' Cathrine repeated, and Uncle Kristen beamed like a bit of a kid who's received a pat on the head.

The mood at the table had taken a dangerous turn. In the space of one fateful moment, I, whose birthday it was after all, had been reduced to a thing of no importance, a passive onlooker as far as what was going on to the right of me between *them* was concerned. I could have wept with resentment. I was no more important at the party than Jo and Gerd, who sat there minding their Ps and Qs on their side of the table, eating, following what went on. They had also seen his hand so familiarly in her lap for a second, and her hand on his as a gesture of thanks. . . . And I, who was now sixteen, who was supposed to be master of ceremonies today, who had woven my plan, I sat there like a spare part staring at a mound of cold mashed potatoes, sick with humiliation and completely at a loss as to how to recapture the limelight.

But then the familiar sputtering of the postman's moped was heard out in the farmyard. So now things were beginning to go right again. I could scarcely sit still, so excited was I about today's delivery and the reaction that was bound to ensue. Everything around me became immaterial and hazy; I sat there on tenterhooks waiting for a sound from the kitchen.

And there it was. I heard her call out as though through layer upon layer of unreality and dreams: 'Peter! There's a letter for you!'

And I shot up from my chair, flew from the table, anxious not to waste a second getting there, for she was no doubt standing there in the kitchen about to open the letter, she might even already be reading it, and I wanted to be there to see all the misunderstandings, all the jealousy, all the reproaches swept away so that life could begin anew at Fagerlund. I leapt across the dining-room floor, still trembling at the knees after the excitement at the table and perhaps a bit over-eager, a little too optimistic, perhaps the effect of the little glass of wine still lingered on in me, for just as I was about to throw the kitchen door open and rush in to her, I tripped on the rug, lost my footing and fell over towards the fireplace. After a futile effort to get my legs back under me again, to avoid the unavoidable, my right knee rammed into the cold iron, then crashed into a corner of the fireplace with all the impetus of my own weight and my speed as I fell, and the pain shot like red-hot needles through every sinew of my body before taking root in the injured knee and behind my eyes, exploding like a shower of white suns.

They all stood round me as I lay there, struggling to hold back sobs through clenched teeth. Uncle Kristen knelt down beside me, placed a hand behind my neck and had suddenly lifted me up as though I was light as a feather, and carried me straight across the floor to the sofa, where Aunt Linn was placing cushions ready. Then my trouser-leg was rolled up and my knee bathed in antiseptic solution. Uncle Kristen felt my knee to see if it had been injured. I held my breath, for I mustn't cry out with them standing there watching, and I saw them through veils of tears, though actually it was already not *quite* as painful as it had been a moment before. . . .

'You're all in one piece at any rate,' said Uncle Kristen. 'The kneecap's all right and nothing's broken. Can you still bend your knee, Peter?'

I nodded, moved my knee slightly and bit my lip. I was furious because he didn't consider it more serious while I lay there in such pain. But the compress that Aunt Linn placed on it did the world of good and would mean that my knee was stiff so long as it remained there, so that no one would be able to forget that I was an injured man; and white-faced anxiety, sympathy and concern, written all over the faces of the others, were also a source of comfort and satisfaction. As an invalid, I had again become the focus of attention and could bring my will to bear upon them.

'Crikey, look how swollen it is!' said Jo.

'Lucky nothing's broken,' sighed Aunt Linn.

Suddenly I remembered the letter. The hullabaloo I'd caused had obviously prevented her from reading it. Now I'd have to wait till the excitement had died down before I could see any result. Everyone looked on solemnly as Aunt Linn put the bandage on. My knee wasn't seriously hurt after all and I felt a little better already – just a light sprain perhaps? But the bandage would give me an excuse for limping the first few days.

I was pleased about that. Now I was impatient to move things along a bit.

'Didn't you say there was some post?'

'Post? Oh yes, I'd clean forgotten about it. There's a letter for you,' said Aunt Linn. 'Just a tick, I'll fetch it.'

She'd just finished putting on the bandage. It was a relief for everyone when my trouser-leg was rolled down again.

'As an acrobat, you sure take some beating, I must say,' said Uncle Kristen. 'You were darned lucky not to break anything!'

'Did it hurt a lot?' asked Gerd, with a nervous smile.

I nodded bravely, feeling that I might perhaps have been able to turn my accident to even greater advantage, cut an even braver figure, make even greater demands upon their sympathy and pity. But it was too late now. Cathrine stood in the background, not saying a word. What did she think of this episode? Had I made a fool of myself in her eyes by slipping over like this bang in the middle of the dining-room floor? Was she standing there in silent admiration of Uncle Kristen, who had lifted me up and carried me over to the sofa as though I'd been no more than a rag doll? The mere thought of it (or was it also that I'd just raised myself up on one elbow and felt the pain throbbing in my swollen knee?) brought tears to my eyes. Had it been a *faux pas* to invite her along to this kids' birthday party? Hadn't the upshot been to increase the distance between us, while it had now become clear to all and sundry how 'well matched' they were, she and Uncle Kristen? She hadn't taken her eyes off him as he spoke, had laughed at all his jokes, squeezed his hand – it couldn't be mere coincidence. . . . A groan slipped from my lips in spite of myself.

'Just lie still now,' said Uncle Kristen admonishingly, 'it'll feel better in a while, you'll just have to lie still.' Said the man with the scar on his leg, who had himself been injured once, *really* injured, had almost bled to death, been nursed back to life by the woman he loved. . . .

'Poor Peter,' said Cathrine finally. At long last a word from her. 'What rotten luck, and on your birthday too. . . .'

Was there a hint of patronage in her concerned voice?

'It'll be better soon,' I whimpered, smiling as much as I could manage. 'Just wait and see – we're going to play hide-

and-seek later. I'll be OK by then, I'm sure!'

The hundred best poems on love. I'd hereby made her part of stage two of my painstakingly prepared plan: hide-and-seek in the barn. Hide-and-seek in the warm semi-darkness, in all the new, dry hay. In the barn, miracles could happen. In the barn, who could deny his innermost realities? And, anyway, my leg felt a lot better already, though I could still remain lying there for a little while yet and wallow in my convalescence.

'Here comes the cake!' announced Aunt Linn. 'And here's your letter, Peter.'

Not a word about the letter to her. Perhaps it hadn't been delivered today? Delayed at the post office? Had I in the heat of the moment written the wrong address? No, that was just not possible. The letter had most likely been left on the kitchen worktop, forgotten in the rush, in all the commotion.

'Come on, then, let's all have a piece of cake. . . .'

The letter was from my mother. She wished me many happy returns and mentioned something about a removal. But I was far too excited to be able to read it through, so I put it to one side.

We ate cake with a strawberry filling. I had opposed any suggestion of decorating the cake with the sixteen candles I was entitled to. That was kids' stuff. And so were cream cakes, for that matter. I was so impatient for this meal to be over as I lay there on the sofa, balancing my plate in my lap while the others sat round the table, talking among themselves and turning to laugh encouragingly in my direction, to cheer me up. Cathrine was seated with her back to me, but turned and smiled quite a bit, two or three times at least. The hundred best poems on love. Aunt Linn sat calmly at her end of the table eating her cake. The little turn she'd had a short while since was forgotten. At long last they seemed to have finished.

'Perhaps you could do a few card tricks, Kristen,' she said.

'Oh yes!' exclaimed the others.

I'd lost the upper hand again. If he got the chance to impress the assembled group with card tricks, he'd soon have reduced me to the role of onlooker again, a guest at my own party.

'No, we're going to play hide-and-seek!' I called from the sofa.

'Do you think that's wise, Peter?' asked Aunt Linn. 'Wouldn't it be best if you took it a bit easy?'

'You're not as right as rain yet, you know,' said Uncle Kristen commandeeringly.

'I'm perfectly OK,' I said, raising myself up and swinging my leg over the edge of the sofa. I managed it all right. The bandage made my knee stiff; it throbbed warmly, but that was just the swelling. 'Course I'm all right!'

'I still think you ought to . . .'

'You can play hide-and-seek later – some other day!'

But it was absolutely essential to play hide-and-seek now, because Uncle Kristen couldn't join in, which meant we were rid of him, then I'd be boss, have Cathrine to myself. Then I'd show them. . . .

It was so warm, so stuffy in the dining-room in the afternoon heat. The potted plants cast long shadows over the rugs. Outside, sun and clouds chased one another playfully, enticing. We had to go outside.

'We're going to play hide-and-seek!' I called. I had Jo's condom in my pocket. Still nobody had opened the letter that explained everything. Still nobody knew that Cathrine loved me and I loved her, and that we would become one in the hay while the others looked for us.

'Oh, but . . .' someone protested.

Even Cathrine's face looked at me in puzzlement, almost in displeasure. Something had gone wrong somewhere. Nobody had opened the letter. Nothing had been clarified. The pieces had not yet fallen into place. But there was still time, I thought, bolstering myself up.

'It's my birthday, and what I say goes! Come on, we're going to play hide-and-seek!'

And I limped out into the kitchen on a stiff leg before the others had got up. I saw my letter to her lying unopened on the shelf above the kitchen worktop. I couldn't be bothered with that now. I hurried out into the sun and the wind: it was now or never!

It was almost dark in the enormous barn. I lay half buried in the hay, in the narrow niche that had been formed between the plank walls when the toolshed had been added on. It was my favourite hiding-place, absolutely safe and difficult to find; you had to crawl close to the wall in tunnels under the hay. Here in the corner there was a natural pocket, which was never properly filled up, even though the hay reached up to the ceiling in other places. Here it was empty; there was space right up to the ceiling. Above me, the light fell in strips through cracks in the plank wall of the west-facing hayloft.

This was the place I'd had in mind ever since Sunday, when I'd invited her to my birthday party. This was where we were to meet, hidden from all, yet with everyone's consent.

We had run away from Jo, who'd been chosen to be 'it', and was standing with his face to the wall, counting aloud to a hundred. With my stiff knee, I had lagged behind. I saw Gerd run up over the broad ramp leading up into the barn, pause and look around undecided. Fine. Let her hide in the hayloft, which would no doubt be the first place Jo looked. But where was *she*? I had to find her, get her in here with me. . . .

I caught up with her in the feed alley. She'd come to a halt, undecided – was she waiting for me? She's waiting for me! My heart rejoiced. I went right up to her, squeezed her hard against the wall, couldn't control myself. . . .

'But Peter,' she said, laughing.

I had my arms round her. I felt everything was improving, coming right as soon as we were together, close to one another. There was no longer anything to be afraid of, because she pressed herself against me too, tense but affectionate.

'Peter, we'll have to hide! He'll be coming in a minute!'

'Come on,' I said, almost unable to let go of her. 'Come on! I know a place where he'll never find us!'

'OK!' Her face beamed. I grasped her hand, wanting to pull her along with me. 'Wait! Wait a tick!' She was holding back. She was giggling and put her hand in front of her mouth. 'I say, I think I'll have to. . . . Know what I mean? I can just nip behind the barn. You go on ahead, I'll follow you. Where is it?'

'On the right when you get to the end,' I whispered. 'Crawl close to the wall. I'll be waiting for you right inside there.'

'OK.'

Then she was gone.

I lay quiet as a mouse, breathing in the sweet scent of the fresh hay. The thought of her peeing in the tall grass behind the barn set my teeth on edge, partly out of emotion and partly out of irrepressible mirth. In just a few moments now, in only a minute perhaps. . . . If I put my ear to the barn wall behind me, I might be able to hear her little hissing sound among the lush green nettles. But shyness held me back. Instead, I suddenly heard the toolshed door being opened and someone (Uncle Kristen?) walking around inside. Shortly after, I heard the grindstone turning on the other side of the wall. Oh, of course; he'd mentioned a scythe which needed sharpening, a few places where there was still grass to cut; you had to bring in all the fodder you could, considering how the crops had suffered from lack of rain this year. But why should he choose just this moment? I came out in a cold sweat all over, for this was a bad omen, a threat. Poor Cathrine! If he went only five or six yards from the grindstone, if he should take it into his head to glance round the corner, he'd see her – see her crouching in that compromising position! I closed my eyes and prayed. I prayed to Providence, to the Powers that be, which had so arranged it that I'd come so close to the greatest goal that a sixteen-year-old had ever yearned for in his innermost desires. Could the consummation possibly be snatched from under my very nose now, and what purpose could that serve anyway? She'd have to get past him on the way back as well – that is, unless she walked all the way round. There wasn't a second to lose. Jo had no doubt already finished counting, or would do so at any moment. She'd have to come this way. It was the safest. Jo was no doubt starting to search at the other end of the long barn, in the hayloft. The grindstone squeaked and grated. He might have taken his shirt off as well, as he usually did when he was sharpening things. Perhaps he was standing there half naked in the hot sunshine showing off his broad, muscular body to advantage, allowing the hairs on his chest and arms to shine with virile sweat, and she had to go so close past him! No, I couldn't think about it, couldn't bear the thought!

But then I heard her coming along the feed alley. She was coming! I heard quick light steps approaching. Then they stopped. She'd done it. No one had seen her. She had come, kept her word!

'Over here!' I whispered, as loud as I dared.

The steps came even nearer, but hesitated. The hay rustled under girlish footsteps.

'Over here!' I was beside myself with anticipation and relief.

'Come here Cath. . . .'

But it wasn't Cathrine, it was Gerd who was worming her way through the tunnel of hay. The last bit, she went down on all fours and crawled over to me, smiling roguishly.

'So this is where you are. I was wondering where I would find you. Oh, Peter. . . .'

Something had gone amiss. The grindstone stopped, pausing in its monotonous scraping for a moment before starting up again.

She crawled close beside me in the semi-darkness, filling my hiding-place with breathing and the smell of perfume, causing the hay to rustle.

'Peter, does your leg still hurt? I thought I'd die when you fell and just lay there. . . .'

When would Cathrine come? What would she say to this? How could I get rid of the brash and pushy Gerd? My plan had gone awry and I was sickened with disappointment, but all the same my arm was round Gerd, my cheek was hot against hers, I could feel her hand undoing my shirt buttons and heard her whisper: 'Why haven't you been to see me, Peter? I've been waiting for you. . . .'

Waiting for me.

But what if Cathrine should turn up after all? What could I say or do then? My thoughts ran wild as Gerd clamped herself on to my mouth and kept on stroking my narrow back up and down with her hand, then under my armpit and over my chest. She was breathing heavily.

'I've missed you, you know. I've been longing for you ever since the fête when we danced together. . . .'

So easy to yield to persuasion, to flattery. But beggars couldn't be choosers. I've been longing for you. . . .

We rolled over one another in the dry hay. She was eighteen and I was sixteen. Had she so much experience that she could come right out with things like that to a boy? With a pang of jealousy I thought of the English chap. What had he taught her? What could I do to measure up to him? The thought of Cathrine faded into the background for a moment. Gerd was closer with her firm embraces, her swollen lips.

'You're so nice, Peter, You're so nice. I love you. . . .'

I sensed confusedly where this was leading, but blocked out all thought of anything but practical things connected with the now seemingly inescapable conclusion of our rendezvous. I pressed my face against her girlish neck, licked the skin, allowing the thundering of my own breathing to drown the faint voices of fear within me, vaguely hoping that all the details would turn out right of their own accord, that the seduction would be the natural result of our little scuffle, this affectionate but breathless battle, without calling for any further ingenuity and courage on my part. Apart from rolling about in the hay, over her, under her, groaning, squeezing, licking, stroking, drowning in my own exaggerations, I had now run completely out of initiative. And the thought of Cathrine was also there, niggling away at me. . . .

Then I heard someone going through the door to the toolshed, voices, laughter. Laughter was coming from there! Uncle Kristen (for it had to be him) and someone else. . . . It was a woman's laughter, soft, intimate, like milk on marble, and I recognized it.

'Shh! It's *them*!' Gerd clutched my arm tight, giggling silently, excited, close to my face. 'It's Kristen and Cathrine!'

It was clear enough without her wide-eyed comment. We could hear them talking quietly together but not distinguish the words. Then laughter again.

'Heavens, how do they *dare*!' Gerd hissed into my ear. 'I thought they might have planned something like this . . .'

'*Planned?*'

'Yes, you surely know they're in love with one another, don't you?'

Yes, I did know. I did know. I'd known it all along. Vain, mad to try to convince oneself of anything else. I merely nodded.

'I was talking to her yesterday – she said she didn't know how it would all turn out, coming here to the party. . . . She was so fond of him, she said, she wasn't sure she'd be able to help herself.' Gerd giggled, carried away. 'She'd been thinking of packing it in two or three days ago, Linn's suspicious of them, you know, but she couldn't face the thought of it now, she said. . . .'

For Gerd it was an adventure, for me it was a death sentence on a dream.

The mumbling in there rose and fell, laughter, sounds, long pauses. . . . Even though my mind had registered the fact that my Cathrine had let me down, deceived me in the most cruel way, this scene seemed totally detached from the incomprehensible facts. We listened excitedly to every sound that filtered through the plank wall.

'Anyway, she was the one who helped me to find you. She said she thought you'd hidden right in here, in the feed alley. She realized I was looking for you, I've told her about us. . . .'

That too. They'd concluded a pact about this, whispered among themselves, haggled over us, me and Uncle Kristen. But I didn't turn to stone and no abyss opened up to swallow me. Instead, I felt anew Gerd's warm closeness, and this time spurring me uncontrollably into action. The soft willingness made me almost brutal: I pushed a hand up under her skirt, feeling silk, elastic and soft, soft skin, and wasn't quite sure where to put my hand, but rested it there, heavy and warm, and in the wrong position. Soon, it was as though every limb in her body was melting; she grew heavy and soft and tearful. 'Peter,' she whispered, 'I say Peter, I'm not "poorly" now, you know. . . .'

Not poorly now. I knew full well what that meant. I'd been given the green light, but it wasn't very easy to know how to set about my assault all the same. I pulled at her silk panties, slipping them down an inch or two, feeling my way carefully forward with my finger: good God, it was her hairs!

'Just a sec. . . .' She twisted helpfully, tugged at her panties, eventually pulling them down as far as her knees. 'OK, now you.'

Yes, me. Numbly, I loosened my trouser buttons. The majestic erection I'd always thought I could count on was there right enough, but less potent, stiff and awe-inspiring than I'd thought and hoped it would be. Yet help was at hand.

'Oh, Peter, *Peter*. . . .'

Unabashed, she went into action, just as the other one, my lost beloved Cathrine, had given me her blessing three days before, but more ruthless, impatient. Did she think she could manhandle it any way she liked? I only just managed to stifle a protest. Was I over-sensitive? Was this the way they did it in England? But I felt the desired response coming on, in spite of my embarrassment and my suppressed lamentation, the desire to do it burned her hand as she pushed and pulled me into position, whispering: 'That's right, Peter. That's right!'

But I was not well acquainted with the capricious landscape of the female paradise, would never, never find any pearly gates in this jumble of limbs, clothes and stiff, prickly straw. It was a fiasco! Black despair. I groaned more heavily than she did, with more feeling too, but for quite different reasons. Why did this initiation test have to be so strenuous? Why couldn't the whole thing be more plain sailing, more straightforward, something concrete which it was possible to know you could do or you couldn't?

But a miracle happened! With a little twist of the pelvis, she got into the right position under me. I felt it slip in. I'd done it! Done it! Yes, I'd done it! I was doing it at this very moment! My get-up-and-go met with an almost cool lack of resistance, surrounding my member like a silken veil, like tepid water. What a relief! I sank down on top of her, heavy, contented, and breathed out as though I would never want to move again. She lay back, moaning and groaning with pleasure beneath me. I must feel heavy on top of her, though it didn't seem that *this* could be what was wrong either, for she writhed, twisted her lower half a bit, as though going out of her way to disturb my sublime peace. But of course! Now I remembered. The movements! Up and down! I'd all but forgotten the only thing I'd known about the sexual act throughout my boyhood: I had to work at my devotion, I had to push in, pull out, push in, pull out, manoeuvre out and in, out and in, into her. Of course!

All right, though it wasn't as easy as all that with a stiff knee, yet I pushed and pulled, pushed and pulled and felt it was so easy, so easy. I invented games, little variations as I lay there, pulled right back, doing a disappearing act before fairly ramming it into the hallowed spot again, then I rode at a jog, slowly, sedately, then at a wild gallop, and her reactions, the sounds, the moaning under me were the yardstick of my performance. It was like mastering complex machinery, an instrument, an organ, and I swelled with pride at my efforts, feeling mastery rather than well-being, knowing that, after this, there was nothing, nothing whatever, that I would find particularly difficult. It was as though the very breathing itself spurred me on as I grew intoxicated by my skills as a seducer: '. . . Nothing to it, nothing to it, nothing to it, nothing to it, nothing to it. . . .'

To my consternation, I suddenly realized that I was perilously close to the fateful explosion. The contraceptive lay in my trouser pocket. Far too late to fiddle about with that now. I felt the sap rise, my blood pound. Up to now, it had been a completely neutral demonstration of my newly discovered talents, now it was other, more powerful commands that spurred on my exertions. My will, sprung from nowhere, to reach beyond the outer limits, beyond all understanding; the urge to break down all boundaries between you and me, yours and mine; being nothing and at the same time everything.

But no, it mustn't happen! It couldn't happen so long as I was in full possession of my faculties and had control over what I did, so long as. . . . But I could already feel a wave lifting me and sweeping me away, an ecstasy, the like of which I thought I'd never experience, leading my will astray, sharpening my senses and making me feel light in the head. I could still 'withdraw' (as the boy next to me in the physics lab called it), but didn't want to, didn't want to. There was still one excruciating second to the end of the world – I wanted to enjoy it to the full, to the full, to the full. . . .

'Oh Peter,' she sighed after a while. 'It was wonderful. I knew it'd be good with you.'

Silence had descended on the toolshed too. No, there was still some movement in there, some whispering. . . .

'Have you done it with lots of girls, Peter?'

'A few,' I said casually. I thought I was entitled to blow my own trumpet a bit, in view of my masterful performance.

'I've done it with one chap before you,' she admitted. 'With David, the bloke from England. And one other chap, but that didn't really count. . . .'

I listened to every single sound coming from the toolshed. I waited, fearing the reaction bound to come the moment it struck me, with full, merciless force, that Cathrine had tricked me, deceived me in cold blood, that she was now having it off with Uncle Kristen behind the thin plank wall, but my new, deep peace, my well-being, my complacency as I lay here in the hay with Gerd Bergshagen was so fundamental that none of all that seemed particularly important. In fact, I felt a kind of comradeship with him, a loyalty, as though on an equal footing with him: you take yours and I'll take mine. . . .

'I say, I'm sorry it happened . . . the way it did.'

A pang of unease as I thought of a possible consequence – but an impossible one all the same. The mere thought of a child, a child by Gerd, was utterly absurd.

'Doesn't matter though. I'll wash it out with some water later.' She knew it all. She impressed me. Never again could she be the big, daft, shapeless Gerd, even though I couldn't say I 'loved' her.

I lay on my back, staring up at the planks above. Here Jo and I had played at cowboys and Indians, clambered up and hung from the beams, dropped head first into the hay; the rope we'd used to climb up still hung there from two years before. I observed the light filtering down through the cracks, making incisions in the dust, saw a shadow move up there, just a hint of one, but there had been a movement, a fleeting shadow in a shaft of sunlight cutting down to us through the half-light. A bird? A swallow in the rafters? No, surely not. But again there was a movement. A dark silhouette lay across several of the shrunken planks in the hayloft; a long, narrow outline cast a shadow where the many shafts of sunlight should have been. But there was still no connection in my mind between this and the fact that someone might be spying on us. Then all of a sudden I spotted a knot-hole, the knot-hole I'd forgotten until now, but when I came to think of it, remembered from numerous summer days spent playing in the barn, the knot-hole we'd used to spy on one another and on 'enemies'. No light filtered through the hole now. An eye was pressed to it. I couldn't see it, but I could sense it.

We'd clean forgotten about Jo. He was wandering around looking for us, for me and Cathrine, as agreed, in order to witness the big love scene. And witness it he had, but not quite as we'd imagined it. Poor Jo. I could well afford to part with a bit of sympathy, as flush as I was now.

'You go first.' She was still whispering. 'Then I'll come a little after you when I've tidied myself up a bit. That way, nobody'll notice anything.'

I could still hear the low voices, the movements, from the toolshed. Above our heads there was the sound of footsteps hurrying quietly away. Jo had had enough. He was off.

'OK, see you later, then!'

I shook free of the warmth, the closeness, the affection that had enveloped me like a tight cocoon. Suddenly it seemed stuffy and nauseating in our secret lair, which wasn't so secret after all.

'I'll be off, then!'

One last smacking kiss.

Then I crawled through the tunnel of hay and hurried down the long feed alley. My knee was forgotten. I was in a hurry, as though something had to be warded off, but what? I emerged in time to see Jo running down the ramp to the barn. When he saw me, he stopped for a moment, and the face that looked at me was completely contorted with hatred, with tears, with outrage. Then he ran on again, straight across the farmyard, climbed over the gate where the heavy, red cows had gathered, wanting to be milked, shot up over the steep path and disappeared among the trees.

My plan had gone down the drain, nothing could be explained or explained away now. I vacillated between melancholy despair and hilarity. After all, it wasn't my fault, nobody could blame *me* because Cathrine was in love with my uncle, not me, but it was somehow my responsibility, because I'd been the one to set the ball rolling, and then it had all gone totally, utterly wrong. I felt naked fear grip my throat, for Aunt Linn had come out on to the steps, at exactly this moment she appeared, and even from a long way off I could see that she was agitated, had something particular on her mind. She hesitated only a second, as though she'd been on the point of shouting, but instead she set off towards the toolshed. In one hand she was holding a piece of paper, a letter, and it fluttered about, rustling with each step she took, each time she swung her arm, white in the midst of the green farmyard, white between the grey and brown buildings. Something had gone wrong, very, very wrong. I had to do something, call out, attract her attention, get her to stop! I tried to shout but no sound came out, then at last I found my voice: 'Aunt Linn!'

I shouted two, three times, and she turned and waved back, waved with the white sheet of paper where it said that Uncle Kristen was innocent, that she had suspected him of adultery which he hadn't committed, that it was highly likely she had also done him other wrongs besides. For she didn't stop, just smiled, had other, more important things to do than engage in idle chatter with sixteen-year-olds. She ran and walked and ran again towards the toolshed where the reconciliation would take place, and there was nothing in the world anyone could do to stop her.

By the wall stood the wet grindstone and from the handle hung the faded shirt Uncle Kristen used when he was mowing the grass. 'Heavens, it's so hot!' said Gerd, who had just come into view, and stood there squinting in the orange glow of the late afternoon sun.

21

I don't remember precisely what happened immediately after this, but Gerd's agitated face stands clearly before me.

'God, if she goes in, she's going to catch them red-handed!' Horrified and at the same time desperately eager to see what would happen. We were in the clear; retribution was for others.

I must have run away from her at that moment. I remember that I ran through the kitchen, where the carry-cot with Cathrine's baby stood in the middle of a shaft of sunlight streaming in through the window – absurd idyll – up the stairs, to the floor above, into the east room, which had always been mine in summers before, when I'd stayed here with Aunt Linn and Uncle Kristen. It smelled musty and abandoned in here. A duvet lay folded on the bed without a cover. Dead flies lay on the window-sill, dead from exhaustion in the battle with the window-pane, the transparency which by some wizardry had become impassable. Here tears overwhelmed me. I threw myself down on the bed, wept for forgiveness, for peace, reconciliation, salvation, everything that could no longer be found in this world. I wept for innocence, for ignorance, for virtuousness in the east-facing bedroom, where I had spent many, many happy hours and days in an earlier existence; my room in the world as it had been.

I fell asleep.

When I awoke, it was almost dark. It must be late. They hadn't found me. Perhaps they hadn't even looked. Things had taken their course, the fire had flared up and burned itself out, the party was over, the guests had gone; now it was just us left on the farm, we who belonged there; now all had been brought to an end, a conclusion. This surely was how it had to be. Everything must be over by now.

I felt cold. I heard voices down below. Hers. His. Serious, accusing, embittered. The embers were still glowing. Would it never end? It had grown cold in the bedroom. I wrapped the duvet round me. My teeth chattered. I listened. A few words were just audible. I heard:

'. . . there's nothing more to say. You drove Marie away. You drove her to certain death, do you understand that? Because you were jealous and imagined things and paid more heed to gossip than to me. Can you grasp what that means? What you've done?'

It was him. His voice was loud and peremptory, but distorted in the passage from one room to the other, sounding like barks, like short wails, like sobs. . . .

Then her:

'I didn't mean to drive her away, didn't want to drive anyone away, but I had to talk to her, I couldn't bear just being a passive onlooker. . . .'

All life had ebbed from her voice, just as her life had lost all hope. And I was partly to blame.

'And don't tell me you didn't try to scare *her* away as well! You knew damn well how easy it was to influence a sensitive girl like Marie.'

'No! No! I didn't mean to! I didn't mean to, I tell you! But as for the other one. . . . Oh, it's *disgusting*!'

They were talking about Cathrine, about their obscene relationship, about suspicions which before had been groundless but were now fully justified.

'You've only yourself to blame. When you drove Marie away, you drove me from the farm as well.'

'*I did not drive her away!* I didn't mean to. . . .' She was weeping now. 'But that *you* could behave like that, run after the girl like a . . . *tomcat*, at Peter's birthday party. What sort of an example have you set him? You know he looks up to you like a father. What do you think he was up to in the barn with that trollop Gerd Bergshagen? Poor Peter. . . .'

That hurt. She had mentioned my name! Even at that fateful moment, she had thought of *me*! She had realized what Gerd and I had been up to, and she was anxious to protect my illusions and concerned about my welfare. . . . My dear, dear Aunt Linn! I could scarcely concentrate, so moved was I, so humbled by the concern she lavished upon me, and after all I had contrived in the way of trickery and intrigue over the past few weeks. I also was guilty. It was excruciating.

'Don't drag the boy into it,' he said gravely. 'He's big enough to understand what's going on.'

I didn't listen any more. What she had just said made me remember something: the contraceptive. An impulse made me feel to see whether it lay safely in my trouser pocket, as it should have done. But I couldn't find it. The pockets were empty! It had fallen out! It must have fallen out in the barn, I thought feverishly. I had to find it before anyone else did, regardless of how small the likelihood of this was. I couldn't stand the thought of how compromising it would be, especially after what she had said, if one of them found it. I had to distance myself from everything which had happened on that dreadful day, at least destroy everything concrete which linked me with events. I would have to stay up here until it grew light. No one would think of looking for me here. Then I would creep out and find it.

'Nothing you say will make the slightest difference now.' His sombre speech continued, slow and ominous: 'I've written to a solicitor and we'll be receiving our divorce papers within a day or two. I can't take any more, do you see, Linn. I can't take any more. It couldn't possibly have gone on like this.'

She was weeping.

I lay waiting for dawn to come. I still couldn't believe that everything wouldn't one day be all right again. Even Uncle Kristen's last words, which hung in the dark stillness around me with their awesome finality, failed to shake this belief in me, the last bastion of the innocence of childhood.

I was wakened by the incongruous sunlight, thinking I'd barely closed my eyes. But it was morning. Already. Was it too late perhaps? Was anybody up? No, I couldn't hear anyone. Not a sound. Just the first birds singing. It might still be early enough after all.

The sun poured in through the east-facing window. It would be a long, warm day. High summer. Golden ears of corn. The tall birches by the gate, with a bit of tired grey in the midst of all the lush green. How familiar it all was to me down to the tiniest little detail, and yet I was a total stranger to it on that still, still morning.

In stockinged feet down the broad stairs, through the kitchen, out on to the doorstep.

Morning. And what a morning! The broad, white sky without a cloud. Dew steaming. Scent of grass, of yarrow. Everywhere the smell of yarrow. The barn still dark and closed, but I knew where I had to look, and I would find it, and everything would be all right.

It was dark in the narrow feed alley. The passage leading to my hiding-place was much frequented by now, after all the use it had seen the day before. I thought of everything that had happened, of Gerd, of Jo, of Cathrine, of Uncle Kristen, barely able to grasp it. I remembered what he had said about divorce papers, and Aunt Linn who had broken down and wept. But that had been yesterday evening. Now it was morning. Sunshine. It would no doubt all turn out right in the end; they would no doubt come to an agreement, I couldn't believe. . . .

But none the less there were facts I couldn't escape: she had frightened Marie, pressured her, threatened her perhaps so that she had to run off, driven her straight out into the forest, or as good as. . . . And he had betrayed and deceived his wife, made a fool of himself running after a girl. It dawned on me that things would never 'turn out right in the end' and once again be as before, because everything we had allowed ourselves to be pushed into had gone so terribly wrong. Here in the dimness of the barn I understood that burdens could only be added to and that the backs which carried them – strong, adult backs – could also reach breaking-point, give way under the weight, collapse and be destroyed. I suddenly saw this so clearly before me during the brief moments as I made my way carefully along the wall to reach my hiding-place and start the search for the ill-fated condom. I shuddered again, for I suddenly realized, with the terror-stricken insight of the sixteen-year-old, what I might find instead. But there was no turning back now; I had to do what I had come here for, fulfil my role as go-between, as the errand-boy of fate.

Then there I was.

Beneath the planks in the hayloft which formed the ceiling of my secret hiding-place lay the beam I'd used as an exercise bar when I wanted to train, to make my muscles as strong as Jo's (I'd never succeeded, never succeeded in lifting myself high enough for my chin to rest on it). This had been the scene of louche consultations. Here the darkest, most intimate secrets had been swopped in whispers. Here we had played at Tarzan, jumped down into the hay, whooping and shouting wildly. Here many an enemy had had to pay with his life.

On the climbing rope we had rigged up two summers before, there she hung. Aunt Linn. A grotesque, elongated figure, her white eyes turned towards the knot-hole in the ceiling. There was nothing to be said and nothing to be done. No tears. No fear even. No longer able to stand, I sank to my knees, inadvertently bumping into the corpse, not hard, yet hard enough to set death swaying to and fro, sending up a cloud of flies from the dark garment – the apron she usually wore, I recognized it – swarming up and out through the hatch set high up in the shrunken plank wall. The flies. They swarmed from the dead body out through the narrow hatch and up into the pale milky morning sky.

22

There's no more to tell.

I went back home a few days later. He drove me to the train. On the way to the station, we didn't say much. The old truck squeaked and rattled along the dry gravel road. The eleven miles seemed endless. All the same, the journey was over far too quickly.

But as we walked up and down the platform together he decided to confide something in me, to give me some information which he perhaps thought I was entitled to, all things considered.

'How senseless it's been, all this, Peter,' he said quietly. His face had taken on a greyish pallor, his eyes were drawn. Hard lines had appeared round his mouth, which had become sunken. He seemed an old man, a marked man, and his smile was a distant memory. 'I don't know what you'll think about this when you've got the whole thing in perspective a bit. But I just wanted you to know that I've asked Cathrine to marry me. She couldn't give me an answer straight away, but said she'd think about it. Well, that's all it was.'

He stood there, tall and stocky in the sunshine. Now it was my turn. He'd placed his cards on the table. Now I ought to do the same: tell him about the letter, tell him I'd shopped him after the summer fête, that I'd been green with envy. But I shied away from it, even though it wouldn't have been dangerous or difficult. Not after all that had happened. What I'd done hadn't been all that important and by no means had it been decisive. Everything would have come to light before long anyway. The separation was a fact. He had proposed to Cathrine.

But it was difficult to find a way of saying it. He stood there unassailable, solid as a rock, the sun full in his face. His black hair was receding slightly at the temples, giving him even more a look of my father. Even now, his face drawn with the strain of grief and loss, he was so much stronger than me. The crow's feet at the corners of his eyes caught the midday light, making him look stern and resolute. At a loss, I searched for some fixed point to look at, glancing down at the brown planks where we stood, over to the birches at the end of the platform and finally up at the sky. I tried, but I couldn't bring myself to do it. No, I couldn't confess to anything. The awareness of what I'd done, the fact that I couldn't admit it, even now when it no longer really mattered, would have to be a millstone round my neck. I tried but I couldn't respond in like measure, especially not after what he had said, especially not after what had happened. For the isolation of the sixteen-year-old runs deeper than any convention about right and wrong, good and evil, moral and immoral. That was why I couldn't bring myself to do it.

The train arrived and cut short the agony. We shook hands. I asked him to remember me to the Bergshagens. Then I was in the compartment with my rucksack and my suitcase, waving, waiting impatiently for the guard to blow his whistle, for the station to glide away and disappear, to become just a memory among other memories, a vague, merciful blur which now and then perhaps might sharpen into pain, a wistful, melancholy pain perhaps; only once in a while, less and less often as I grew up and got older: the last summer at Fagerlund.

When I got home, the removal men were there, fetching the last few things. In her letter Mother had mentioned in passing that we were going to move. We were moving to a smaller flat in a slightly cheaper district. Mother was rather agitated, organizing the entire exhausting operation, ordering everybody this way and that. 'Peter!' she cried. 'There you are! How are you? Oh my goodness, it must have been terrible for you! How dreadful for poor Linn, for all of them!' Anaesthetizing me with her perfume.

But Dad wasn't there. He'd had to go off somewhere 'to rest for a while', as she put it. The firm had gone bankrupt. We were to visit him when the removal was over.

'But he left something for you. A surprise for your birthday. Here you are.'

I unwrapped it. It was a wrist-watch. A good make as well. Just what I'd wanted!

'Eat up now, love,' she coaxed. 'Just imagine all you've been through!'

It smelled of paint in the new flat. The furniture had been left higgledy-piggledy. It would be some job to arrange it all. I noticed a case full of books, my books. Suddenly I remembered that the book containing *The Hundred Best Poems on Love* lay forgotten on the sideboard in the deserted drawing-room at Fagerlund. It didn't matter much to me now. I'd never managed to get to the end of a poem before anyway and as like as not wouldn't manage it in future either; there were so many distractions, things that interfered and stole one's attention from the short lines which were supposed to say so much, provided one discovered 'the key'. . . . No, poetry was not for me, there were other things besides, things to touch and feel that appealed to me more. From now on I would set about cultivating such things. Something had ended and something new was beginning.

I ate Mother's apple pie. I looked around me in the flat, heard the noises from the street, thought it seemed like only yesterday I'd left, thought that the whole summer at Fagerlund seemed to be drifting away like clouds before my inner eye. Poems on love – who cared?

I looked at the case containing the expensive watch. I opened it. It was a beautiful watch with luminous figures, a second hand and leather strap. Waterproof. Just what I'd wanted. I had felt it in my bones, known for certain that I'd get a watch for my sixteenth birthday. I'd take good care of it, take it off when we had gym, be careful to avoid getting a single scratch on the sparkling quartz glass.

Dad's present to me. His acknowledgement that I was sixteen. The days of sheath-knives, playing at cowboys and Indians in the forest, rural romanticism, all were things of the past. The wrist-watch was a sign from him to me that I was grown up.

And I still have it, in a drawer somewhere.

Printed in Great Britain
by Amazon